I0584625

Through the Heavens and Earth

Book Three of the Blood and Hexes Trilogy

by
ALEXANDER FERNANDEZ

Edited by
Trana M. Simmons

Book One: Above the Ashes
Book Two: Below the Darkness
Book Three: Through the Heavens and Earth

Chapter One

A Beacon of Hope

Deep in prayer with the Moon Goddess Selene, Sybil's body floated on a cloud. Lunar mist surrounded her, cool and bright in its embrace. The deity had just promised to send her flying chariot so Sybil could take her companions to Athens. The city had fallen under a brutal assault by Umaq and his demons, their goal to destroy the Greek sun god, Helios. Selene would not accompany the chariot as the moon deity struggled to evacuate civilians. No time to falter, the team of horses would provide the quickest method of travel.

However, the last time Sybil had transported her friends across the world, everyone almost died.

Instead of exhilaration over soaring aboard a celestial chariot, anxiety from a terrible memory froze her. On the way to Machu Picchu to stop Umaq from murdering the sun god, Inti, she had ruptured a ley line while attempting to travel across it. Sybil's friends had nearly perished because of her ineptitude in controlling the earth energy.

For Athens, she had expected the moon goddess to open a portal or provide teleportation. The last thing Sybil expected was to be in charge of transport yet again.

1

What if she made another mistake on this flight and something terrible occurred?

Making haste is the utmost importance, Selene implored through the prayer. *My brother Helios and I await your arrival.*

We…we shall be there promptly, Sybil managed to respond.

After receiving your brave offer for assistance, renewed hope has awoken inside of me, the goddess continued. *Courage and strength abound inside you and have stirred the heavens. Together, we will stop Umaq and erase his tyranny from our world.*

Even as Sybil listened to Selene's optimism, she failed to suppress the awful memories from the hilltop in Machu Picchu: Marcelo bathed in fire as the sun's rays pierced him, demons tearing Salix to pieces as she protected Marcelo, and Johann unable to maintain his werewolf form while monsters pummeled his body. Sybil's ley line disaster broke her self-assurance and trust in her abilities for traveling in this magnitude. Weakness numbed her, and she desired to fall into a dark pit away from responsibility and heartache. How could she face Umaq and his army in this faltering state? How could she protect her friends?

Sybil ventured to communicate in return, her words propelled by heartfelt emotion. Ashamed, she didn't want to disappoint the moon goddess, yet her insecurity proved steadfast. *Goddess Selene, of a truth, I am moved by your words and your faith in me. However, hesitation hath converted my heart into ice. Hitherto, concern for my friends' wellbeing fills my soul with uncertainty. I do not wish to see them harmed again, I warrant.*

She remained unable to view anything through the surrounding white haze, but the deity's unseen presence spoke clearly. Selene's tone came strong yet tender, full of authority but laced with kindness. Each word from the goddess symbolized a gentle hand on Sybil's back, a sweet caress on her cheek.

Your emotions are powerful, and through this prayer, I can feel them as my own, Selene observed. *The Maiden of the waxing moon conveyed to me what occurred in Machu Picchu. Great fear of past failure weakens your resolve. The weight on your shoulders is heavy, so allow me to diminish your worries.*

In anticipation of your prompt arrival, Helios has manipulated the sunlight within the city limits, and it will not harm Marcelo. In a sign of the utmost skill and bravery, you have cured the werewolf of moon sickness. The dryad has also grown anew, her roots deep and unbreakable. You have accomplished much, but the best protection for your friends is belief within. Demonstrate to them, and especially to yourself, that your most powerful gifts will always triumph—strength of heart, compassion, and the power of a young witch that traversed time and space to end Umaq's evil.

At the mention of Umaq, another torrent of dreadful memories assaulted Sybil. Her mother, Olivia, lay slain at the dock while trying to escape witch persecution all across England. Sybil's dearest friend, Constance, trusted and beloved housemate, swung dead at the end of a rope. Umaq's malevolence had started long before modern day Salem. His dark schemes robbed Sybil of her childhood and had nearly cost her life. Not long ago, those gruesome circumstances had shattered her conscience and pushed her to grow as wicked as the demon master.

Yet through deep love from Marcelo and her companions, she had surpassed those atrocities and continued to battle in the face of unspeakable danger. And now Selene, an omnipotent goddess, had been inspired after hearing Sybil's prayer. Her self-doubt seemed minuscule compared to what would happen to the world if Umaq completed his twisted goals. The situation proved to be more than just protecting those at her side. Grace remained Cessani's prisoner. Innocent people had already perished in the struggle against Umaq's demons, many more certain to follow.

Some of the weight lifted from Sybil's tired shoulders. The stress constricting her chest lessened, and she breathed easier. In her gut, a spark lit the furnace of determination. Her heart beat free, and love for those around her burst outward. Through the prayer, she projected tears of relief and a warm hug for the deity.

Thank you, dear Goddess Selene. I shall journey forth and strive for those dearest to me, for those who still hope, and for the innocent who have already lost it.

Selene's final words glided through the lunar mist. *Then come, Sybil! Fly the stars, and sail on the moon. May the lunar light shine upon you in faith and her celestial glow provide a beacon for those who despair.*

***

"Sybil?"

The soft voice calling her name sounded from a great distance. Exhausted, she moaned and rolled over on the cloud, warm and content in her rest.

"Sybil!"

The much louder call worked to open her eyes. Marcelo's concerned gaze hovered as he knelt next to her. Awake, she recalled her surroundings as reality returned. A hard floor underneath her sprawled body replaced the fluffy cloud. The ceiling and walls of the witchcraft shop, The Cauldron Black, emerged as the last of the sleepiness wore off. In this area of Salem near Derby Waterfront District, she had just finished praying to the moon goddess and must have swooned.

Marcelo helped Sybil to her feet, and she stared at the destroyed interior of the store. Magical items lay scattered about, the remnants of spell casting used to free Johann from the moon intoxication. Merchandise and broken chunks of wood cluttered the floor. Shelves lay stacked against the front door to barricade the entrance from gun-wielding citizens outside. The armed residents, terrified and angry about Cessani's violent occupation of Salem, had managed to corner Sybil and her friends inside the shop.

"Are you all right?" Marcelo asked. He took Sybil into his arms, and she eased into his comforting embrace.

"I seem to fare well," she answered. "My prayer to yonder Goddess Selene caused me to strive more than anticipated."

The dryad, Salix, drummed her long fingernails against a patch of cherry-colored bark on her thigh. Though she lacked a mouth, the clicks on the wood communicated her words. *It is good to see you awake and thankfully unharmed, Spell Weaver. You only lost consciousness for a few minutes. I am relieved.*

"Thank you, dear Salix," Sybil replied. "Truly, the situation in Athens is dire. I am not conversant on how long it shall take Selene to comply so we can make haste to yonder city."

"Oh, I dare say the goddess responded quickly," Johann said from the window. The werewolf, currently in human form, peered outside as a bright light grew in the night. His wide eyes then stared at Sybil. "You're not going to believe this!"

She moved to the window alongside the others. Bullet holes from earlier in the evening had pierced the glass, a reminder for everyone to stay low and lift their heads just enough to peek.

Sybil gaped at the promised chariot and team of horses parked outside. Six illuminated white steeds stood proud in two rows of three. The majestic beasts shook their heads, and legs stomped the ground in anticipation. Long, gorgeous manes shone like white fire between their pointed ears and down the back of muscular necks. The large, two-wheeled metal chariot sparkled with pearls, glittering diamonds, and a coat of gleaming lunar dust.

"Selene's chariot," Sybil said in awe. "Truly, I have heard a sundry of stories about it since I was a child years agone."

"And I recognize a taxi when I see one," Johann remarked. He sniffed close to one of the bullet holes. "I don't smell the gun-toting cowboys anywhere. They must have run off."

"Let's get out of here," Marcelo said. "Umaq has already destroyed Inti, and Helios is in danger."

6

Through the Heavens and Earth

About to comment, a sudden bout of coughing doubled Sybil over. She gasped, her throat on fire as she turned her back to the others and coughed into her hands. Marcelo's concerned voice called out, but she waved him off and stepped further away until the fit subsided. Breathing heavily, she glanced at her palms in shock. Black, watery residue coated her skin. Fighting panic, she quickly wiped her hands on the top of her jeans and pulled her blouse down over the stains.

She turned back around and forced a small smile. "Forgive me. The little nap hath dried my throat. I fare better forthwith."

Marcelo returned a loving smile, then worked with Johann to shove aside the barricade in front of the shop entrance.

The odd blackness spewing from Sybil's body terrified her. She dreaded to know what had caused it, but no time remained for worrying over the unknown. If Marcelo discovered her condition, he might wish to cancel the mission or try and have her stay behind. Saving Helios—and the world—proved too important to debate other distractions.

With the barricade removed, Johann carefully opened the door. After a cautionary sniff of the air, he led everyone to the chariot and they climbed aboard the open-backed vehicle. Sybil glanced over the dangling reins, then at Marcelo.

"Hey, don't look at me, I'm not driving." He laughed. "Your prayer, your ride. Go on, love. Take us to Athens."

Sybil now stood in the front of the chariot. She gripped the reins and hesitated, staring at the flowing manes and strong backs of the white horses. The steeds

7

neighed and shook their heads. Lunar dust floated from their bodies in a glittering mist.

"Everything good?" Marcelo asked.

"Yes, my love," Sybil responded. She had taken a moment for herself, one last breath to prepare for the fight ahead. "Night dwells hither in Salem, yet the sun blazes in yonder Athens at this hour. But fear not. We shall be under Helios' protection."

Confidence radiated through her renewed touch on the reins. Her heart beat in strength of purpose, her mind soothed and prepared. In response, the horse team stamped and snorted in eagerness.

Sybil flicked her wrists. The harness jingled, and the chariot launched forward. Six sets of hooves thundered loudly on the concrete. Shining white manes whipped back and forth after each powerful stride.

The horses lifted from the street and pulled the lunar chariot into the sky. The magnificent creatures' legs pounded the air to provide thrust, and Selene's celestial mode of transportation burst forth in speed. Like a comet, the glowing vehicle painted an icy white streak across the black sky.

Sybil glanced at her friends as the wind swept her hair across her face. Wonderment ignited Marcelo's green eyes, twin emerald stars shining in the heavens. Awe split Johann's face in a wide smile as he gaped in all directions, his blond ponytail fluttering. Intense happiness radiated from Salix. The rush of air rustled the leaves on her small body, each bend or twist of foliage an expression of joy.

No fear occupied their rapt gazes nor doubt over Sybil's ability to lead them. No terrible memory of a disastrous ley line ride existed here. Their love and trust powered Sybil's heart and fueled her emotions. The overwhelming sensations brought tears of bliss. She felt as if she could fly without the chariot and soar to the moon itself.

She whooped in delight and gave the long reins another flick. The chariot burst ahead with increased speed as the land disappeared beneath in a sea of lights. Frost streamed from the steeds' nostrils, and their hooves clawed along the heavens. Marcelo grinned and pumped a fist high. Salix hopped up and down. Johann transformed into a werewolf and howled in elation.

The chariot flew east across the Atlantic Ocean. The massive body of water appeared black beneath the star-speckled sky. The team of horses plowed through a knot of clouds and tore them apart. Further ahead, a giant beam of moonlight suddenly flashed into view. The steeds galloped even faster and charged toward the celestial column of light.

"Sybil, what's going on?" Marcelo asked, his gaze set forward.

She pulled hard on the reins to maneuver, but the horses ignored the attempt to alter course. "I know not. Forthwith I am no longer in control!"

The chariot continued toward the moonbeam. Soon the vehicle flew into the illuminated pillar, and the entire scenery changed in the blink of an eye. The surrounding night above and dark ocean underneath vanished. Sybil squinted at the appearance of sunlight and a sprawling city landscape below. In panic, she whirled to check on Marcelo.

Also caught off guard by the abrupt blast of sun, he threw his arms over his head and dropped to a protective crouch. After a moment, he rose and glanced about, then offered Sybil a reassuring nod. "It's just like you said. Helios diminished the sun's power, and I'm not turning into barbeque. We made it to Athens, and Umaq hasn't won yet."

"But he's close to hoisting the trophy," Johann observed as he gestured toward the distant city. "The moonbeam warped us across the planet to hasten our arrival, but the situation on the ground looks grim. We need to hurry."

Chapter Two

Greek Tragedy

Sybil looked out over Athens in dismay. Several columns of black smoke rose from raging fires. Many structures blazed or had been reduced to rubble. Everywhere, demons of various shape and size ran through the streets or scaled buildings. Other monsters flew about to rain destruction and attack the fleeing citizens. Cars and busses raced while trying to escape. In the sea south of the city, hundreds of boats sped away from the bedlam. A multitude of people crowded the docks, desperate to board a vessel and flee.

Sybil now realized the immediate danger to the citizens trapped at the docks. She worked the reins and the horses descended while she scanned for a safe place to land. A bright light on the water caught her attention, and she gasped. A glowing figure ran across the surface of the sea, dodging several attacks and pummeling flying demons in blasts of lunar light.

"'Tis Selene!" Sybil exclaimed over the wind. "She strives to protect yonder boats while they escape. We ought to split up. Thus, we can aid the goddess and search for Umaq at once."

Salix scraped her bark-covered toes on the floor to communicate. *By branch and leaf, soil and stone, the lunar deity will have my aid. I am angry.*

The brave, fired-up dryad gripped the edge of the chariot and vaulted over the side. Like a parachute, a huge leaf grew from her narrow back and slowed her descent.

"I love my little plant face!" Johann shouted. He glanced at Sybil and Marcelo. "Leave the evacuation of citizens to the dryad and wolf. You two find Umaq and bust his teeth out before he murders Helios."

He leapt over the side and transformed into the werewolf. Salix grasped his hand just as he plummeted toward her, and the two floated down toward the docks.

"Looks like it's you and me," Marcelo said as he scanned the bedlam. "We'll have to move fast."

"Where shall we search?" Sybil asked. "The city is vast, and a sundry of demons are everywhere."

Marcelo pointed as the chariot swooped in an arc over the vast metropolis. "There's a swarm of them gathered around the Areopagus, or the Hill of Ares. I remember that place from a visit long ago. Might be a good place to start."

Sybil guided the flying chariot closer to the huge outcropping of rock that overlooked much of the city. A horde of monsters smothered the stone surface of the hill, flailing about and moving with agitated postures.

"Truly, I can feel a rather dense concentration of mystical energy yonder," she said. "Thereof it is similar to the celestial plane from where the Mother and Crone tended our injuries. I warrant that may be the entrance to where Selene and Helios dwell."

"That's good enough for me," Marcelo replied. "The beasts are definitely excited about something on that rock. Let's go down!"

Sybil wrapped the reins around her hands and sent the chariot into a sharp dive. She then pulled on the harness, and the moon vehicle leveled out just above a green forested area near the Areopagus. The agile steeds reacted smoothly, confident at Sybil's touch as they galloped lower through a break in the green canopy. Strong hooves pounded the earth as the chariot touched down between a cluster of trees. The horses soon halted in a busy chorus of snorts, tossing manes, and heaving flanks.

Sybil stepped off the vehicle and bowed before the team of mighty steeds. "You are home, noble steeds of the moon. My heart thanks you for your selfless aid."

Marcelo joined her as he patted the necks of the lead horses. "I'm certain the demons spotted us soaring over the city. Follow me."

Sybil glanced back as she ran beside Marcelo. The horses and chariot dissolved into a cloud of white dust that lifted through the thick treetops and vanished. Elsewhere in the woods, piercing howls and guttural roars warned of demons on the move.

Marcelo suddenly changed direction as Sybil's legs pumped at his side. He darted among the trees and occasionally stopped to listen, then sprinted off along a different path. He finally halted, his young face devoid of sweat. As an undead, his mouth did not open for lack of air and his chest did not heave in gasps.

Meanwhile, a gasping Sybil nearly collapsed as she leaned over and pressed her hands on her knees. Sweat moistened her skin. Hot air rushed in and out of her throat as she tried to catch her breath. She yanked the collar of her blouse up over her nose just as a violent cough burst past her lips. She knew the black goo peppered the inside of her shirt, but the important thing was for Marcelo not to notice. The coughing stopped, and she wiped her mouth.

"Sybil, are you really all right?" Marcelo asked. "You've had that awful hack since Salem."

"Nothing ails me," she lied. Besides the cough, her lower right side burned and throbbed. Just a stitch from running, or something worse?

"Look over yonder," she announced, pointing to change the subject.

Not far beyond the last line of grouped trees, they observed the riled mob of demons atop the rocky hill. The creatures parted to let someone or something through, and Sybil gasped. Umaq labored up the stone incline. The cacophony from the monsters grew louder. He reached the peak and raised a glowing, teal-colored staff.

Sybil realized the shiny staff had been crafted from hardened ley line residue; no other material on earth could match the color and radiance. How did Umaq obtain the rod, and more importantly, how did he and his demon army travel here so quickly?

A sudden stab of guilt answered her question—the ruptured ley line. Again, her error had gifted the demon master piles of ley line shards and liquid earth essence as it sprayed from the temple by the sun god's altar. An intelligent and powerful man, Umaq must have somehow solved how to open a ley gate and also travel through it.

14

From the hilltop, the demon master shouted in a strange language and gestured in spell casting. The monster horde grew more agitated. Growls ruptured and roars boomed as impatient, clawed feet scraped across the stone like bulls ready to charge.

A faint vibration tickled Sybil's chest. She felt the stored mystical energy surrounding the Hill of Ares increase as Umaq chanted. The boost allowed her to confirm the source of the distinct spiritual hum.

"Yonder location is truly the entrance of the celestial realm, and he strives to break in," she said in distress. "Helios is in danger forthwith!"

Concentration dominated Marcelo's features as he studied the scene. "We'll have to wait for the right time to charge. Stay behind me as we go up the hill."

This moment presented their chance to end Umaq's quest of smothering the world in darkness after uniting this realm and the demon one. While Johann and Salix battled to save the civilians, only Sybil and Marcelo remained. Their last encounter against Umaq ended in disaster, and he had grown more powerful since then. Would their effort be enough to stop the demon master?

Doubt, fear, and hesitation needed to be thrust aside. Sybil met Marcelo's reassuring gaze, and he nodded as if reading her mind. So many things to say between them, but no time for words. All they had was an instant; in that moment of eye contact, the love between them carried an eternity of conversation and expression of heartfelt emotion. She trusted him with her life. Returning the nod, Sybil bent her knees and leaned forward as if crouching at the start of a race.

Umaq waved his arm, and a bright flash of light burst from atop the pinnacle of the Areopagus. A large shimmer appeared next, and he stepped through the makeshift doorway into the celestial realm. The demons crowded in and began to file through.

"Now!" Marcelo urged.

He charged toward the rocky hill, and Sybil sprinted behind him. Reaching the incline, Marcelo crashed into unsuspecting monsters from behind and sent them tumbling down the slope. Preternatural speed blurred his powerful strikes. Hard kicks and punches opened a path as bodies fell. Other demons howled, arms and legs thrashing as he lifted creatures and threw them off the Hill of Ares.

Prepared, Sybil rushed forward through the wake of cleared demons. She leapt over the sweeping arm of a fallen monster and dodged a tail swipe from another. Her thighs burned as she struggled up the stony incline. Her lungs worked overtime in ragged breaths. She slapped away sweaty bangs from her face and spit a glob of black residue onto the hill.

Marcelo reached the shimmering doorway. He turned and exchanged hard blows with three, multi-eyed demons as the beasts approached. Behind, Sybil maintained her awkward sprint up the hill. Reaching the combatants, she charged into the melee like a rugby player and tackled Marcelo through the portal.

In a tangle of limbs, Sybil and Marcelo rolled across a cool, tiled floor deep in the celestial realm. A fountain churned somewhere nearby. No time for sight-seeing, Sybil concentrated on the gateway they had fallen through and launched into a spell.

"Divide now the earth and heavens above, low crawls the snake and high flies the dove. Sever yonder path from the hill of rock, the doorway in-between I slam and lock!"

The glimmering portal vanished. Earlier, several demons had already rushed through the opening with Umaq, but Sybil succeeded in cutting off the rest of the mob. Marcelo helped her up, and they both ran further inside.

Sybil only had a moment to admire the gorgeous environment around her while she continued through a remarkable Greek temple. The décor reminded her of characteristic scenes from *moovys* about ancient Athens she had watched with Marcelo. White marble benches, leafy potted plants, and jeweled ornaments dotted the area. Tall, impressive columns stretched to the high ceiling. Rich green vines twisted around some pillars and dangled between other ones like curtains. Bubbling marble fountains surrounded by gold statues adorned spacious patios.

An explosion rocked an adjacent hallway, and Sybil nearly fell over as the temple shook. She followed Marcelo into the passage and stepped over debris from a blasted wall. Ahead, shouts and the uproar of combat grew louder. The pair finally entered an expansive oval surrounded by tiered seating and discovered the source of battle.

Helios, the Greek sun god, and Umaq darted, dodged, and exchanged fierce blows in the center of an amphitheater. No scene of performing arts or discussion of politics took place on the stage. Instead, a deity and a demon master struggled for the world's fate.

17

Solar energy glowed around the golden-haired Helios as he wielded a spear and shield. Cinched at the waist, a white linen chiton draped from one shoulder and swirled around his ankles. Sandaled feet pivoted in agile maneuvers, the god's white-hot eyes fixed on his opponent.

Contrary to Helios' light, a dark luminescence radiated from Umaq—the power of the netherworld. Sybil could hardly recognize the old Inca. Blackness replaced his former yellow, phlegm-colored eyes. All his hair had fallen out. The deranged man had always been malevolent, but now something worse emanated from the demon master. His twisted expression revealed a despicable monster, someone physically and mentally transformed, where humanity scarcely remained.

The rabid demons that had entered the celestial temple alongside Umaq also rushed to attack the sun god. Sybil then recognized Zelaenah, the golden-eyed and obsidian-skinned creature having four arms and six breasts. The female demon led her team of growling beasts. Claws swiped and sharp fangs chomped in a flurry of relentless attacks.

"Focus on Umaq," Marcelo called as he raced into battle. "I'll handle the demons."

Trying not to worry, she charged at her nemesis, the man who had murdered Constance and struck Sybil unconscious for centuries. Even after waking from her lengthy slumber, Umaq continued to terrorize, harm, and threaten her and her loved ones. The chance to end it all had arrived.

Nearing the fray, Sybil uttered a spell and leapt high across the amphitheater stage. Her feet slammed onto the tiled floor and opened a large crack between

Umaq and Helios. A jagged wall crafted of stone exploded from the fissure and rose to separate the two riled combatants.

Sybil peered through the dust and blasted Umaq using a hardened knot of air. The demon master grunted and tumbled onto the debris-cluttered floor. She waved both hands and another barrage of air battered him. Umaq skidded, rolled, and slammed into the first row of benches surrounding the oval stage.

Riding her momentum, Sybil shouted and cast a roaring jet of fire. Umaq vanished. The flames scorched the stone seats and extinguished after the miss. She glanced around in bewilderment, then motion caught her eye on the far side of the amphitheater. From the other side of the melee, the demon master patted dust from his clothing and smiled.

Sybil quickly scanned the action to check on Marcelo and Helios. Two demons appeared dead, but the ruthless swarm had taken its toll on the Greek sun god. The deity had dropped to a knee. The spear lay broken on the ground, and his dented shield moved wildly to block attacks from four monsters. Marcelo struggled against another group of three, his clothes shredded and skin torn open in several places. Zelaenah suddenly dashed forward and pummeled him, her four fists knocking Marcelo flat.

Alarmed, Sybil ignored Umaq and ran toward the battle—a mistake. The demon master teleported to her side and clubbed her using his ley staff. The blow sent her crashing onto the floor, dazed. She watched through half-lidded eyes as Umaq created a large black sphere fashioned from nether essence. He thrust out his arms, and the round projectile rocketed toward Helios.

19

The spell shattered the sun deity's shield and plowed into his chest. Helios cried out in severe pain and collapsed. Umaq and the demons closed in. Marcelo recovered, but Zelaenah intercepted him and the pair traded a fury of thunderous blows.

Wincing, Sybil struggled onto her feet and chanted. *"Searing heart and flaming soul, the heavens crush within a black hole. Bathed in light my will and desire, oh sun god of yore, consume my inner fire!"*

She raised both arms, and a brilliant rose-gold hue of spiritual energy burst around her after the incantation took effect. The light parted from her body and rushed toward Helios in a huge, sparkling wave. Although Sybil remained still, her heart hammered in exertion and sweat poured. Tired muscles throbbed as if she had lifted weights for hours. She gasped, trying to catch her breath. The demanding spell had scraped her internal energy reserve, manifested it into a physical phenomenon, then transferred her vigor to the sun god.

The wide, iridescent enchantment slammed into Helios and absorbed into his beaten flesh. As renewed strength surged, his exhausted countenance switched to that of a fresh player on the field. Brow furrowed in anger and his jaw set, the sun deity bolted to his feet. Shouting, a powerful swipe of a muscled arm battered Umaq and the demons to the ground.

Helios glanced at Sybil and shouted a warning. "Take cover!"

A sizzling, white-hot light erupted around the sun god. A drained Sybil could barely crawl away as her arms and legs felt like jelly. The light burned her skin as she reached the stone wall created by her earlier spell. She rolled behind the barrier as intense brightness filled the large amphitheater. Closing her eyes tight, she covered her head to defend it against whatever deity-powered attack loomed.

"All galaxies tremble before my supernova!" Helios shouted. "A star's birth and death begin and end in fire from Hades."

A cool body then smothered Sybil; Marcelo had arrived to protect her. "I don't know what's about to happen, but hold on. I think the sun god is really pissed off!"

A tremendous blast rocked the entire area. Wind howled and the temperature soared. The protective wall crumbled. Dirt roiled and rubble flew about. Sybil and Marcelo held each other as the supernova tossed them through the air…and out of the celestial realm.

The pair landed in a thick forest beyond the rocky hill of the grand Areopagus. Marcelo had broken Sybil's fall as he lay beneath her, although her body still throbbed from the impact. Between the treetops, she spotted a glowing crack low in the sky just before it vanished. The blast had ejected through that fissure, but at least the celestial realm had sealed once again.

Marcelo helped Sybil to her feet, his face full of apprehension while he inspected her. "Are you in one piece, love?"

"Just barely," she managed to say, winded and dizzy. "What hath occurred to Helios?"

Marcelo boldly stepped into a patch of sunlight. "The protection is still activated, which means he's fine. Otherwise, I'd be in flames right now."

A frenzied flap of wings rose overhead. Above the trees, Zelaenah sailed away clutching Umaq in her bird-like feet.

21

Marcelo cursed. "It looks like Umaq survived, and they're heading for the Acropolis. We can—Sybil!" He touched beneath her nose and drew back a finger covered in black residue. "What is this? You are far from okay and need help. Helios is safe for now, so we can rest."

"No," Sybil replied, wiping her moist nose on a sleeve. The ferocious fire of pursuit burned in her gut. Unbreakable resolve pumped her heart, and great desire charged her spirit. She would catch her prey and snuff out her nightmares once and for all. "Umaq hath now been separated from his demonic forces, and hitherto he appeared injured. 'Tis our behoof to continue lest he escape once more. His evil must end forthwith." Not waiting for a response, she broke into a jog.

Marcelo caught up and shot her a concerned glare. "You're right, we won't get another opportunity like this one. But the second you cough, stumble, have another nosebleed or whatever that was…we are done. I'm taking you home."

Sybil nodded while trying to stay focused and not display her own deep concern. The blackness still frightened her and seemed to be growing worse, but Marcelo's anxiety motivated her to stop Umaq even more. The demon master, murderer, and wrecker of her life would be stopped at all cost.

Following Zelaenah's flight path, they ran into one of the most ancient and renowned locations in the world. Recalling scenes from a *moovy*, the Acropolis of Athens contained the amazing Parthenon, the Temple of Asclepios, the Theatre of Dionysus, and several other incredible sites packed together in this elevated part of the city. As within the celestial realm, Sybil only had moments to admire the breathtaking architecture and historical significance of the Greek ruins.

The tall, white fluted columns, wide steps, and carved friezes impressed even while partially crumbled. The size, shape, and layout of the multiple structures of the Acropolis created a city inside a city, a sparkling gem embedded in the ring of Athens. She wondered how glorious this place was during the height of Greek influence and power.

Yet time—and a demon infestation—had further tarnished the beauty. Sybil moved around rubble and stepped past hundreds of discarded personal items that littered the area. In their panic to escape from Umaq's attack, the fleeing citizens had dropped cameras, purses, backpacks, sunglasses, souvenirs, and numerous other belongings.

Peering ahead, she spotted Zelaenah and Umaq descending into the central area of the white-columned Parthenon. Having once served as a treasury, the ancient structure had been built to celebrate a great victory over Persian Empire invaders throughout the Greco-Persian Wars. Nearing the large building, Sybil and Marcelo slipped between the aged pillars and into the grounds. The roof had collapsed long ago, leaving sunlight to stream onto large pieces of broken marble.

A visibly wounded Umaq struggled to remain standing. Zelaenah glanced about the area, then froze when Sybil and Marcelo approached. Umaq labored to raise the ley staff, then struck it using a blue stone hanging from around his neck. The staff vibrated and a shrill, haunting tone sang in the Parthenon. A gap split the ground, and bluish light from a ley gate blasted forth.

Running, Sybil spread her arms to summon miniature lightning on her hands. The tiny bolts danced between her fingers, across her arms, and down over her body until the sizzling light wrapped her. In a surprise rush, she teleported to Umaq's side and drilled a sharp elbow into the side of his head. He dropped to his knees, and the ley staff clattered beside him.

Marcelo launched forward in a blur of speed. He lowered a shoulder and plowed Zelaenah to the ground in a hard crash. The demon's wings molded into her body and two extra arms grew in their place. She grabbed Marcelo's shoulders and rolled on top of him, then used her other free hands to bash his face.

Umaq groped for the ley staff. A violent cough prevented Sybil from stopping him as she choked on black sludge. The rod swung in a wide arc and struck the back of her knees, buckling her legs as she toppled. Umaq moved away in a frantic crawl and dropped into the ley gate to escape.

"Curse you!" Sybil shouted.

She sprinted toward the edge of the hole, but her adversary had vanished in the blue light. Turning back to help Marcelo, something tightened around her midsection. From inside the breach where Umaq fled, a tether of black nether essence had coiled around her waist. A moment later, it yanked her into the ley gate. As she fell through the opening, a roar of earth closed the gap and cut short Marcelo's frantic call of her name.

Chapter Three

Weeping Willow

"Sybil!" Marcelo shouted as the hole rumbled to a close.

Helpless while struggling against Zelaenah, he had watched in terror as Sybil tumbled into the opening. Still lying on his back, he growled in renewed effort and hammered a knee into the demon's side. He shoved her away and ran to where the hole had been. Angry and desperate, he dropped to a knee and beat a fist on the ruined floor of the Parthenon.

Zelaenah laughed. "That's too funny. You look like a child throwing a tantrum." One hand wiped blood from the demon's nose while the other three brushed dirt from her body.

Marcelo ignored the senseless taunt as he stood in frustration. Sybil vanished and he had failed to protect her. Where could she be? Would she be able to hold off Umaq on her own?

Zelaenah's sudden, fierce kick knocked Marcelo several feet away. He snapped out of his troublesome thoughts and blocked two of her punches. However, the demon's four arms placed him at a disadvantage. The other fists bashed into his jaw and ribs. He dodged another kick and slammed his forehead against hers. She countered by squeezing his torso using two arms while the other pair of elbows pummeled his face.

Returning the bear hug, Marcelo lifted Zelaenah and sprinted to the nearest pillar. Both fighters crashed into the column in an explosion of dust and stone. In a wild scrap, they rolled through debris, stood in a fury of blows, and fell back onto the ground during an epic wrestling match that would have impressed ancient Greeks from the Olympic Games of yore.

The longer this situation dragged on, the less time remained to locate Sybil. Intense fear for her wellbeing panicked Marcelo. He couldn't waste any more time fighting here. Worried thoughts about Johann and Salix also rattled his mind. Were his friends all right? Had the civilians escaped?

To worsen matters, the demon soul inside him abruptly spoke in its usual scorn. *Look at you, whining and crying. Without me, you fight like a human—weak and useless. Remember when you allowed me to come forth on the beach in Salem? You smashed Daiyu's face as she teased about putting you on trial. Let me take over again and you'll finish Zelaenah in an instant!*

No. Never. Although Marcelo did have limited success against the ancient vampire, Black Jade, he would not resort to becoming what he loathed most—a mindless, blood-thirsty monster. That same monster had nearly caused the death of an innocent civilian in South Boston when Marcelo lowered his guard. In Salem, he had managed to regain control after allowing the cursed demon soul to take over. However, what if the internal beast discovered a way to hold on and block Marcelo from reclaiming his body?

26

He shuddered at the thought as a wild bloodbath would ensue. The creature would feast on humans and drink to its content...all while wearing Marcelo's face. Allowing the dangerous and unpredictable demon to emerge was not the answer. For the moment, Marcelo would have to find his own way out.

Still thinking of Sybil, he welcomed the fear gripping every cell in his body. He focused on the terror of her vanishing and used the sentiment as leverage against Zelaenah. Surging panic pumped his muscles. Dread hardened his bones and anxiety sped his reflexes.

The female demon's attacks soon failed to stop him. Her moves grew predictable, the feints and pattern of fighting easily countered. Her strength no longer matched his. Her high intellect and guile did nothing to aid in combat.

Marcelo rained more punches on Zelaenah. He dodged strikes and drove knees and elbows into his opponent. He threw her far across the Parthenon and kicked the demon back down when she tried to stand. She eventually grew weak and breathed in gasps. Blood ran from her flesh, and one arm hung broken. In a final act, the demon molded two arms into her body and leathery wings burst forth in their place. She flapped them in a thunderous clap, and a powerful gust pushed Marcelo backward. Screaming in rage, Zelaenah leapt into the air and flew away.

Finally free of her, Marcelo realized he lacked the ability to go after Sybil. Having fallen into a ley line, she could be anywhere in the world right now and would have to fight alone. The thought pained his cold, unbeating heart. Jaw clenched in anguish, he turned and fled the Parthenon.

Burning cars and debris from ruined buildings cluttered the streets of Athens as he sprinted toward the coast. His feet crunched on glass. Dark smoke clouded the sky. Squealing tires and screams echoed in every alley. He reached the area where the Moon Goddess Selene had been protecting ships as the populace fled the demon horde.

The bedlam had not subsided. Citizens packing the docks stampeded to fill small boats, fancy yachts, and fishing vessels. Clothing, bags, shoes, and other personal items littered the ground as families grabbed whatever they could in haste. A multitude of ships raced away from the harbor. Other damaged crafts had capsized or bobbed half submerged, swarms of people flailing in the deep water. Combat and panic exploded everywhere to the backdrop of a once beautiful city in flames.

Selene, bathed in a celestial white glow as she battled on the wharf, swung her lunar lance and tore a knot of beasts in half. Moon powder burst from her palm and blinded two scaled demons. Her weapon impaled a snarling, four-legged creature and she flung it into the sea. The goddess's golden hair hung in ringlets that bounced in each action. Crafted from folded fabric, her long white peplos gown rippled as the deity turned and leapt in a furious struggle.

Nearby, Johann's sharp werewolf claws and teeth ripped open monster flesh. Blood from returned slashes matted his fur. Saliva flew from his maw, his dark eyes narrowed in a savage frenzy. He bowled into groups of demons to knock them flat or spun in a whirlwind of thrashing limbs to strike.

Salix danced in a rhythm of music. The wind, ocean waves, and even the shrill cries of startled gulls represented her full orchestra as it played a sorrowful melody of the planet in turmoil. Notes became her weapons, each crescendo and change in tempo driving the dryad's varied attacks. Her razor-sharp leaves and branches peppered the enemy. She swayed, hopped, and twirled between vicious creatures in a smooth ballet of nature's fury.

And Helios, the ancient Greek sun god, had burst on the scene after Umaq fled. No longer in danger from the demon master, Helios had returned to Selene's side to vanquish the remaining demons and aid the populace. A yellow-orange glow blazed around the deity as he created a giant, glittering raft of starlight. Muscled arms gripped an illuminated oar made from a sun ray. He propelled the shiny vessel through the water and rescued dozens of citizens from the ocean. When a flying monster drew near, the oar doubled as a weapon. The deity swung the hardened sun ray and crushed the demon before it could harm anyone.

Marcelo registered the chaotic environment in an instant, but his fear only grew. Although his friends fought valiantly, the relentless horde of demons would prove too much to handle. Their sheer numbers seemed far higher than expected. After having been blocked from entering the celestial realm, the monsters who followed Umaq to the Areopagus returned to the coast to join the fray. The demon master may have escaped, but the frenzied creatures remained under his control with the sun god still targeted for elimination. For the moment, Marcelo had lost Sybil, but he vowed to stay close to his friends and defend the sun god.

"Johann, Salix, rally around Selene!" he called out.

29

The companions battled their way to the moon goddess, and the group formed a defensive perimeter around the main pier. The demonic mob closed in and intensified their attacks. Selene blasted the area with sizzling moon beams. Marcelo punched and kicked. Johann swiped and bit. Salix launched bone-crunching branches and piercing leaves.

During the fray, Marcelo chanced a quick peek over a shoulder. Helios had safely placed the civilians from his raft onto other vessels. The deity rose into the air and sped over to join his sister at the dock. He landed next to Selene and the others, but immediately dropped to a knee. The sun god appeared exhausted, his eyes squeezed shut. The glow surrounding his body had diminished. He tried to stand, but collapsed once again.

"The supernova," Helios panted. "It took nearly all my strength to expel Umaq from the celestial realm, and I'm spent. I…I can scarcely remain awake."

As if to drive the point home, Marcelo's skin suddenly began to heat from the sunlight. If Helios lost consciousness, the protection from the celestial rays would vanish—the daylight would incinerate Marcelo as it did in Machu Picchu.

The sun god's feebleness rejuvenated the demon horde. The creatures pressed in, a mighty wall of fangs, horns, and muscled flesh stomping their way forward to a chorus of snarls and roars. Marcelo cursed as his strength also left him, and smoke began to rise from his undead skin. Realizing their advantage, the enemy exploited the weakening side of the perimeter and knocked Marcelo to the ground in a coordinated rush.

Sets of hooves and clawed feet pounded him in repeated blows. The crush of bodies over him provided shade, the one thing Marcelo felt grateful for. However, he wouldn't last too long under this furious attack. His wrist snapped. An ankle popped out of place. Black, dead blood spurted from a broken nose.

Out of nowhere, Salix's sweet, melodic voice floated to him in her dryad language. *Worry not, Marcelo. I will end this now. The sun god, and all of Athens, will be safe. I am ready.*

Skittering leaves, lapping water from the sea, and crackling fire were nearby sounds that represented her words. Each resonance carried Salix's emotions—fear, contentment, grief, and pleasure. The sentiments mixed together in a giant heartbeat that thundered not only to Marcelo, but across the entire planet. The phenomenon characterized a beautiful heart filled with deep love, no regrets, and satisfaction.

"No, Salix!" Marcelo pleaded.

The hard blows continued to pelt him, but he sensed nothing. The only pain he experienced came from what he anticipated—the loss of a beloved friend.

Salix jumped high and sailed outward far past the encircling mob. Her olive-green figure, the size of a child, landed in a grassy and wooded area beyond the docks. In a bright flash of light and sudden howl of wind, the dryad transformed into a small tree devoid of leaves. The trunk began to grow, stretching, groaning, and wide as a house. In a breathtaking wonder, the tree shot upward and exploded in size until it towered high over the city. Foliage sprouted on hundreds of branches until each hefted thousands of long, narrow leaves.

The rough bark appeared gray and ridged. The long, elegant limbs swept down in arches toward the ground. Narrow leaves blazed light green on their top side and showed a hint of silver dazzling underneath. The rounded, open canopy and drooping branches provided the familiar gracefulness of the classic and gorgeous weeping willow.

The giant willow trembled, and a moment later the cement beneath Marcelo shook as the tree radiated massive amounts of subterranean energy. All around the area, hundreds of roots burst from the ground in sprays of earth and concrete. Each gnarled root pierced a demon through its back or punctured the monster's chest. From the branches, rattling leaves broke off to swarm the flying beasts in dark clouds and slice the creatures into pieces. Everywhere, not a single demon escaped Salix's wrath of nature.

The towering willow grew still, and the shaking stopped. After the hectic din of battle, an odd, heavy silence blanketed the docks. Even the interior of Athens lay quiet as no vehicles moved, monsters roared, or terrified citizens shouted.

A wide, cool shadow loomed over Marcelo as Johann's large form protected him from the sun. The werewolf stared at the tree and cried in silence, each tear matting the fur beneath his eyes.

Selene tended to her brother. She pressed a hand against Helios' chest and directed lunar waves into his body. The sun god opened his eyes and stood, groaning. He gestured to the sky and restored the protective filter effect over the city.

Marcelo observed the lofty weeping willow and swallowed a shout building in his throat. Oh, beloved dryad, child of the tree. Why? He knew the reason and would have done the same to save his friends. But Salix's noble gesture didn't make the pain any less. In fact, the agony bore into his unbeating heart even more. It gouged his chest and bled his cold insides in grief.

Johann reverted to his naked human form. Still in tears, he picked through a pile of clothing that had spilled from a broken suitcase left by a fleeing citizen. He donned a mismatched outfit then placed both hands over his face, his shoulders sagging in grief.

Marcelo stepped over and embraced his friend. "She saved us, the brat," he said in a thick voice.

"Salix babylonica," Johann replied, referring to the species of tree she had become. He wiped his eyes. "Easy to grow and quick to take root. My little plant face pulled out all the stops."

The dryad belonged to *Salix delnortensis*, or Del Norte willow, a species native to the massive Klamath Mountains of southern Oregon and northern California that only grew one or two meters tall. However, the dryad's selflessness converted her into the magnificent, mystical version of weeping *Salix babylonica*.

"Her yellow flowers will bloom in late winter or spring," Marcelo commented.

Johann suddenly glanced about, his expression frantic. "Where in the hell is Sybil? I lost myself in the fog of war and assumed she arrived with you. And then Salix…" He trailed off. "Is Sybil all right?"

Salix's fate lay before Marcelo in the form of an enormous, elegant tree that had saved not only Athens, but the world. The pain of her loss had not subsided—it festered in a deep wound of sorrow, anger, and regret. As for Sybil, he could only shake his head at Johann's inquiry. The tired gesture represented vulnerability and additional ache he dared not accept until the truth stood before him.

"Umaq dragged her into a ley gate when he escaped," Marcelo explained. "She could be anywhere by now."

He wiped away the dried blood from his nose and looked away into the distance. His broken wrist had already started to heal. The bones moved beneath his skin, grinding, molding back together. His crooked foot where the ankle had separated worked to repair itself. The injuries would take time to fully recover, as did the horrible breaks in his arm that occurred during his fight against Daiyu.

Johann raised a trembling hand and gripped Marcelo's shoulder. Already distraught from losing Salix, the werewolf's eyes had grown fierce amid pale features. "We can't do anything about our dryad, but we will find our witch. That crazy powerful girl is still fighting, I know it."

"As do I," Helios proclaimed as he approached with Selene. Soiled and torn from combat, his white tunic barely clung to a shoulder. Snapped leather cords dangled from both of his ruined sandals. However, after Selene's treatment, solar energy bathed the renewed sun god, his white eyes glowing and alert. "If not for young Sybil, I would not have been able to defeat Umaq. She's an amazing witch, the strongest I've ever met."

Marcelo bowed to the deities. "I wish we could stay to help restore your beautiful city and aid the people."

"Selene and I will ensure the health and safety of everyone around," said Helios. He frowned at the dead demons. "Not to mention cleaning this place up."

Selene smiled and placed a hand over her heart. "This victory could not have taken place without all of

34

you here," the moon goddess said. "Unfortunately, more work remains for everyone. I must toil here while you search for Sybil." She exchanged a knowing look with her brother. "But before you depart, Helios and I have a present for you, our method of giving thanks."

The deities lifted their arms, and heavenly light illuminated their bodies. A flaming ball representing the sun appeared between Helios' hands, and a white moon came to life between Selene's. The round lights zoomed toward the sky and hovered over the giant weeping willow. The pair of spheres danced around each other, opposites in meaning but together in purpose.

A gray cloud formed over the tree canopy. Rain poured, and glistening water trickled down each leaf and branch. Refracted beneath the real sun, rainbows burst from each drop that fell to the ground like tears as the weeping willow characterized its name.

The sun and moon spheres joined. Light burst from the new ball and dried the moisture from the tree. An enchanted breeze swayed the drooping branches, and a small object fell from one of them. The wind scooped up the item and dropped it into Marcelo's outstretched hand. Resembling a large green caterpillar, he recognized a catkin. These slim, cylindrical flower clusters had ordinary petals or none at all, and were usually pollinated by wind or insects.

"Your beloved dryad turned into the Salix babylonica," Selene began. "The full transformation is permanent, and here her soul will remain. However, a fraction of her spirit lives inside the catkin gifted to you. Take the flower and plant it in her native region. Allow the willow to grow, and the Salix you knew will be born again. Years may pass before the process is complete, but after sweet patience and bitter time, the dryad will once again dance through the forest."

Johann sniffled and wiped his red eyes for the second time. "My emotions can't take much more of this. I'd rather fight the demon horde." He bowed to the deities. "I have no words to express my gratitude."

"Nor do I," Marcelo said in a near whisper. Guilt pricked him. He had allowed hope to diminish when Sybil tumbled into that hole. Yet Salix's pending return renewed the flame of optimism. In times like these, he missed the skipping of his heart when emotion overwhelmed him. "This is truly wonderful. I am in your debt."

Helios inclined his head toward Marcelo and Johann. "And Athens is in yours. The names of Sybil, Johann, Salix, and Marcelo will forever be remembered here, like the Acropolis."

Smiling, Johann gestured toward the massive tree dominating the landscape. "I suppose the city will have a new tourist attraction for everyone to remember our little dryad."

Marcelo also smiled and bobbed the catkin on his palm, then slipped it into a pocket. "Time to go, Johann. Let's extend this moment of good fortune and use it to find Sybil."

"You will reunite with her, I'm certain of it," said Selene. "Take my chariot, Marcelo. Fly beside the sun and moon. Use the celestial bodies as beacons to guide your heart."

The moon goddess waved both her arms, and the glorious chariot materialized on the dock. The white horses stamped and snorted. The long manes on the steeds' necks danced. Shining like a gem, the wheeled chariot beckoned a rider to soar into the heavens.

Marcelo rotated his damaged wrist and flexed his fingers. His grip would remain weak for a while longer, but he'd manage. In regard to his broken heart, no cure existed until he found Sybil safe.

"I only hope I can fly as well as Sybil," he said, climbing aboard.

Johann stepped up beside Marcelo and squeezed his shoulder. "Let's bring her home, old man. Where are we headed?"

"To where it all began for us," Marcelo replied. "Machu Picchu. Umaq took a beating, and I bet he'll return to his fortress to hide out and recover."

He gripped the reins, and the team of horses stirred. A mental and emotional connection to the beautiful steeds surged through him. Marcelo marveled at the feeling; every hoof stomp, tail swish, and snort carried an expression of joy, anticipation, and empathy. Sybil had also experienced this wonderful sensation. He imagined her next to him as they both laughed into the wind.

Soon. Soon his beloved would be by his side.

Marcelo flicked his wrists. The glowing moon chariot shot forward as six sets of hooves pounded the dock. He pulled the reins, and the vehicle lifted into the sky. Despite all the daylight, Selene's giant moonbeam flashed into existence ahead—the warp gate to Machu Picchu. Peru was ten hours behind Athens, and plenty of night remained there to find Sybil.

Chapter Four

Reap What Is Sowed

Standing atop the underground ley line, Umaq watched as Sybil plummeted through the opening above and landed at his feet, stunned. He reeled in the lasso and extinguished the black nether energy issuing from a sweaty palm. The effort to pull her inside winded him. Shrapnel from Helios' blast had pierced his side; pain surged and nearly toppled him. The deity's supernova had also scalded Umaq's left arm and leg. Gasping, he leaned on the ley staff and took a moment to recover.

All around, the subterranean darkness pressed in. The only light source originated from the river of earth essence whisking the pair of combatants through the underground. As Umaq performed his ley line travel experiments, he had learned to respect—and fear—the unending, living darkness. Unseen eyes watched. Open mouths breathed. A distant heart thumped. Forever lost in the flows, an inexperienced ley traveler might scream or weep in loneliness. The untried explorer would beg for immediate death or risk a slow, painful digestion in the earth's foul belly.

Sybil and her friends had probably experienced something similar when they attempted to use a ley line and surprise Umaq inside of Machu Picchu. Clearly

38

unprepared, the group had appeared in a chaotic mess of ruptured terrain and fractured earth energy. They had more than likely been lost down here for quite some time before arriving—in sheer luck—at the right place.

As for Umaq, he had had more than enough time to practice ley travel before heading to Athens. His fervid research, intense desire, and sense of urgency allowed him to master the earth flows and transfer a demon army across the planet in moments.

But it had all been for nothing.

He looked down at Sybil and trembled in fury. How many times had this insolent witch ruined his plans? After discovering her abilities in Salem Village, he had waited over three hundred years for her to wake in the prime of her power. The first part of his project had been successful; the crafty witch restored her youth and attracted the false vampire, Marcelo. However, Umaq's spell to control him had failed. The witch's potent love—and other unforeseen factors—had freed Marcelo.

And here she was again, using the very power he had bestowed her to stop him from killing Helios!

Sybil moaned and began to stir. Lying on her side, she suddenly motioned to launch a spell. Umaq kicked her arm and smashed the ley staff against her forehead. She tried to rise, then fell back in a daze.

Pain abruptly flared from Umaq's injuries, and he slumped to his knees. Sweating, he hissed in anguish and struggled to his feet.

"Harming people with magic is fun, but there's nothing like old fashioned physical violence," he told her, out of breath.

Sybil eyed the ley staff as he raised it over her. "Then finish me forthwith," she said weakly, her face

39

bloody. "Truly, you have already lost, and my heart is satisfied. Helios lives, and yonder demon army shall be annihilated."

Not long after obtaining the dark power of the netherworld, Umaq had desired to renew his attempt to control Marcelo and turn Sybil into a demonic undead. However, his recent downfall and subsequent rage obliterated that idea. Only their violent deaths would satisfy him now.

He stared down at the witch and ran through a few scenarios. Crush her skull. Incinerate the girl in a magnificent blaze. Feed her to the worker demons at Machu Picchu. So many options, what should he do?

Sybil rolled over and threw up. Some black liquid poured from her open mouth and splashed onto the shimmering teal ley line. She coughed, gagged, and retched again. The witch struggled to her hands and knees. She trembled in place, head lolling as she spit to clear her mouth of the dark residue.

"That's dark nether essence spewing from your body," Umaq observed in wonder.

He recognized the same blackness that coursed inside him ever since he took it from the portal to the netherworld. How could the dark energy reside within Sybil? He hadn't struck her with any such spell, and she had certainly never set foot in the demon realm to absorb the power.

Wait…could it be?

Umaq grabbed the bottom edge of her shirt and yanked it up halfway. An ugly wound festered on her lower right side, the spot where he had stabbed her with the enchanted black dagger. In Machu Picchu, he had crafted the weapon from raw nether essence that poured from Inti's ancient altar. The blade had been used to exterminate the Inca god of the sun, but Umaq had also wielded it to fend off Sybil as she attempted to stop him.

The dagger must have infected her body with the foul energy of the netherworld. Her symptoms must have been gradual and certainly unexpected. It seemed the illness had fully manifested now, and it couldn't have been a more perfect time. The methods he had pondered over how to kill her would prove too easy and quick. Afterall, there could be no good pleasure without torment.

"O happy dagger!" he sang, quoting *Romeo and Juliet*. He used the bottom of the staff to tilt Sybil's face in his direction. "I could kill you now, but I'd rather you suffer here in the earth's bowels. You navigated the ley line once but are in no condition to master it now. Choke more on your black vomit. Bleed out the nether darkness and drown in it. Ride the ley flows until you shrivel in agony and death. From the surface, I'll hear your cries for help that will never be answered."

Sybil reached out in a feeble attempt to grab his leg. He stepped away and laughed, then winced in pain. Time to take care of himself. Good thing returning home to Machu Picchu would be simple.

Umaq adjusted the ley staff in his grip. He had named it World Key, as the device allowed access to any ley gate throughout the planet. Smiling, he admired the rod he had fashioned himself after an incredible amount of labor and sweat. Two prongs extended at the tip, one just longer than the other. The shoulder-height length and odd fork design allowed the right frequency to emit when he struck the tines. The double rich tones had been the secret to splitting the terrain and accessing the twisting

41

rivers of earth energy. Once underground, manipulating the ley flows became routine after he had mastered the use of World Key.

After a final glance at Sybil, he lifted the staff and plunged the end into the ley river. He spent a few moments twisting the shaft left and right a few degrees, searching until the rod glowed bright. This signified his destination had locked into place. The teal-colored river split, and a new channel coursed in a curve to the left. He removed World Key and hopped over to the correct current. Looking back, he watched Sybil rush away in the opposite direction until the darkness swallowed her.

"Die!" he hollered. "What goes around, comes around."

A short time later, Umaq used the staff to swirl a portion of the ley river in a small circle. The earth energy swelled beneath his feet, and a column grew to lift him toward the surface. Holding the blue ley stone tied around his neck, he struck the tines on the end of the rod and a pair of sonorous notes rang.

Overhead, a loud rumble shook the layer of soil and stone blocking the way out. A crack yawned open, and pre-dawn darkness and starlight filtered into the underground chasm as the rising column reached the gap. He stepped off the makeshift elevator and into the temple ruins near the altar of Intihuatana in Machu Picchu.

The hole closed behind him as he strolled into the elevated courtyard on a hill overlooking the ancient city of the Incas. In minutes, Umaq had left the midday sun in Athens and returned to a spectacular, star-filled sky on the other side of the planet. As the mountain stood away from the bright lights of a modern city, here the endless celestial bodies blazed in their glorious explosions against the black canvas of space.

Below the hill among the ancient structures, the shadowy forms of many lesser demons on patrol moved throughout the dark, silent paths. With Umaq's vicious guards and magical defenses, the foolish human armies had long since given up on attempting to retake Machu Picchu from his grasp.

He ran a finger along World Key to stimulate the ley energy it had been crafted from. A bluish light brightened from the pronged tip, and he held it before him as a lamp. Leaving the temple, he crossed over to the altar and admired the stonework; carved shelves and benches had been worked into the large rectangular base. Several intricate surfaces and angles had been cut, features that served to study astronomy, provide a seasonal calendar, and for worshipping the sun.

Umaq lay a palm on top of the altar. The stone vibrated from the immense mystical energy saturating the mountain. Through his touch, he absorbed some of the natural force and manipulated it to heal his body. Torn flesh molded together, and bruises faded. Cracked ribs mended, and smooth skin replaced burns.

Refreshed, he left the courtyard and descended several steps into the Sacred Plaza. Under his control, the worker demons had completed a remarkable job of restoring the ancient buildings. Original stone and new had been meshed to rebuild the strong walls of temples and walking paths. Historically, this principal area had characterized the political center of Machu Picchu, as well as hosting various celebrations and festivals.

The Temple of the Three Windows represented the most important structure in the Sacred Plaza. Umaq

43

stepped inside and snapped on a few battery-operated lamps. A simple one-room structure, the demons had fashioned a new roof, thick pillar, and stone-tiled floor. Along the back wall, the three windows overlooked the Central Plaza, a grassy strip that divided the city in two. Each window could be utilized as a portal, and Umaq had made extensive use of the opening called Uku-Pacha.

Here, the portal to the netherworld had been activated. His demons had poured through the gateway, lesser and higher-tier monstrosities that aided him in killing the sun deity, Inti, and nearly destroying Helios. Splashed across the floor and over the windowsill, blood stains tarnished the old stone from when Umaq murdered one of Cessani's witches to activate the portal. Yet having had insufficient mystical energy to sustain the opening, Uku-Pacha randomly flashed on for minutes at a time or only seconds. Currently, the window sat dormant; only the nighttime darkness and shining stars displayed.

Umaq moved to the corner of the temple and knelt before a heavy wooden coffer. He threw back the lid and revealed a collection of items used for spell casting. Tools, potions, powders, jewelry, and various artifacts lined the bottom. He extracted dozens of odd-shaped bones he had unearthed from the soil beneath his ancient home, then laid them on the floor until the skeleton of a demon took shape.

Hundreds of years ago, this monster had marked a significant advancement—and disappointment—in Umaq's quest to become a master of his work. He had performed a new, complicated experiment to fuse this demon's soul to a human body. Marcelo had been the unwitting participant; unfortunately, the test failed and turned him into an odd, blood-drinking, undead creature similar to a vampire.

Umaq had recently uncovered the old demon's dusty bones for another future experiment. However, he never expected to use the skeleton out of necessity. With his global plan of conquest shattered for now, this long-dead creature provided the ace in his sleeve, a final chance at redemption.

While Sybil rotted in the darkness beneath his feet, he could now focus on eliminating Marcelo. After the witch and copycat vampire were gone, Umaq's goal of uniting the demon realm with this one might still see fruition. The portal to the dark netherworld continued to operate, although randomly. Many more beasts could be summoned to destroy another sun god. After Inti, the second deity's bloody death would smother the world in darkness and permanently destroy the mystical barrier between realms.

But first, the bones. Umaq dove into his work. He manipulated every tool and magical ingredient in the coffer. When those items depleted, he collected from his house more objects and components for spell casting. Several tomes spread on the floor, the ancient pages turned to the darkest of magics. Incense wafted and candles burned. He swayed in trance, spoke in dead languages, and moved in formal ritual around the demon skeleton.

The most critical of ingredients poured out from Umaq's heart. His hatred, malevolence, and longing for revenge fueled each spell, gesture, and forceful word. He envisioned Sybil suffering greatly from her illness and screaming in the fathomless underground. He visualized Marcelo torn to pieces and cast into a roaring blaze.

At some point the sun rose low, and new light filtered through the windows. Sweat poured and Umaq gasped in exertion; however, the most difficult portion had not commenced. He took several deep breaths and mentally prepared himself for the certain pain to come.

His arms spread wide, he shouted commands in a demonic tongue. Black nether energy burst from his skin in smoky tendrils and hovered in a cloud. The dark mass then descended onto the skeleton. Bones rattled on the floor. Candles burned hotter, brighter. Book pages fluttered. Incense smoke swirled in fast eddies throughout the temple.

Tendons, ligaments, and muscle began to grow on the bones. Veins and arteries stretched and snaked around limbs and torso. Gray flesh formed and spread over the body. Razor-sharp teeth and claws emerged. Bony spikes rose across the creature's shoulders, and leathery wings sprouted from its back.

The demon drew a breath, its first in hundreds of years. A misshapen head lifted, and six slanted eyes blinked once. The monster pushed itself up and stood on clawed feet, its height towering above Umaq. The demon inspected its long-fingered hands and flapped its wings. Its gray skin glistened, and muscles flexed in movement.

Umaq's magnificent new experiment had been a success! Intense pride swelled as he studied the demon. The first time he had summoned this creature centuries ago, it had crawled out half-dead from a crude portal of fire in his hut. Now the demon stood tall, strong, and ready to—

The monster charged and batted Umaq to the ground. He grunted as the beast pinned him beneath its muscled arm and sniffed through tiny slits above its maw. Saliva glistened and drooled between its bared teeth.

"I don't have what you're looking for," Umaq said, straining beneath the beast. "But you know who does."

A growl rumbled in the creature's chest as it stared. Umaq observed the absolute emptiness in its eyes as no soul occupied the body. Only sheer madness lurked in its gaze, a rampant confusion and longing to be complete. Devoid of its soul, the demon existed in a half-life internal prison of despair. Marcelo possessed the demonic spirit, the beast's missing half and key to alleviating the insanity. The tortured demon would stop at nothing to repossess it. The crazed monster would scour the earth for Marcelo and rip him open to extract the prize.

Umaq had resurrected the demon for this very purpose, to finalize his revenge and clear the way to total victory. Killing Sybil and Marcelo signified an enormous satisfaction following the debacles in Salem and Athens.

The creature roared and ran out of the temple in long, bounding strides.

"Happy hunting," Umaq called out as he stood with effort.

A sudden wave of dizziness swayed him, heart hammering trickles of sweat moistened his forehead. Fatigue nearly buckled his legs. The spell to resurrect the creature had severely weakened him. It felt as if every drop of blood had been sucked from his body. He closed his eyes and remained calm until the worst of the sensations disappeared.

Feeling somewhat better, he began cleaning up the items scattered along the floor. He then froze at the

47

unexpected appearance of a woman in the doorway. Had one of Cessani's witches returned to Machu Picchu for something?

The old woman sagged against the stone frame as if exhausted. Stringy gray hair hung unkempt, and strands partially concealed her withered features. Her clothing appeared too baggy for her skinny body. The patterned, short-sleeved tan shirt wrapped a narrow torso, the exposed skin on her arms like shriveled tree bark. Worn jeans draped loose over a thin waist and two scrawny legs. The designer sneakers and colored laces—

Umaq gasped in shock. He suddenly recognized the outfit because he had just seen it about an hour ago…on Sybil Radella Cotterill!

Impossible. How could this old woman be the young witch or at least someone wearing her clothes? A short while ago, Umaq had exiled the girl to darkness and despair deep underground. She would soon die in serious agony from the black sickness. If she somehow managed to survive that, starvation would take her life in a matter of days.

"Who are you?" Umaq demanded.

She didn't speak or move. Unease prickled his skin as he slowly approached the woman. She remained in the doorway, breathing deep and slumped against the frame in effort to remain standing. Her head hung low, frail arms loose at her sides.

"What do you want?" he asked.

When she refused to answer, he reached out and parted the greasy strands of hair from her forehead. The woman strained to lift her chin and finally met his gaze. Umaq stepped back in disbelief. A volatile mix of fear and anger boiled in his gut.

It was Sybil!

Somehow. Even much older, no mistake. That face and those piercing eyes belonged to the witch he had tormented back in Salem Village over three hundred years ago. The look belonged to the same young girl he had captured and fought in modern Salem, battled against in Athens, and left below ground in what seemed minutes ago.

"What...h-how?" Umaq stammered.

Sybil only stared. After a moment, she found enough strength to walk inside the temple. She glanced around in confusion, her odd expression a million miles away, as if she had no idea where she stood or why she had come.

Inspired by her weak and distraught manner, Umaq moved to study her more closely. Black stains he recognized as nether essence covered the front of her blouse. Dark smudges tainted her hands, mouth, and chin. Each stain appeared old, as if her skin and clothes had been dyed many years ago. Her outfit also seemed aged. The colors had faded, and the material appeared threadbare in places.

During Umaq's experiments using the ley line, he had discerned that time could bend in the eternal flows of earth energy. Yet he dared not tempt fate with such a dangerous phenomenon and had steered clear of further studies. If someone incorrectly manipulated the ley line, they could lose or advance hours, even days in the tunnels.

But for Sybil to have aged *decades*...

Umaq could only just imagine what she had gone through below ground. Since returning from Athens, an hour had passed for him and nearly a lifetime for her.

49

This was the second time he had robbed her of youth and stolen her life. Well, he wanted her to suffer and she had. Sybil seemed a shell of herself, lost in madness and confusion like the demon he had unleashed moments ago. What a perfect pair the monster and witch made.

Umaq smiled and resumed tidying up the area. He thought of telling Sybil all about the demon and its deadly purpose, but refrained after another opportunity presented to continue the girl's torture. He didn't doubt she would soon reunite with Marcelo, and afterwards, Umaq's demented monster would tear Marcelo apart right before her eyes. Escaping from the ley tunnel did not mean an end to her nightmare. Umaq might as well sit back and enjoy that moment when it came.

"Umaq," Sybil uttered in a hoarse voice.

He turned and stared in surprise. "So, you are slightly cognizant after all. Yes, it is me. You won the battle in Athens, but my work here is not finished. The nether portal is still functioning, my bastion remains untouchable, and darker times are coming your way."

Sybil lifted an arm to try and cast a spell, but nothing happened. A black drop oozed from her nose and dripped on the floor as the illness still gripped her.

Umaq grinned and stepped close to place a hand on her shoulder. "No gas left in the tank for magic? It seems—"

A coil of dark nether essence suddenly wrapped his wrist. Umaq shouted in pain as his skin burned. Had Sybil...no. This attack came from elsewhere. From his wrist, he saw a long tether of dark energy stretching back to the activated portal in the Uku-Pacha window. The cord had originated from within the demon realm.

50

Like a snake, another black coil burst from the portal and encircled his opposite arm. Startled by the mysterious assault, Umaq grunted and struggled to pull away. Two more cords snapped forth to ensnare his waist and neck. Pain overwhelmed him and he fell to his knees. In tears, he glanced into the dark abyss on the other side of the portal.

Someone wanted him inside.

A prior conversation with Cessani flashed in his mind, one that took place before his invasion of Athens. Full of greed and pure arrogance, he had siphoned—or stolen—the dark power through the portal and had grown more powerful than ever.

You don't realize how dangerous this is, the old witch had said. *You've already achieved triumph over Inti. Our plan succeeded, and the new era will begin. What more do you want?*

To be a true god, Umaq had replied, smug and nonchalant toward any consequence over his actions.

Zelaenah had also warned him about stealing from the demonic gods, but for centuries, Umaq had long disregarded the strength and influence of irrelevant deities. During an argument with the demon, he had again boasted about his newfound power.

I take what I want, he had told her.

And pissed off the underworld gods while doing so, she had responded. *Using black nether energy to defeat Inti is one thing, but taking it into your body for personal advantage while claiming equivalence to the deities? That's another level of stupid entirely. Do you believe your egotism will go unpunished?* I can't wait to see the dark gods rip your flesh off.

Cessani and even Zelaenah had been right…and Umaq a total fool.

He screamed in raw panic. Having just mocked Sybil, it seemed he had no gas left in the tank either as several attempts at magic did nothing. The black tethers dragged him closer to the window. He thrashed and rolled on the floor, kicked out and clawed the stone tile.

"Sybil!" he cried out in desperation. "Help me, please! Free me and I can cure your sickness, I swear it. Your youth…I can restore it." Near death and half out of her wits, would she even believe or understand him at this point?

The coils lifted Umaq from the floor and jerked him onto the windowsill. He threw his arms out and gripped the edges of the stone. He strained to hold on, muscles trembling. Behind him, the vast darkness of the demon realm awaited. He felt is icy and scalding breath on the back of his neck. Remaining still, Sybil gave no sign of wanting to assist.

"The Inca sun god can be revived!" he pleaded. "The dark gods keep Inti's spirit like a trophy. Save me and kill three birds with one stone—your sickness gone, youth returned, and the sunlight restored."

He promised Sybil everything she could desire on a silver platter, but his words sounded hollow and useless. He had deceived and harmed this witch for hundreds of years. And now, the evil man sobbing for help would say anything. But his offer held truth; Umaq really could do all three of those things. He would have added stopping the resurrected demon from harming Marcelo; unfortunately, that proved impossible as the creature functioned out of his control.

Sybil only stared. Although part of her mind seemed to remain, her expressionless face and vacant eyes reminded him of the senseless demon raging in madness. Did she even register anything he had said? She appeared very confused and not in touch with her surroundings as the decades lost to the subterranean gloom had unleashed its toll on her wellbeing.

Umaq's grip along the stone edges weakened. Unable to hold on, the black coils yanked him into the portal. He left in a cry of terror and anguish, his body tumbling backward into a madness of his own.

Chapter Five

Reunion

Sybil watched Umaq vanish into the portal. His scream faded as the window flickered between the demon realm and this one. After several moments, the gateway closed and the scenery through the opening displayed the darkened meadow of the Central Plaza in Machu Picchu.

It was finally over. Umaq had been defeated, and Helios remained safe.

But…where had she arrived to, and why? Who was the strange man that just disappeared through the window? Hadn't she just known him a moment ago and felt relieved about something?

Ongoing weariness buckled Sybil's legs, and she collapsed on the stone tile. A million thoughts and flashes of memory whirled in her head. She floated and fell. She laughed and cried. Pain. Distress. Grief…and more pain. Insanity. Clarity.

Umaq…yes, Umaq had been defeated. Sybil had fought him in Athens and inside the ley tunnel.

She suddenly screamed. Nightmares and terror. Tears spilled, and she curled into a fetal position on the floor. A darkened and powerful trauma pummeled her distraught cognizance. Lost and lonely. So terrified and desperate. Unanswered pleas and far, empty voices. No human contact for years.

The black trauma wrapped around Sybil and squeezed. She shivered and sweated under the strain. Her mind contracted and threatened to rupture. Her heart bled emotion and she struggled to breathe.

"Marcelo," she called weakly.

She had gotten lost in a subterranean hell. The never-ending ley flows had carried her across the planet for what seemed an eternity. She had aged, but returned to the near present time from when she first fell into the hole. How did she escape the underground? What had kept her from completely losing her wits? Some blind spots remained, but for the moment, she had regained enough presence of mind to somewhat understand her whereabouts and situation.

Sybil struggled to stand. She headed for the exit, swayed on her feet, then steadied herself against the doorway. Outside, the stars in the night sky blazed in a gorgeous glitter of white fire among the heavens. She hadn't seen the sky or felt a sweet breeze in years. The sensations equaled a loving caress, and she immediately thought of her beloved Marcelo and dear friends. Were they still in Athens? Were they safe?

She sneezed, and black nether residue sprayed from her mouth. The illness hadn't gone away, which brought another question—how had she not died from the sickness? In Athens, it seemed like she had been fading fast. The unexpected infection had worsened by the hour. It didn't seem possible she had somehow survived underground for decades.

She thought about Umaq's desperate bargaining before he had vanished. Could he really restore Sybil's youth and end her sickness? Did a small chance exist to revive the sun god, Inti?

Too tired to ponder the unanswered inquiries, the overwhelming exhaustion demanded she rest. She headed for the grassy lawn of the Central Plaza and lay down on the cool blades, not caring if Umaq's demons still prowled. It didn't matter if one of them mauled her in the middle of Machu Picchu. Age and illness plagued her. Withering health drained her body and soul. Her mind persisted as a fragile mess; the trauma had eroded her mental and emotional wellbeing.

She truly loved Marcelo, a deep and unyielding adoration that would endure forever. Nothing would change that, but perhaps the time had arrived to say farewell. Better he remember her as a spirited youth in his arms and not a broken, emaciated shell lying at his feet.

A four-legged demon eventually came and woke her from a doze. Sybil lay still as the beast sniffed along her body. It pawed the ground next to her and smelled her face. The creature growled, then trotted away into the shadows.

Sybil sat up in surprise. The demon had seemed only curious. With Umaq gone, the creatures he had loosed upon the world may no longer be under his control, but that didn't explain why this monster hadn't ripped her to shreds. Having a free will, the beast had passed up an easy meal on the grass. Could it be the blackness inside her? If true, then that might explain why the demon had left Sybil alone.

She lay back down and sighed. More questions, more fatigue. Umaq had been defeated, and that's all that mattered. Time to sleep.

The wind roared and pulled her out from a nightmare. Grogginess dulled her senses and fractured her awareness again. Where was she? A light flashed in the sky, and Sybil sat up for the second time. The light grew larger and approached. Confusion stunned her as a glowing white chariot and team of horses touched down on the grass. The brightness lit the surrounding field as if the moon itself had floated to Earth. A few demons bolted from spaces that no longer held shadow.

Had she died? Would this odd vehicle transport her to the afterlife? Two men emerged from the chariot and sprinted to her side. One of them appeared to be a vampire and the other a werewolf in human form. She wasn't sure how she knew that, but something about the men seemed familiar.

The black-haired vampire held her, his green eyes wide and face stunned. He possessed the look of a very young man; however, lifetimes of emotional stress dominated his timeless gaze, the weight of the world etched into his smooth features. Bathed in light from the chariot, he seemed to be an angelic figure—so she had died after all. He called her name over and over. Panic, concern, and profound love saturated his tone. He caressed her face and kissed her mouth. His touch felt even more familiar...she knew him, somehow.

The other man knelt next to Sybil and gripped her withered hand in both of his. A blond ponytail hung down his back, wispy bangs low near his eyebrows. He cried, a torment of his own lurking in his dark-eyed stare. Pain dwelled in his soul, a deep, repeated agony that threatened to blacken a heart filled with so much life and love. She knew him, too, and wished to soothe his discomfort.

The men spoke to each other, but Sybil only half-listened. Her interrupted sleep left her even more tired. Before she knew it, the vampire lifted her in his arms and carried her to the chariot. Inside, he sat next to her and wrapped a cold arm around her shoulders. Yet the cool embrace calmed her, the gesture wakening more memories a fraction at a time.

"Take us home now to California, Johann," the vampire said. "She's not well at all. The questions and answers will come later. For now, we need to get her somewhere safe."

Johann's face twisted in a comical expression. "Pilot this thing? No way. Dogs don't fly."

"I need to keep an eye on Sybil," the undead answered.

Not an undead. Not a monster, blood-drinker, or a stranger. Marcelo. Her true love and partner in life. Her best and brightest memories of him returned. Exhausted and barely conscious, she leaned in and held him.

"Sybil?" Marcelo asked in surprise. He pulled back and studied her, his expression eager, eyes full of hope. "Are you all right?"

Battling the fog in her mind, she started to rise, and he helped her stand on unsteady feet. Sybil moved to Johann and embraced the speechless werewolf. His warm, emotional hug spoke volumes as he also waited for her to say something, to see if she was all right. She released her good friend and stepped to the edge of the chariot.

"Where is our dear Salix?" she asked softly, avoiding Marcelo's question.

She almost dared not inquire about the dryad. While Sybil had lain in the grass and Johann held her

58

hand, she recognized something in his tears, a prior pain that made sense now as the werewolf's face fell.

Johann explained what occurred in Athens, of his little plant face's heroic sacrifice. Marcelo showed her the catkin and explained it may be years before Salix would revive.

Sybil took the green cylindrical flower cluster and kissed it. "I shall see you again, dear dryad," she whispered, her heart wrapped in emotional ache. Her trembling hand returned the catkin, and she turned away to look over the Central Plaza.

"My love, what happened to you?" Marcelo pressed, certainly desperate for answers and concerned about her welfare.

Sybil chose to remain quiet. Marcelo touched her shoulder, but she moved away. She wasn't ready to talk. Her distressed, broken mind hadn't healed from the black ley line trauma—it may never achieve true recovery. The dark, unknown gaps of memory from her decades-long underground experience terrified her into near paralysis. She couldn't close her eyes without a harrowing nightmare ripping her apart.

How longer would the problems continue? Worrying would not make the situation any easier. For the moment, Sybil had made a promise to a cherished friend she would not break. It signified the one thing under her control when everything else had spiraled into madness and despair.

"Grace," she said, looking up at the stars and changing the subject. "Hitherto, she is a prisoner in yonder Salem. Please take us forthwith. Cessani hath claimed she would release Grace after Umaq's defeat. I had a fair sight of him, and he was forced into the netherworld. 'Tis no longer necessary to feel disquieted about that man."

Sybil glanced between Marcelo and Johann. She lacked the energy, or the willpower, to explain anything further. Hopefully her short oration had been enough to satisfy them for now.

Marcelo's eyes pleaded for more. *My love, what happened to you*, he had asked. His desperate, pained words had expressed volumes. Sybil knew he wanted nothing more than to hold her close to him and make everything better. She loved him for that, but at the moment, all she could offer was a reassuring nod.

Marcelo acknowledged her gesture. He returned a soft smile that signified, *I am here whenever you're ready*. He stepped to the front of the chariot and took the reins. The horses sped down the meadow and lifted the vehicle into the air. A moonbeam transported the group to the darkened skies over Salem, Massachusetts.

Only one hour ahead of Peru, night stretched over the city as the team of horses touched down onto the verdant park of Salem Common. Sybil climbed out, grateful for Marcelo's supporting arm as they strolled across the thick grass near a large white gazebo. The illumination from the chariot winked out as the steeds disappeared.

"We landed right in the middle of one of my worst experiences," Johann said, frowning. "Thanks, Marcelo."

Sybil recalled a moon-drunk Johann in his werewolf form, fighting amid a makeshift arena in the center of the park. A rowdy throng of witches and monsters had captured intoxicated werewolves and placed bets on the helpless creatures in forced battles.

Salem Common now rather stood quiet, although a few supernatural beings moved along the shadowed tree line near the street.

"Sorry," Marcelo replied. "It's the best area to land close to the Salem Witch Museum."

The group left the park and crossed Washington Square Street where it intersected with Brown Street. Just ahead stood a castle-like structure with large towers and a brown brick façade. The former Salem Witch Museum had been converted into Cessani's headquarters for her new witch-rule. After Inti's fall, the imbalanced darkness had strengthened witches who worshipped the moon deities. Cessani's followers and expanding covens revered the Maiden of the waxing moon, and Mama Quilla, the Inca Moon Goddess.

The mystical shake-up across the planet had also emboldened supernatural entities. When Sybil had last visited this place, an array of demons, ghosts, vampires, sirens, centaurs, and other creatures flooded the sidewalk and street in front of the museum. They had all come to celebrate the darkening and revel in the presence of a deity, the Maiden, who made a special appearance upon Cessani's rise to power.

The occasion also marked a period of injustice and terror for normal human citizens. Witches and their zombies patrolled the streets and had pacified Salem under both threat and brute force. Grace attempted an uprising against Cessani's punitive rule and had been imprisoned, her coven scattered.

Still leaning on Marcelo's sturdy arm, Sybil approached the building and halted before the guarded entrance. Just as in Salem Common, a few supernatural beings loitered in the area, but nowhere near the amount as before. Small fairies floated in circles, chatting. A knot of witches shared a smoke. Three vampires leaned against the wall of the building and studied Sybil's group. One of them whispered something to another. The undead nodded, then sprinted out of sight.

Two witches in red robes blocked the door. A silver pin in the shape of a waxing moon gleamed on each of their left shoulders.

"Inform Cessani that Sybil hath returned," Sybil told the pair.

One of the witches entered the building. A few moments later, he reappeared to usher everyone inside.

They walked through a newly furnished and freshly painted lobby. Paint cans and tools lay beside unfinished sections of drywall. Other construction and renovation materials sat on tables or spread on the floor, signs of ongoing work for new offices and meeting rooms.

Sybil entered Cessani's office, where this time it lacked the Maiden sprawled on the couch eating a tub of ice cream. A wide shelf held a mess of disorganized books, folders, and loose paperwork. The new carpet appeared clean and the coat of paint bright.

Behind a computer, Cessani bolted to her feet the moment she saw Sybil. The older witch— well, technically Sybil was older now—had silver streaks in her loose black hair. Her robe swished as she moved around the desk to approach. Dark eyes pierced Sybil in a stunned face.

"The guard who announced your arrival said you appeared to have lost your youth, but I didn't believe him until now," Cessani remarked. Her eyes moved up and down, inspecting. "What happened?"

Sybil ignored the question. "Umaq is no more. Release Grace forthwith as your aforesaid promise."

Cessani clucked her tongue. "Not much for chitchat, are you? Well, at least Umaq really is gone. Mama Quilla informed me the moment it happened. As the Inca Moon Goddess, she sensed a...how to describe it...a *calming* of the mountain at Machu Picchu after he vanished. That's quite a victory, so well done." She eyed Marcelo and Johann, then headed for the door. "Follow me."

Sybil stumbled in the hallway, but Marcelo's strong arm kept her upright. Her eyelids had grown heavy, and she could barely concentrate anymore. She required a long sleep to feel better and hopefully restore her spell casting ability. She remembered how no magic had produced when she tried to blast Umaq in the temple.

A few hideous, twitching zombies stood guard in adjoining rooms and other short hallways. Witches also observed the visitors, their hands ready to cast spells. Cessani reached the room that held Grace. The woman launched into a series of gestures and mumbled some incantations to remove the complex enchantment barricading the open doorway. A faint hum stopped the moment the spell dissolved.

"You're free," Cessani said to Grace. "Get out."

Grace emerged. Her long, disheveled blond hair had been tied in a slackening bun, a few escaped strands bobbing. Her wide smile and bright blue eyes fell on the group in the hallway. As expected, she hesitated in shock when she recognized Sybil. Grace exchanged a look with Marcelo, who returned a solemn nod.

The loving, kind woman smiled and took Sybil into her arms. "Thank you, my dear friend. I never doubted you. I worried and cried while thinking of you, but I always knew you'd return." She pulled back and cupped Sybil's face. "Whatever happened to you, dear, we'll find a solution together." Grace exchanged hugs with Marcelo and Johann. "Let's go to my place. All of you look ready for some tea and bourbon."

"Your house, and anywhere within city limits, are the only places you'll go," Cessani remarked.

"Just what do you mean?" Grace asked angrily. "You said I was free."

"You are free from imprisonment, yes," Cessani answered. "But consider this a probation. I can't have you plotting with your coven again. I'll keep watch on you for a period of my choosing. When I'm satisfied you no longer pose a threat, I'll lift the restrictions."

Sybil lashed out and grabbed onto the front of Cessani's robe. Although her grip felt weak, her fatigue vanished as adrenaline surged. "Hitherto you persist, hag! Your prattle and the suffering you have caused Salem irks me so."

Her outburst had caught everyone by surprise. Marcelo tensed, and Johann appeared ready to brawl. Grace pivoted toward the witches down the hall as they moved much closer. The zombies clicked their teeth and snarled.

"Oh, do you think I'm evil?" Cessani asked, her face flustered. "How dare you judge me. From what I understand, you nearly killed a woman to restore your youth the first time." She stepped close and a fierce glare impaled Sybil. "Will you do so again, hypocrite?"

Sybil's hand fell away from the robe. Her spirit withered as the crushing guilt from her early days in Salem returned tenfold. She had not only placed a

64

woman in a coma, but tried to drown a man in front of his entire family as well, both acts of vengeance for Constance's death.

Her gaze lowered to the floor, and she shuffled away in silence. Marcelo reached for her arm, but she pushed his hand away. The others fell in behind her, their footfalls on the tile loud and awkward in her dejected wake.

More anguish—and rage—waited outside. The vampires that had been hanging around by the front wall now approached. The one who left in a hurry earlier had returned accompanied by a fourth vampire, one that stopped Sybil's heart in cold shock.

Daiyu. Black Jade.

On a high rooftop in Salem, the ancient Chinese vampire had attacked Sybil, drank her blood, and left an ugly ice-burn scar on her wrist. The undead woman had also threatened to hurt—or even kill—Marcelo through some kind of trial. However, the crisis in Athens hadn't allowed a moment to discuss the situation about Daiyu.

The vampire grinned at everyone, her light skin almost shining. A thick, black braid hung in front of a shoulder down to her slim waist. A jeweled choker wrapped her neck, equally gemmed bracelets on her wrists. A yellow buttoned blouse and faded jean skirt completed her outfit. No shoes covered bare feet. Black lacquer painted the nails on her fingers and toes.

The other three vampires kept their distance from Black Jade, and it didn't surprise Sybil. Although Daiyu stood short in physique, a dense, freezing, and powerful aura surrounded the woman. The immediate atmosphere around her seemed to crush anything in its path. If she walked too close to someone, the mere proximity would inflict injury or unconsciousness.

Daiyu took a step forward and Sybil retreated out of instinct. Marcelo did the same, but not before grabbing Johann and Grace's shirts to pull them back. Grace and the werewolf hadn't met Black Jade, but both may soon wish they never had.

"The triumphant return," Daiyu announced as she studied the group. Her eyes stopped on Sybil. "Or perhaps not so triumphant. You've seen better days, witch." She flicked her gaze to Marcelo. "Umaq is gone, but your trial is not over. I owe you a judgement."

"Then make it," Marcelo replied, irritation in his voice. "You have no idea of what we went through in Athens..." He glanced in compassion at Sybil. "And elsewhere." He fixed a hardened glare on the vampire. "I'm out of patience and tired of your games. Your test was for me to convince you I'm not a danger to society. I had hoped stopping Umaq would suffice since I don't know any other way."

Daiyu applauded in a mocking gesture. "So you saved the world from a maniac, but does that eliminate the threat from you?"

A blaze of fury ignited inside Sybil, far stronger than what she experienced toward Cessani moments ago. Her gnarled hands curled into fists. She trembled, ready to explode into action. Marcelo was right. Sybil and her friends hadn't suffered in Athens and claimed victory over Umaq only to return to a sneering Daiyu. The ancient vampire enjoyed teasing and torment. As a beaten Sybil had discovered on the rooftop, Black Jade's amusement came from the desolation of others.

But an aged Sybil had no strength to fight and no magic. How could she stop the vampire and end this now?

Luckily, a phone call did it for her. A ringtone of "Sugar" from Maroon 5 boomed from Black Jade's pocket. Smiling, Daiyu took out her phone and glanced at the screen. Her casual attitude and indifference to Sybil and her friends indicated the vampire had no fear of those around her.

Daiyu brought the lavender phone to her ear. "Hey, Ricardo!" she said. "Long time—"

Black Jade's wide smile slowly faded. She froze, listening. Her face melted into shock, a blank stare and wide eyes in a faraway place as the caller apparently told her something dreadful. With her petite frame, youthful outfit, and bare feet on the sidewalk, Daiyu seemed like a teenage girl lost in the city. Hearing the unexpected news, she now appeared vulnerable, almost human in this fleeting moment. Sybil never expected to see that type of look on such a powerful creature, one rivaling the force of a deity.

Her voice strained, Black Jade spoke in Spanish, then ended the call and turned to the other vampires. She gestured, and her crew followed her to a black Cadillac Escalade parked by the curb. Black Jade and the vampires climbed inside the large vehicle, then disappeared down the street.

"Well," Grace said, her face pale. "Seemingly, I've been locked up for too long and we have much to discuss. That was rather unpleasant." She turned to Johann and extended a hand. "I'm Grace, by the way. Thank you for being part of my rescue team."

67

Johann stepped past the hand and embraced the blond witch. "I'm Johann, werewolf and victim of Sybil and Marcelo's exploits. Never a dull moment with those two." He pulled back and smiled. "Grace, I remember you saying something about bourbon? I think we can all use some of that now."

The group found Grace's battered Prius parked further down the street. The bumper sat askew, a crack marred one headlight, and several dents covered the hood. Grace sighed while she inspected a busted-out window.

"I caused most of this damage myself, but I certainly don't remember this window being broken," she observed with a frown.

"At least your ride is here," said Marcelo. "I'm not even sure my car is still parked near Crater Lake in Oregon. For all I know, the thing could be impounded on Mars."

Sybil recalled his poor Aston Martin Rapide left in the underbrush on the side of the road by the lake. Marcelo had taken the group there so she could open a ley gate at the top of a dormant cinder cone on Wizard Island.

Everyone settled inside the Prius. Heading out, Grace recapped her failed attempt to liberate Salem from Cessani and Nastasiya, the foreign necromancer responsible for all the zombie patrols in the city.

"If the Maiden deity hadn't come to Salem and interfered, my coven might have been very successful," Grace finished. "At least Nastasiya isn't here tonight. I don't think I can take much more drama."

For the rest of the short drive, the group rode in silence to Grace's house in south Salem. Too much had happened. Exhaustion sapped everyone's strength and will to converse. In the backseat, Sybil leaned into Marcelo and could barely keep her eyes open. The car eventually pulled onto Cleveland Road and into the asphalt driveway next to a white two-story home.

Large potted plants flanked the steps to a raised wooden porch. Once inside, Grace started preparing a large meal and welcomed Johann's help. While the two worked in the kitchen, Sybil led Marcelo to the couch and pressed her frail, liver spotted hand to his lips. Worry filled his eyes as he glanced at her. A stern gaze reminded him the days of protesting the offering of her blood were long past. Marcelo bit the pad of her thumb and drank while Sybil's opposite hand gently caressed the back of his neck.

The food ready, everyone dug into their plates, followed by hot tea and bourbon. Marcelo spoke of his violent encounter against Black Jade on Dead Horse Beach and the ridiculous trial for him to prove he was not a threat to society. Sybil then added her own brutal experience with Daiyu and how her injured wrist had resulted from their conflict. Afterwards, Johann filled Grace in on the details of what occurred in Athens.

Sybil then narrated what happened to Umaq in Machu Picchu. However, she remained quiet about her experience in the ley tunnel and how she ended up so aged. Additional memories continued to surface, yet she didn't feel ready to share nor desired to remember more. Receiving warm words of support, Sybil loved how her friends respected her decision and in no way pressed for details or made her uncomfortable.

However, her sickness presented one topic she couldn't avoid. During dinner she had hacked black residue into a napkin and sneezed dark droplets into a handkerchief. She explained that the infection resulted when Umaq stabbed her using the dagger crafted from nether essence. Neither she nor anyone else knew of a spell, potion, or other remedy that could treat such a unique disease.

"Do you think Umaq was telling the truth about being able to cure the illness?" Grace asked.

Sybil shrugged. "Facing death, he gave forth desperate prattle. Yet he is gone, and I shall never know the truth. More importantly, to our behoof the world is safe from him forthwith."

Conversation continued without Sybil as her head bobbed in weariness. She picked up random words about Athens and her illness. Later, she grew vaguely aware of being carried, then tucked into a warm bed.

Chapter Six

Shattered Mind

Awake, well fed, showered, and refreshed, Sybil stepped outside into the shade of Grace's porch to say farewell to Johann on this warm day in late July. He stood by the others, backpack slung over a shoulder. The werewolf had a plane to catch, a flight home to Nevada City in California, while Sybil and Marcelo had their own flight later that evening.

Grace embraced Johann and slipped a sandwich into his backpack for the road. Marcelo clasped hands with his friend, then extracted the catkin from a pocket. Sybil took the little willow pod and caressed it before handing it to Johann.

"Take care of Salix," she told him. "And please, send forth greetings to Dom for us."

Sybil had only met Dominic Rossi one time, but Johann's love interest and partner at the nice bed and breakfast in Nevada City had been extremely amiable. She wished to see him again one day.

Johann handled the catkin as if it were made of glass. He placed it safely in a small round container and hugged Sybil. "I will set up my little plant face in the warmest, comfiest spot in her home in the Klamath Mountains. Dom and I will make the trip together. I'll pass on your greeting, as I know he'd love to hear about you and Marcelo. After Salix is home safe, Dom and I will be close by after you settle in Avila Beach. Don't you and Marcelo dare be strangers, or I'll come looking for you. Call me for anything, I don't care how trivial it may seem."

"Same with me," said Grace. "Once you're all in California, I may be far on the east coast, but never hesitate to reach out. Cessani claims she's keeping an eye on me, but the favor works both ways. I'll keep you posted if there are any developments."

Johann's maroon Uber pulled up to the curb. The werewolf waved a final time and climbed inside. All of them watched until the car disappeared around the corner.

Afterwards, Marcelo spent over an hour on the phone making various calls to Oregon to inquire about his abandoned car. In the end, he discovered the Aston Martin had been taken to Shady Cove Towing and Recovery in the city of Shady Cove, about an hour from Crater Lake. He secured payment to release the vehicle from impound and made arrangements to have the car transported to his residence in Avila Beach.

Following some tasty lunch, Grace kept busy washing everyone's clothes while Sybil and Marcelo cleaned the house. Sybil resisted calls for her to rest and plowed ahead with the chores. She might be old and weak, but helping out proved the least she could do to repay sweet Grace for hosting three unexpected—and somewhat messy—guests. But by late afternoon, she couldn't help falling asleep on the couch.

Past sundown, Marcelo woke her when the time to leave had arrived. New memories of her ordeal in the ley tunnel had trickled into her head during horrible nightmares. While preparing to leave, she did her best to hide distressed feelings from her face. Adding to her sorrow, no magic returned after believing sleep would recuperate her spell casting ability.

A lengthy farewell of hugs and kisses to Grace occurred on the porch. Sybil and Marcelo then climbed into an Uber and headed for the airport in Boston. The overnight red-eye flight took them to San Luis Obispo in California, and they finally landed around two in the morning local time.

Another taxi brought them to Avila Beach on the central coast. The yellow cab pulled in front of the long, curving driveway stretched before Marcelo's beautiful home in the beachside community. Sybil stepped out of the vehicle and inhaled the nostalgic, salty air. She observed the gorgeous, star-filled sky, unable to recall how many times she had dreamed of living in peace here with Marcelo. Her last reverie had been shattered by a demon that burst into the master bedroom in an attempt to kill her. Umaq was gone, but her wrecked mind and tired body almost expected something worse to happen.

Marcelo held her hand as they walked through the front door, and a motion sensor brightened the crystal chandelier high above their heads. They crossed the spacious foyer covered in white marble tile swirled with blue. Attractive, smooth granite counters adorned the kitchen. Polished wood flooring and luxurious furniture decorated the large living room, the best features a gas fireplace and huge flat screen television. Sybil never stopped enjoying the pleasant modern accommodations; everything from nice cars to an electric toothbrush had amazed her ever since she woke up in the twenty-first century.

"Are you hungry?" Marcelo asked. "I'll prepare something for you."

"No, thank you," Sybil replied, then hesitated. "Of a truth, I fancy some coffee."

"Coffee? It's three in the morning. You should be crashing by now."

Deep fatigue had settled over Sybil, but it felt different than sleepiness. In fact, her cognizance blazed wide awake with memory and thought. The long flight had allowed more recollections to stew in the pot. Quiet and pensive, she had stared out the small round window while looking at nothing. Marcelo had tried to engage her in conversation, but her silence had thrown up a thick wall.

She glanced at the sofa where Marcelo had told her his life story, of how he died by Umaq's hand as a young Spanish Conquistador. The sofa beckoned for another tale, this time for Sybil to recount her life-changing experience in the ley tunnel.

Ever since Marcelo found her lying in the grass at Machu Picchu, she had witnessed desperation on his face, wanting to know the truth of what happened to her. The worry over her shocking condition must be driving him crazy. She had noticed his constant glances during the chariot ride, while at Grace's house, and now at home. No matter how hard he tried to hide it, his concerned expression and tone revealed apprehension within. Sybil owed the man she loved the truth, and the time had arrived no matter how much it might pain her.

74

"After yonder coffee is ready, come hither and sit down, love," she said. "Forthwith I shall tell you my story."

The anxiety on Marcelo's features returned as he gaped at her. Yet overpowering the worry, his love for Sybil burned the brightest in his green eyes. He went in the kitchen and prepared a mug, then returned holding the steaming drink. She grasped the coffee and sipped, relishing the mountain of sugar and cream he knew she liked.

They settled on the sofa, and Sybil melted into his arms. Another sip, a deep breath, and the haunting words followed.

***

Deep underground, Sybil watched Umaq speed away on a new branch of shiny ley line and disappear. Undaunted over being left alone in the tunnel, she had ignored his boasting and threats. The bleeding knot on her forehead where he struck her with the staff became her only concern. She cast a curative spell to reduce the swelling and halt the blood.

Sybil climbed to her feet on the surface of ley energy. The blue essence partially obscured her shoes as if she stood upon a patch of low mist. Above and all around her, a suffocating blackness pressed in. She knew the ley river flowed at a brisk pace; however, the lack of visible features in the area made it impossible to sense actual movement.

Time to return to Athens and seek out Marcelo. Together, they would finish off Zelaenah if he hadn't already. Sybil lifted an arm and hovered a palm over the mystical river. She closed her eyes and focused her spiritual energy on Athens, visualizing the grand city landscape of docks, buildings, the Hill of Ares, and the sprawling Acropolis. With the scene in her mind, she prepared to manipulate the ley flow to her destination.

A flash of unexpected fear opened her eyes. She lowered her arm as confidence seeped from her heart. Once again, a memory of her previous venture in the ley tunnel during the trip to Machu Picchu made her hesitate.

That first journey had started out well enough. Although not precise, she had manipulated the earth flows to guide her and her friends to Peru. Ley lines shifted as states, countries, and ocean passed overhead. The surrounding threat of eternal blackness faded to insignificance as the initial experience had grown from apprehension into elation. Her initial attempt at ley travel had been a success…for a time.

In the end, the very powerful earth energies had overwhelmed her. The ley lines slipped from her grasp. She lost track of space and time in the endless deep. She tumbled helplessly alongside her friends through visions and nightmare. Her body burned and froze. Intense pressure crushed the breath from her lungs. She floated in emptiness, blind and terrified. How long had she screamed?

A hot surge of anger shattered the recollection. Frustrated, Sybil closed her eyes and performed several calming breaths to try and settle her nerves. She gritted her teeth and raised an arm over the blue river, fingers splayed. Summoning courage, she used her prior failure as fuel to rekindle her determination. She remembered Selene's inspiring words and envisioned her friends' smiling faces. After a few moments of internal conflict, the fear melted and indecision shattered. Athens sprang back into her mind, the citizens in danger as the sun and moon deities fought to protect the city.

The straight ley line suddenly curved to the left. It dipped, rose, then turned to the right. Sybil rode the river while channeling a spell through her palm onto the flowing earth essence. Encouraged by the progress, her revitalized will boosted the magic. The desire to rejoin her friends provided a beacon for her destination.

Sometime later, a trickle of sweat down her left temple signified a big problem. She hadn't detected the Athens ley gate—or any ley gate—in an hour. Or had it been several hours?

Time passed. More sweat beaded her forehead and moistened her clothing while she traveled around aimlessly. Borders, deserts, mountains, and bodies of water passed overhead. She also skimmed underneath random cities, trembling in effort and concentration. She no longer possessed Salix's twig, the magical object that had helped focus her spellcasting on Wizard Island. Even Umaq had a device to aid him as he wielded the staff cast from ley energy.

Sybil realized opening the way out proved far different—and more difficult—than forcing her way in. She had only gained access to the underground once while opening the ley gate housed at Crater Lake. As for escaping the tunnel, only luck had brought her and her friends to Machu Picchu. A fluke opened the way out, but she had not been in control at all.

The problem with luck is that it hadn't let her measure and record the experience using the ley line. Upon reaching Machu Picchu, an immediate battle for her life prevented the chance to learn anything about the travel. Her near-fatal injuries and subsequent five-day sleep also diminished what little knowledge she gained. Even if Sybil somehow managed to pass near a convergence, the fast-moving ley line averted enough time to cast an effective spell to open a gate.

To worsen matters, a strong cough doubled her over. Black nether droplets sprayed from her mouth onto the blue river as she struggled to remain standing. Wiping her mouth, she straightened, planted her feet, and fought the ley line for a while more.

Sometime later, Sybil found herself lying on her side in the blue ley mist, breath ragged. When had she collapsed? How long had she struggled to escape the underground? Her throat ached, dry and sticky. Cramps flared and muscles throbbed over her arms and legs. Her joints creaked and bones trembled under strain. A growl churned loud in her empty stomach. Vertigo and fatigue held her down in a heavy grip. She napped, woke only to cry, and slept again.

Do not despair, child!

A boom stirred Sybil awake. She rose to her hands and knees as the ley line carried her nowhere. Another loud thud echoed in the encircling darkness. Not an explosion, falling rock, or her imagination as a third boom turned into a steady rhythm of beats.

A heartbeat.

"Mother?" Sybil called out weakly.

Delirious, she addressed the Earth Mother, an omnipotent nature spirit that dwelled inside the vast planet—or rather, was the planet. Did the Mother truly dwell here? Had the disembodied voice been a trick of her warped mind?

78

I am here, young Spell Weaver. Now allow me to sustain you.

Some wisps of ley essence rose around Sybil. The thin tendrils entered her nostrils, mouth, and ears. A rush of vitality surged through her. Raw ley energy quenched her thirst and hydrated her body. It filled her belly and served as nourishment. The essence soothed her worn muscles and sore bones. It reduced fever and eased illness. She slowly stood and gazed out into the darkness. The Earth Mother's heart pulsed all around, each beat a soothing caress and whisper of hope.

"I am forever in your debt," Sybil uttered in disbelief, grateful beyond expression.

Her head then lowered in sudden shame. After her previous and disastrous attempt while using ley line manipulation, Salix's words still haunted: *The Earth Mother has been wounded by our effort. The Ley line essence spills like a ruptured vein. I feel Her distress. I am in pain.*

Guilt flooded Sybil's insides and saturated her core. She lowered to her knees and stared at the blue glow of the ley river. "I apologize, dear Mother. My harmful use of ley lines has caused you pain, and once again I am trying to alter forces beyond my ability."

Sweet child, all wounds heal in time, the Earth Mother responded. *But you have many that still trouble your dear heart, both in the past and present. Your exhausting, three-hundred-year battle against Umaq had darkened your spirit and turned you to evil. But you rose above the torment and now fight to liberate the world from unimaginable devastation and terror.*

For that, I am the one in your debt. I heard the heavens sigh when you saved the Greek sun god. But

79

your pursuit of Umaq the Betrayer endures, and I fear new wounds may be inflicted upon you. Dark filth from the demon realm already poisons you. My ley healing can abate the illness, but I am unable to cure it. The deities also cannot help you. The black essence of the netherworld is foreign, very powerful, and beyond their ability to influence.

In addition, the death of the Inca sun god, Inti, still blankets the planet in mystical darkness, and I grow weaker by the day. The negative effect threatens nature's stability and may give rise to new dangers. You must continue the fight, young Sybil. My true pain comes from asking this of you.

Despite multiple dangers, the earth spirit's plea had bolstered Sybil's resolve. Comparable to when the Goddess Selene inspired action through prayer, the Earth Mother stimulated Sybil's passion to protect her loved ones.

Her cheeks flushed, and her heart skipped. She lifted her eyes to the blackness and placed a hand over her chest. "Please do not be troubled, great Mother. I shall strive until Umaq is no more and the balance hath been restored." She glanced around the vast emptiness, uncertainty furrowing her brow. "Hitherto, I am trapped in the tunnel. I have toiled some hours to find a way out, I warrant."

Dear one, you have wandered the ley tunnels for two days. I have been trying to reach you all this time, but the earth trembles under nature's imbalance and inhibits my power.

Sybil's blood froze in astonishment. Two days! How could that be? No wonder she had collapsed. She had learned that time and distance can somehow warp in the underground, but the notion still stunned. What had happened outside in those two days?

"Not conversant of my whereabouts, my friends must be very disquieted," she commented. "And what of Umaq? I must escape hither forthwith!"

I am too feeble to open the way for you, and prayers to the deities will go unheard. The underground exists in a realm of its own and behaves contrary to reality on the surface. You must find the strength, and the will, to accomplish escape on your own.

Sybil imagined Marcelo traveling everywhere, feeling terrified over her disappearance. She pictured her friends assaulted and hurt by Umaq. The horrible ideas frightened her, but she managed to shove all the wild thoughts away. Worrying more about those things meant distraction and more time wasted.

She took a deep, calming breath and expelled the negativity in a rush of air. "Truly, I am grateful for your efforts and guidance hitherto, Mother. I conceive what I must do."

She turned away from the ethereal voice and focused ahead on the direction of ley flow. She spread both arms and set her feet on the river's surface. Spells and chants flew from her mouth in repeated waves. Her body spun in rhythmic, ritual dancing. Her head rotated and long hair whipped in tune during a spirted song of magic.

The blue ley lines reacted to her efforts. Paths shifted, and many new branches opened. Sybil sped down rivers, curved around the wide open abyss, and swooped through the earth.

"Forthwith to yonder Athens!" she screamed at the darkness. "To my dearest friends and the love of my life!"

Ahead, a knotted twist of ley lines signified a convergence. Sybil's heart thundered in anticipation. Sweat drenched her clothes. Her shoulders ached and throat burned, but she held on tight for a final spell.

"Heavens fall and nether rise, I seek spirits of yore and implore the wise! From rock to tree through land and sea, take me forth from the earth I flee!"

The ley line beneath her feet increased its speed. Hair waving, Sybil whooped in joy as she neared the bright blue junction of earth essence. She closed her eyes and flew into the mass…then exited on the other side. Her eyes opened. She stood on a different ley river surrounded by darkness. No rocky surface approached, no sun and blue sky welcomed. She turned around and rode backwards, watching the convergence shrink from view.

"I…I shall try again," she whispered.

And again.

One more.

Another.

How many times did she attempt and fail? How many ley gates missed?

New spells launched from cracked lips. Nether essence leaked from her nose. Breath expelled from a raspy, dry throat and overworked lungs. A weary body trembled. A completely exhausted—and terrified—mind screamed.

Sybil fell over, and the Earth Mother nourished. Sybil lost consciousness, and the alert Mother prodded, encouraged, and fed her.

More time passed. Sybil's hair grew longer. The fatigue approached quicker and rest periods increased in duration. Her will faltered, determination died.

She toppled over and refused to stand. "Take me far," she told the emptiness.

The Earth Mother's heart boomed a loud drum of inspiration. *Look upon your friends, Sybil! They join you out of love, in grief, and everything in-between. Welcome them into your arms. Use their spirit to guide you.*

Sybil peered down the ley river and saw her friends approaching. Marcelo, Johann, and Salix waved and smiled. Her beloved companions cheered and clapped. Sybil struggled to her feet and ran toward the group. She leapt into waiting arms and cried against shoulders, buried her face in chests.

Marcelo's cool, familiar embrace wrapped her. Johann's sweet smile glowed. Salix sang in delight, the leaves fluttering on her arm and shoulders in a sign of emotion. Sybil's spirit shone, bliss overflowing from her heart. Tears flowed and she sobbed in happiness.

She rejoiced in the moment, but it would soon pass because her beloved friends didn't truly exist here. As a life-long witch, she recognized an illusion when confronting one.

She noticed the tiniest blur of color on their clothes. A near imperceptible, bluish hue surrounded their bodies like a warm aura. Her friends had been fashioned from the ley essence she stood upon. The Earth Mother, in a loving gesture of compassion and encouragement, had created the illusion to rescue Sybil from black despair.

It worked. Sybil renewed her effort to escape. She conjured, danced, and chanted across the world in endless ley streams and bottomless tears. How long had she dug into her reserves to maintain the effort? She lost weight. Her brown hair faded to gray. Varicose veins and liver spots appeared. Sweaty and feverish, she choked on black vomit and sneezed dark essence.

But she did not die.

The Earth Mother repeatedly saved Sybil's life. Though weak and drained of energy from the mystical imbalance, the Mother continued to pour her remaining tenacity and vigor into sustaining Sybil over the long decades. She bathed her in ley streams, soaked the spiritual earth essence into her flesh and bones. The ley energy sustained and healed, for Sybil would have perished from lack of water, starvation, and illness.

But who would nourish the Earth Mother? The poor, tortured spirit always suffered alongside Sybil. The mystical darkness squeezed the life from the planet's soul. The Mother wept in the underground, fighting to keep Sybil alive, her only hope.

A deep with no end. A perpetual fall. Blackness dark and terrifying. The days, months, and years ticked by. Flesh shriveled and skin tightened. Hair thinned and receded. Her fragile bones and dry joints ached. Several teeth loosened and vision blurred. Her memory faded, whereabouts unknown.

A heart struggled to beat.

Old and frail, Sybil glanced down the ley line as her friends once again appeared on the blue river. She had seen them hundreds of times over the years, always whenever the worst depression overwhelmed her. They hugged and caressed her, but this time she paid them no attention. Their false arms felt hollow, their impassive smiles flat. The laughter seemed forced and words of comfort empty. After several moments of disgust, Sybil waved her arm in anger and the illusions vanished.

Happiness would not help her escape. Relief did not hold the key. Warm feelings had become a curse.

"Earth Mother!" she shrieked. "Make me hurt. Make me bleed. Sorrow shall be my strength!"

My dear child...

Profound grief reverberated from the Mother's voice. Love saturated each of those final three words to Sybil, a parent watching her baby suffer...and knowing nothing more could be done.

Some new individuals appeared on the ley line. Olivia, Sybil's mother, strolled down the river. A burly man stepped up behind her, a knife in his grip. The brute reached over Olivia's shoulder and slammed the blade into her chest. Her bright smile twisted in pain. Terror widened her eyes. Blood soaked the front of her dress and reddened the ley essence.

Sybil fell to her knees and cried out. The trauma of witnessing her mother's murder over three hundred years ago rushed outward in an instant. The pain and emotional torment had not subsided over the centuries. Numbness turned her limbs to stone. A vice squeezed her chest and crushed her heart.

Constance Chandler suddenly appeared. Sybil's beloved friend, fellow witch, and housemate in Salem Village stood high on a ladder. A noose wrapped her throat. Terror blanched her sweet face. Her wide, empty eyes gazed at nothing as shock dulled her senses. A man kicked the ladder away and Constance plummeted. Her body jerked at the end of the rope in death.

Relentless agony lashed Sybil. She wept in hard gasps and nearly fainted. She wrapped arms around her midsection and suffered in raw anguish. Constance's execution had broken Sybil all those years ago. The intense level of pain had reduced her to a shell devoid of emotion. Any humanity had dissolved in her fire of black rage and thirst for vengeance.

Reliving both traumas ignited a new fire. Sybil soaked in the pessimism and used her suffering as fuel. Each tear of agony enhanced her magic. Every enraged shout exploded in renewed energy. She relished the torment and welcomed the dark memories staining her past.

The Athens from years in the past vanished as a destination. Marcelo and her friends disappeared from her thoughts. Only Umaq, the origin of her incredible ache, burst forth in her mind. His malevolent presence served as an anchor as she worked to target his position aboveground.

Sybil screamed an incantation—her last. Just as youth had left her worn body, her magical ability slowly faded into ineffectiveness. The last of her mystical stores poured into the spell to locate the source of her hate. Her voice seemed to echo across the planet, the vibrations trembling the earth above. Abhorrence laced every word, each syllable sharp and penetrating. The spell roared across space and time. Barriers melted, years bled together, and reality shattered. Ley lines split apart in shreds or crashed into each other in sprays of blue essence.

A fierce dance gripped Sybil and thrust her body into action. Arms flailed and legs stepped in a chaotic, yet coordinated rhythm. Her head rotated, shoulders rolled, and hips swiveled to a furious clash of mystical music. She leapt, spun, and landed in tune to pulsing notes and speeding crescendos.

The ley river beneath her feet swelled. The blue energy propelled Sybil toward the surface as she spread her arms. Above, a rocky ceiling rumbled open in a smooth gesture of complete control.

She passed through the circular opening and stepped off the ley river onto stone tile. Behind her, the ground moved in a gentle shake as the gap closed. Sybil didn't care where she ended up—she had escaped. Fresh air filled her lungs as she collapsed on her side, exhausted. A sweet, gentle breeze caressed her skin. The darkness of night instead of the deep underground wrapped her in peace.

However, her success produced bitter tears as she started to cry. Love had not triumphed, but hatred. In the tunnel, Sybil had rejected her friends and crushed their warm affection. She found their intimacy weak, an obstacle to her freedom. Instead, she chose to welcome revulsion and fury. She had wrapped herself in pain to find the strength to break out. Sybil loathed what she had done, but it proved necessary to survive.

After a long while, she rose in an oddly familiar place. Partially crumbled walls and a ruined ceiling surrounded her. Sybil recognized the temple at the top of a hill in Machu Picchu, the same one she had burst into—via broken ley line—the last time she appeared at the ancient structure.

She walked out into the small courtyard where a dazzling, star-studded sky and brilliant moon stretched overhead. The celestial bodies brightened the isolated mountain in an ethereal glow. Centered in the area, she observed the impressive stone altar of Intihuatana. Sybil recalled her bloody battle against Umaq while trying to prevent Inti's death. In what seemed ages ago, she—

Ages. How much time had passed since then? She glanced around in confusion, then studied her frail, liver-spotted hands. She grabbed her thinning hair and rubbed the unkempt, gray strands between her fingers. She looked down at a wraith-like body beneath baggy clothes and gently touched her wrinkled face. The years pressed on her shoulders and her bones ached. Fatigue weakened her muscles, and she only wanted to sleep.

She pondered how many decades had passed in the underground. What year was it now, and how much had the world changed? Were her friends alive? The terrifying concept of lost time overpowered Sybil. She stumbled against the altar and cried again, helpless and near mad after her ordeal.

But this wasn't the first incident where several decades had been misplaced. Sybil had awoken in modern Salem after slumbering for over three hundred years. Her youth destroyed, she found herself a wrinkled old hag, frightened and mentally broken. Now Sybil lived as an old woman again…emotionally wrecked for the second time.

The tools for her to escape the underground had been soaked in rage. But in the deepest and darkest part of Sybil's mind, she realized she had found something greater than those raw emotions—acceptance.

Perhaps Sybil's recurrent aging had resulted from the inability to avoid her fate. This represented her punishment for having stolen that woman's youth and placing her in a coma, a sentence for a crime of the blackest magic.

Fate. Punishment. Whatever the situation called for, Sybil accepted her condition. She had picked up where she left off, right after Marcelo opened the lid on her coffin in the museum storeroom. Her new life began now, however short it may be. She stood alone, lost in a foreign time as disease ate her body.

Sybil headed for the stone steps leading down into another wide courtyard of temples and ancient structures. Dark moisture trickled from her nose, and she wiped it away. Out of breath, fatigue clung to her limbs and dulled her senses. Mass confusion fogged her already ruined consciousness, and shattered emotions wavered between grief and horror.

She tried to focus on something positive, like her friends—wait, only what friends? She thought she remembered a couple faces but didn't recall any names. And where in the world was she? *Who* was she? Memories rioted and feelings warred. Scenes of people, places, and jumbled events cracked in her head. The recollections grew whole, then shredded again. She remembered and forgot in a harrowing, nauseous cycle.

Adding to her nightmare, a terrifying roar broke the stillness. She stared across the courtyard and an appalling, winged creature barged out from one of the buildings. Six slanted eyes in a misshapen head swept the area. Sharp bones grew from its broad shoulders, its muscled body gray-skinned and scarred. Claw-tipped fingers flexed repeatedly. The demon lacked a nose yet moved its face as if sniffing the air.

The three sets of eyes darted onto Sybil. An odd sensation burned through her head as she held its gaze. Did she know this beast? How could that be possible? It seemed unlikely, but one fact stood out—the creature had gone completely insane.

Terror froze her. The demon's stare alone would make anyone scream. She perceived its madness like sandpaper scraping her skin. The creature's foul odor personified its frightening mental sickness, putrid and immeasurable. Yet despite everything, she somehow recognized the monster or at least sensed something familiar about it.

The demon approached. It studied her from head to toe, then suddenly lifted toward the sky in a flurry of wing beats. The peculiar encounter twisted Sybil's frail thoughts and emotions even more. Shaken and numb, she moved toward the temple where the demon had exited. Old, lost, and broken, she didn't care if another beast waited inside to rip her apart.

***

"And then I had a fair sight of Umaq inside yonder temple," Sybil continued. She shifted on the couch against Marcelo. "My consciousness was most distressed. I soon conceived that only a short time had passed since the events at Athens—although aforesaid I had aged decades underground."

Marcelo caressed her hair, and she glanced up at him. His stern silence weighed heavy. Her long story's impact hardened his expression. While staring across the carpeted living room, his green eyes blazed in a distant, penetrating gaze.

"Your words had me living every moment with you in that lonely tunnel," he finally uttered in a strained voice. "I am so deeply sorry, Sybil. You've gripped this darkness inside you, and the trauma must have been unbearable." He clenched a trembling fist and closed his eyes. A deep breath loosened his hand and softened his features. "I failed you. We got separated in the Acropolis, and I should have been more careful. I could have—"

Sybil pressed a tender finger against his lips. She stroked his cheek, then turned his distressed face to hers. She smiled and projected love through her adoring eyes. Remembering the clichéd expression people used when lamenting a situation gone bad, she found the term humorous after Marcelo had explained it to her while watching a *moovy*.

"Woulda, coulda, shoulda," she recited.

Marcelo's eyes widened in surprise, a comical expression. She laughed softly and he smiled in return, the emotional relief evident in his young features. He wrapped her in his arms and kissed her forehead.

"You didn't even have to cast a spell to make me feel much better," he said. "And how pathetic am I? You're the one who suffered alone, and I'm just here moping."

"Do not worry so," she replied. "Of a truth, you comforted me by listening, and your presence forthwith is medicine for my heart and soul." Grunting in effort, she stood from the couch and stretched, sighing in contentment when her spine popped.

"Sybil, I felt your elevated temperature while you recounted your story." He frowned, eyes full of concern. "Love, you're not getting any better and we couldn't find a remedy while at Grace's house. The Earth Mother was unable to heal the black illness, and she mentioned the deities cannot help. There's also the question of your aging." He stood from the couch and paced the carpet. "I

91

can't just sit here and watch you suffer. There has to be a solution!"

Sybil approached and gripped his shoulders. She gazed into his eyes and felt the desperation troubling him. Her lover would swim through fire and tear down mountains to save her. If the roles had been reversed, she would also feel helpless and not rest until finding the answers.

In sympathy, all she could do was nod and offer some hollow words of reassurance. "Fear not, Marcelo. Hitherto we endured too much to lose hope forthwith. Greater things have striven to defeat us and sap our resolve. You and I remaineth standing. Nothing in this world or yonder one shall break our will, I warrant."

They held each other. Hollow words indeed, for it seemed that her willpower had already shattered in the underground. Her acceptance of her condition had been planted. In Machu Picchu, she had even lain in the grass to die. How could she convince Marcelo to feel better if her confidence had already failed?

While they readied for bed, an idea came to her. The plan involved sneaking away from Marcelo, but that would not be easy. To improve her chances, she had to ensure he ingested her blood before settling down. With sustenance inside him, Marcelo tended to doze for longer periods, and that's what Sybil needed most of all.

As predicted, he fussed when she offered him her hand to bite. She had to grow stubborn in return and insisted he eat something, just as he sometimes pestered her to have food when she wasn't hungry. After a small spat, he finally drank.

They climbed into bed, and she waited. As an undead, Marcelo didn't breathe, so she couldn't listen to his rhythm and judge when sleep took him. However, she had gotten used to how he rested. An odd stillness would come over him as if he truly lay dead. That familiar moment finally arrived after twenty minutes. She allowed five more minutes to pass before carefully slipping off the mattress.

Hurrying, she quietly grabbed some clothes and exited the bedroom, then tiptoed down the hall. She dressed in the kitchen and slipped some cash from Marcelo's wallet on the counter. Grabbing her phone, she paused while staring at the device.

No. No phone. Once the front door closed behind her, a single call from Marcelo might crush her plan. She would probably wilt to his frantic plea for her to return home. Sybil needed to remain strong and committed, no matter how much pain leaving him caused. She needed guidance, and most importantly, inspiration. Even though she loved and trusted Marcelo, Johann, and Grace, their returned sentiment would not provide the direction she required.

Only a dryad may have the answer. A little plant face.

Depending on the advice Sybil received, the resulting task may prove impossible to complete while Marcelo remained at her side. She needed to journey alone, as he would unleash hell to stop her. Love didn't always mean fighting together. In this chaotic world, sometimes the best way to display affection meant leaving the other person behind.

Sybil wrote Marcelo a note and left it on the table. She glanced toward the bedroom one last time. Sighing, she stepped through the door, uncertain if she'd ever see her love again.

Chapter Seven

The Downside of Winning

Sitting in her office at the converted Salem Witch Museum, Cessani stared at the computer and clenched her teeth in frustration. Dozens of e-mails crammed her inbox, and most of the letters blared complaints from witches outside of Salem. Irritated, she gripped the mouse and clicked through a few messages.

From Rhode Island: *I have received unclear instructions about establishing a new coven here in Providence. Many witches are wondering what's going on, and I haven't heard from you.*

From Connecticut: *I drummed up just enough support to open a new coven in Hartford, but our group lacks cohesion. I certainly don't want to be stuck as the leader. This new magical power from the moon is great, but we need proper management.*

From London, England: *The Moon Goddess, Mama Quilla, has been amazing in establishing our coven. She is very supportive, active in our community, and to our delight, speaks well at our gatherings. Unfortunately, multiple commitments have her traveling often to other cities and countries. We don't see her as much as we'd like, and the coven doesn't want to lose focus. Should there be a schedule for her visits? What about you, are you coming to see us soon?*

And the most exasperating e-mail of all, from nearby in Boston: *What a blessing it is to have the Maiden, Goddess of the Moon, preside at our coven meetings! However, all she does is eat our food and avoids offering any direction for the group. We are a bit lost, and I can only hold off the grumbling members for so long. Where do we go from here? Please help!*

The destruction of the Inca sun god had eroded the mystical barrier between the mortal plane and the supernatural. The spiritual balance of light and dark had tilted toward darkness. Ordinary people were unable to notice such a dramatic shift; however, Inti's death had incited the paranormal world.

After the barrier thinned, witches had achieved new abilities governed by the lunar deities and the power of the moon. Cessani's goal had been to use these skills to influence society and revitalize witch authority. Inspired by Mama Quilla and the Maiden, Cessani's followers had instituted covens in several cities in the US and beyond.

However, the rapid growth had avalanched out of control. Cessani was only one person, and it seemed even two moon goddesses would not be enough. Too many covens required proper guidance. They needed methods of development, teaching, and encouragement to instill devotion and maintain enthusiasm. The expansion beyond Salem had brought Cessani tears of happiness, but the emotion quickly soured into stress and loss of sleep.

Needing a break from the computer and some fresh air, she rolled her chair away from the desk and winced as she stood. Hands in the small of her back, she groaned in a stretch and rotated her neck until it popped, then bent her knees a few times to get the blood flowing.

Halfway to the door, her smartphone buzzed. She fished the device from a pocket and growled at the Maiden's request for a video chat. From the app, the young deity's silly icon of a kitten eating an ice-cream cone danced on the screen.

Cessani's thumb hammered the answer button. The Maiden's smiling face filled the screen, a bit of chocolate or other food soiling the corner of her mouth.

"Why are you video calling me, Persephone?" she barked. "I asked you to come in person several times. We have a hundred things to discuss!"

"Jeez Louise, nice to see you too," the Maiden replied in a pout. "No need to attack me."

"Apologies, Goddess. It's just that I'm losing my mind here," said Cessani. "You can teleport here in an instant. Please do so that we can have a much more comfortable and productive conversation. Sometimes it's hard to talk through these things."

"Nah, using this technology is much more fun. Watch!" Persephone fumbled with the smartphone. A moment later, her face turned into an animated cow's head. Perched on the cow's ears, birds chirped and flapped their wings. She laughed and the camera shook. "Now you try one, Cess!"

Cessani curled a hard fist at her side, her limited patience already gone. "Persephone! Can you please be serious for just a moment? I've received nothing but complaints from the new members. You promised to travel to each coven and provide supervision. What exactly have you been doing? Meanwhile, Mama Quilla has been working her tail off."

The Maiden blew a raspberry. "Mama the Moon Babe needs to slow down and enjoy the moment. We all worked so hard to achieve this, and things will take care of themselves. No need to stress, Cess, or you'll get more white hair and wrinkles."

Cessani pinched her thigh and tried to speak in a more calm manner. "You are the goddess of the waxing moon. You represent innovative beginnings, expansion, youthful enthusiasm, and birth, to name a few. We have fresh moon powers, new covens, and expanding witch power. I figured this role would be perfect for you. Why aren't you taking it more seriously?"

The cartoony cow face vanished and revealed a more somber Maiden. "I was goddess of the waxing moon. That term is associated with the Triple Moon Goddess, which I am no longer part of, remember? I left the stiff and by-the-book Mother and Crone out of boredom and a chance to do something…well…*new*, as you pointed out. I enjoyed teaming up with you and Mama Quilla. Battling Inti proved exciting and fun. Meeting witches from all over is also cool."

The young goddess stated she *enjoyed* teaming up, as in past tense. "I have a feeling there's a 'but' coming," Cessani replied.

Should she be worried? Angry? The young deity had been unpredictable since the beginning. Cessani had discussed this sort of behavior with Mama Quilla. Worry or anger might represent the stronger emotions; however, Persephone's change of heart did not surprise at all.

The Maiden's shrill laughter exploded from the phone. "You said a *butt* is coming!"

97

After a few exaggerated clears of her throat, the goddess regained her composure and began anew. "*But* I'm terrible at this role. I can't do this type of thing alone. Throughout history, the Mother and Crone provided help and guidance for every action or decision I ever made. The three of us have unique traits, yet we work together to administer the different phases of the lunar cycle. Lately, I've felt lost without them. No offense to you and Mama Quilla, as you've been super great. But I miss the Mother and Crone. After all, what's a Triple Moon Goddess without the triple?"

Unexpected sympathy touched Cessani. Any prior notion of apprehension or fury over what the Maiden might say vanished. The goddess of the waxing moon may be thousands of years old, but Cessani only saw a confused teenager on the video chat. The young girl felt lost and didn't understand her place in life. Pressured and uncomfortable at home, Persephone had run away. She explored, experimented, and met new people. In the end, she found herself and realized the answers had been at the beginning all along. Sometimes it took a rough journey of loneliness and hardship to find truth. The Maiden had just experienced life, a phase very similar to what Cessani had gone through in her younger days.

"Hey, why are you smiling?" the deity asked with a hurtful expression. "I'm spilling my guts here, and my heart, too."

"I know, sweet Goddess," Cessani replied. "I'm smiling because you painted a picture of my own adolescence. Your story is my story, dear Maiden, and I'm sorry for what you've been through. Your heart is bigger than this world, larger than time itself. You've had

98

generations of people from different places and cultures relying on you for everything. I can't imagine the stress and responsibility of carrying that title. When things grow too arduous, everyone needs time to search within, even deities. Should you wish to return to the Mother and Crone, you have my support and blessing."

For once, the Maiden failed to reply in a snappy retort or jest. Surprise overcame her features. She stared into the camera, lips parted, emotion swimming in her teal-colored eyes. The next moment she vanished.

Cessani shrieked in surprise when thin arms suddenly wrapped her from behind. The pleasant scent of fresh flowers and warm honey revealed the Maiden after an unexpected teleport. Cessani turned in the grip and returned the loving embrace. She stroked the deity's long white hair, which sparkled as if filled with stars. Persephone sighed in contentment and melted into the hug.

"Thank you, Cess," said the Maiden. "Like any rebellious teen, my decision is not yet made and it may change ten times in the next day or so." She pulled back and smiled. "But for the moment, I'll head back to Boston and teach the coven a thing or two. Besides, they have the best cupcakes at their meetings."

"I'm delighted to hear you'll still give it a shot, even if it's only temporary," Cessani responded. "Those witches really look up to you, whether it's the new Persephone branching out on her own, or the Maiden of the Triple Moon Goddess."

"I do love them," the deity said affectionately. "Whatever hat I end up wearing, I will not let them down." She offered a determined nod. "Well, I'm off!" The Maiden winked and disappeared.

The computer chirped, signifying a new e-mail. Earlier, Cessani had been ready to throw the darned machine out the window, but the tender moment with the Maiden had calmed her. She returned to the desk to read, bracing herself for yet another disaster in a different city. Instead, a welcoming surprise appeared from Mama Quilla.

Dear Cessani,

Warm greetings from South America! I must admit using this technology to communicate is intriguing. I had been dormant for so long, these wonderful devices of your time had almost passed me by. I probably sound like the Maiden, as she is thrilled by using things like the smartphone.

Anyway, I have great news! The covens in Cusco, Rio de Janeiro, Bogota, Quito, and Managua are booming. It's been tough juggling the new groups, but the members are very enthusiastic and patient. They love learning new skills, and their strong devotion is admirable.

I've somewhat neglected the covens outside of South America, although not intentionally. It's been quite a challenge visiting each location around the world and providing mentorship to so many new groups. The growth is wonderful, but I'm afraid a bit too much at the moment.

As the Inca Moon Goddess, I admit my heart lives with my native Peru and the covens of South America. I share a deep bond with the local brujas and chamáns. However, I will continue to make the rounds, as they say, to the best of my ability.

I hope this message finds you well, and that the Maiden is not causing too much trouble! I will try and visit you as soon as possible. Take care and best wishes.

Cessani placed an elbow on the desk and held her chin in thought. Good news indeed, yet the problem of rapid expansion became increasingly evident. She praised Mama Quilla's effort and felt terrible for asking so much of the goddess. At least the deity had made heartfelt connections in her homeland, and the potential demonstrated by the South American covens looked promising.

Now for some fresh air. She rose from the chair and nearly bumped into one of her aides rushing in the doorway.

"Cessani, the mayor is here to see you," David announced, his red robe much too loose for his small frame.

She groaned, her respite once again thwarted. "I told her to make an appointment! What does she want now?"

"Well, she wouldn't tell me. Should I send her away?"

Cessani rubbed her tired eyes. "No," she said in defeat. "Have her come to my office." Why add more pain for another day? Might as well cram it all into this hellish one. She returned to the desk and plopped heavily into the chair.

David reappeared in the doorway with the mayor, Ava Deque, at his side. She strolled into the office and took the seat opposite the desk. A light blue business suit covered her lithe frame. Beneath curly black hair, green eyes scrutinized Cessani, a slight frown on her painted lips. The mayor crossed her legs and set a notepad on her knee, pen ready in her right hand.

"You've been avoiding me again," Ava began. "You're rather stressed, judging from the look on your face. You've taken over Salem and carried the mantle. Not so easy, is it?"

It seemed the mayor had come for an argument. Cessani shrugged, exhaustion soaked in her bones. "It's not just Salem I need to worry about."

"That's not my problem," Ava stated. "At the expense of Salem, your attention has been fixed on the new covens outside the city. The neglected citizens under your nose are angry. *I'm* angry. Despite your takeover and witch rule, I thought we had an agreement when you allowed me to remain as mayor. Remember, I lack the ability to cast spells and am unable to do anything about the monsters causing havoc in the streets. That's your responsibility."

Cessani closed her eyes, fists tight on her lap. The supernatural creatures running amok in Salem presented *another* problem she hadn't had time to deal with. Ava was right about one thing. The monster responsibility belonged to the witches.

Following Inti's death, what started out as a raucous celebration party for the new era had turned into utter remorse. The mystical imbalance benefitted witches, but had created an unexpected downside. Werewolves had been thrown into severe bedlam as a suddenly potent, lunar body affected their mental state. More vampires appeared and began to act in ways dangerous to societal norms. Ghosts, ghouls, fairies, and a plethora of other supernatural beings emerged, not always in peace. Worst of all, the remnant of Umaq's demons from Salem proved to be even more reckless under the spiritual darkness.

Cessani and her witches had managed to thwart Grace's wild attempt to wrest back control of the city. Mass destruction, zombie corpses, countless injuries, and chaos had ensued in street-to-street fighting. Imprisoning Grace had been a victory; however, the protests continued in different fashions.

In the wake of dangerous monster activity, the citizens of Salem had gathered in front of the witch museum to voice their concern over safety. Bullhorns, signs, and chants had been the extent of the protests, a lingering discontent that forced Cessani's hand. With her local witches already stretched thin across the city in a method of control, she had asked them to do more while driving out fierce golems and shooing away banshees.

"The matter will be taken care of soon, Mayor," Cessani offered with no plan in mind. "I'll even hit the streets myself. Salem's well-being is just as important as my new covens, and the local citizens are not forgotten. My witches are just as fatigued as I am, but we'll do our best to clean up our own mess."

The mayor jotted something down onto her notepad. "Well, I sure hope so. You said something similar during the last meeting we had." A moment of silence passed as Ava studied Cessani.

"At the very least, I must say your witches have done some good for the people," the mayor continued. "Crime has nearly vanished under your watch. Things like lost pets, misplaced items, and even missing people have been remedied after a spell cast or two. You've even managed to create new jobs in your governing. The hitch, of course, is your new witch tax. But I suppose nothing is free."

"Nothing pays for itself," Cessani agreed. She stood and stretched again, then motioned the mayor toward the door. One way or another, she would have her fresh air. "I'll send you a progress report in a week. You'll see improvement, I promise."

Ava scribbled another note. "Spoken like a true politician. Good luck, Cessani." The mayor stood and departed the office.

A nap suddenly seemed more desirable than fresh air. Or better yet, a vacation. How much more of this could Cessani handle? The constant, stress-induced headaches and upset stomach threatened to drive her bonkers.

As of late, the only thing positive turned out to be Umaq's defeat and apparent death. She had privately hoped for Sybil's success against the demented man, and the younger witch—or rather older now—did not disappoint. Cessani couldn't imagine how much worse the planet would have been while Umaq stood in power. His dark magic and demonic army would have annihilated the world.

Thinking about her local trouble, did a simple solution exist? Cessani had started this mess of witch rule and coven expansion. Looking back, teaming up with Umaq to defeat a sun god seemed easier. She had to figure the situation out, and fast. Having no answers, she hurried outdoors for a break before another e-mail chimed, the phone rang, or an assistant blocked her path.

Chapter Eight

Trail of Blood Tears

Outside the second-floor apartment, cars honked and engines roared through the narrow streets of Managua, Nicaragua. Police blew whistles to direct the flow of vehicles and pedestrians. Citizens whistled for taxis and bartered in Spanish for goods over the noise of traffic. Shops and wood booths lined the road in a characteristic evening of the city's bustle.

In the living room, Daiyu knelt beside four dead members of her kin. Their heads had been crushed into unrecognizable shapes. Torn open chests revealed that someone—or perhaps something—had pulverized each vampire's black heart into jelly. Around the apartment, broken furniture, caved-in walls, and doors knocked off hinges signified a terrible struggle.

"The murders continue," Daiyu whispered.

Emotional ache stung her own black heart. The absence of her soul didn't mean she proved incapable of sentiment. Grief—and increasing rage—churned in her twenty-five-hundred-year-old body.

Black Jade turned away and slowly moved around the dwelling. The pattern of crushed heads and destroyed hearts had been repeated here in Nicaragua.

105

The same grisly murders had occurred in Panama, Colombia, Ecuador, and traced all the way back to Peru.

The vampire deaths had originated in Peru near Machu Picchu. The assassin had then headed up north across multiple countries through South America and into Central America. The trail continued northward in a definite sign of heading to Mexico and possibly the United States.

Clara, the old woman who owned the apartment building, approached carrying white linen sheets. Daiyu retreated a few steps as her dense, powerful aura would harm the elderly female. Clara leaned over to tenderly cover the four undead.

"These vampires were always well-known in Managua," she said in Spanish. "They were our friends and never hesitated to help humans in need."

"I appreciate you calling me about this," Daiyu replied in Spanish, her tone somber. She placed a wad of cash on the cracked coffee table. "Please ensure the victims are properly laid to rest."

Black Jade left the residence and stepped onto the night-darkened sidewalk. Her revelry in Salem had been shattered after she received the first horrific notification about the slayings. It had all started with Ricardo's frantic call from Peru, then Marcus' agitated video chat from Ecuador. By the time Ruth left a voicemail from Colombia, Daiyu had already boarded a flight for South America. The disturbing calls continued after she began her investigation in Machu Picchu. Finally, Clara's tearful plea had brought Daiyu to Nicaragua and more dead kin.

What did the killer want? Numerous species of supernatural beings roamed the planet, so why only hunt vampires? After several centuries of existence, Daiyu had built a massive network of contacts that spanned generations across the world. Always alert and efficient, her informants had done their part to report the murders, but a sudden lash of guilt cut Daiyu deep.

After waking from her twenty-year nap, the mystical barrier between the mortal plane and the netherworld had thinned after Inti's death. The world had become interesting once again and entertainment awaited. She grew complacent while partying alongside witches and a moon goddess in Salem. She also wasted time mocking Sybil and toying with the false vampire, Marcelo Flores, by placing him on trial.

Unfortunately, complacency had resulted in the slaughter of her fellow undead. Twenty-two vampires had been murdered under her watch. While laughing at the spreading darkness, Daiyu failed her family. Guilt burned red-hot in her stomach. Sorrow lowered her head, and ire clenched her fists. She trembled on the sidewalk as pedestrians kept their distance.

She screamed and plowed a fist into a building wall. Chunks of brick peppered her face and clattered on the sidewalk. She bolted down the street in a burst of preternatural speed, rocketing past structures and vehicles while heading away from Managua. Human observers only witnessed a blur of color or felt a gust of wind as she raced by.

Chasing a few phone calls and texts in a reactive manner would not stop the terrible murders. She had to maneuver one step ahead and wait for the killer. But where to lay the trap? Honduras, Guatemala…Mexico?

"Mexico City," Daiyu said into the roaring wind. She had a much larger network there to aid in the snare. "Come find me, and I'll rip you to pieces!"

Ditching the cumbersome and near-impossible task of finding a last-minute plane ticket, she sped on foot through the night. During the day, she hired a van driver while she sat in the back wrapped in protective clothing from the sun. As evening returned, she leapt out of the vehicle and zoomed onward. A focus on vengeance fueled her journey. She crossed borders and did not stop, feed, or rest until reaching Mexico City.

An hour before dawn, Daiyu completed her trip and slipped into the darkened streets. The densely populated, high-altitude capital of Mexico was known for its magnificent historical locations and beautiful architecture. The Templo Mayor, a thirteenth-century Aztec temple, had been fashioned in the late postclassic period of Mesoameria. Very close to the temple, the Palacio Nacional housed the President of Mexico and had served as a palace for the country's ruling class since the Aztec Empire. A large portion of the current structure contained building materials from the original design that belonged to the sixteenth-century leader, Moctezuma II.

Having no time for pleasantries or the modern etiquette of a Blood Studio, Daiyu fed on a drunken vagrant and left him sleeping in an alley. Full but dissatisfied over the taste of alcohol-laced blood, she crossed the Plaza de la Constitución, the enormous main square also known as the Zócalo, and approached the Catedral Metropolitana de México.

One of her favorite locations in the country, this grand cathedral never failed to impress. Its foundation began soon after the Spanish conquest of Tenochtitlan and took nearly two-hundred-fifty years to complete. Due to the long period of construction, its architectural styles included Gothic, Baroque, Churrigueresque, and Neoclassical. Throughout that time, generations of social classes of architects, painters, sculptors, and gilding masters had incorporated various ornaments, paintings, sculptures, and furniture for the building's interior. A number of church authorities, governmental officials, and different religious orders had also been involved in managing the cathedral in a method of social unity.

Daiyu passed through the large wooden doors and experienced the familiar silence of entering a place of worship. An unexplainable, but very beautiful *hush* always smothered her whenever she entered a cathedral or even a smaller church. A tangible sensation, she seemed to cross into another world, one of breathtaking exquisiteness, solemnity, and wonderment. This hidden world in plain sight brought hope and tranquility to millions of people in every corner of the planet.

For Black Jade, the cathedral offered a place to rest while the sun burned outside. It also provided a meeting place for her contacts and kin.

She strolled down the tiled floor, polished to a glassy finish that reflected light from a large golden chandelier above. Wide, fluted columns stretched to high arches supporting the ceiling. Flanking the aisle, dozens of pews faced the large white marble of the High Altar. Beyond that, various niches in the immense golden Altar of the Kings held canonized statues of kings and queens, as well as paintings and angelic figures.

Daiyu neared the front pews and smiled at two vampires and three humans who rose from their seats to greet her. "Thank you for meeting me," she said to the group, maintaining enough distance to not harm them. "I'd love to roam the city with all of you and chat like old times. Unfortunately, time is short and we have work to do."

"We received your messages," said Martha, a young local and one of Daiyu's human associates. "I am very sorry for your losses, Black Jade. This strange attacker you spoke of will not leave Mexico City alive."

"We are all ready to fight," added Amoxtli, a vampire and Aztec who fought the Conquistadors during the fall of Tenochtitlan. His lovely name meant 'book' and ironically, he adored reading them by the truckload. "How much time do we have to prepare?"

"I'm grateful to have you all by my side and appreciate your courage," Daiyu began. "I have been tracking this beast since Peru. It travels fast and doesn't remain still for long. If the creature moves equally fast during the day and after dark, I estimate it will arrive tonight. It only hunts vampires and seems to locate them easily, so I'm using myself as bait to lure it here. My strong and old-as-hell presence should provide enough of a beacon."

"What else can you tell us about this monster?" Emanuel asked, another vampire Daiyu had known for centuries. Emanuel meant 'God is with us', a name fitting for their current surroundings. "I still can't believe that thing had been able to overpower several vampires so easily."

"I'm afraid I know very little," Daiyu answered. "The attacks are quick and chaotic. Unfortunately, those two elements had spawned conflicting witness accounts from the people I interviewed on the streets. But I do believe this creature can fly, based on some evidence in Nicaragua."

"The sun will be up any moment, so let's talk strategy," Martha suggested. "I'll call my friends in the southern cities of Pueblo, Chilpancingo, and Oaxaca. They'll establish a spy network throughout the region. Nothing will get through without their awareness, even if the beast takes to the sky."

"Perfect," Daiyu responded as she gazed at Martha in admiration. The young woman had always proven flawless, one step ahead in any situation. Her sharp mind and dominant personality worked well in this grave scenario. "Communication and teamwork are key. Our battleground will be the Zócalo across the street. Amoxtli, make sure the plaza is cleared of people tonight. I'll meet the creature there. The rest of you prepare for an ambush."

"My group has a stash of excellent weapons," Martha offered. "I can't wait to blast this monster in half."

Daiyu smiled. "Are you sure you don't want to be a vampire, Martha? I'd love to spend the next few centuries with you."

Martha grinned. "You've been asking me that for years, and I always say no. Will you ever give up?"

Loud footsteps approached from a side door, and a voice called, "There will be no vampire-making or blood-drinking in my church."

Daiyu recognized Father Torres, an elderly priest. He wore a black, ankle-length cassock with long sleeves, and dark eyes peered above a salt and pepper beard. He halted and stood rigid, hands folded behind his back.

"Well, then it's a good thing my victim turned me down," Black Jade replied.

"Years ago, I told you I don't like the undead using the church as a hangout," Father Torres stated. "It's disrespectful."

"I don't intend to be," Daiyu said. "But if you're offended, I guess I'll have to increase my donation to the church coffer next year."

Father Torres' stern gaze broke into a wide smile. "Then all is forgiven."

Daiyu laughed. "I wish I could hug you, old man. It's been a long time. I'd love to catch up, but there's serious work to be done."

"Of course," the priest replied in a solemn tone. He embraced everyone else in the group, all of them long-time acquaintances. "Amoxtli, you are an honored Aztec warrior who has protected this city for centuries. You bravely fought the Conquistadors and must now face another great challenge." He gazed at each human and vampire. "I've heard enough of this mysterious monster to know it should not thrive in this world. The church is your sanctuary, and I pray for your success."

"Thank you very much, Father Torres," said Daiyu. "Hopefully, everything will end tonight."

The priest nodded, then turned to leave. "Don't break anything, clean up your messes, and most of all…come back safely." He strolled back down the aisle between the pews and disappeared through a door.

"Let's get to work," Daiyu told the others.

Using a large map of the city, the discussion and planning continued until sunrise. Afterwards, Martha left with the humans to ready the weapons and look for advantageous positions for the assault.

Restricted by sunlight, the vampires remained indoors and trained in the large foyer. None of them had ever faced an aerial adversary. They practiced tactics, sparred, and worked on coordinated attacks to take the powerful beast down. After a late afternoon doze stretched out on the pews, night fell and the undead stepped outdoors to meet Martha in the plaza.

Amoxtli went ahead to scout the permitter for pedestrians and spread word of the looming danger. As the plaza cleared, Martha informed Daiyu of where the humans would be stationed. Daiyu instructed the vampires to remain nearby on the adjacent street.

The preparations set, Black Jade stood alone in the center of the darkened Zócalo. Night smothered the area, but her supernatural vision spotted fine details in every nook. Vendor booths sat empty in the wide square of old, concrete tile. A few discarded cups and napkins littered the ground. A cat sprinted across the bordering street. Realizing the imminent battle, most of the buildings in the neighboring area had shut off their lights as residents fled to other parts of Mexico City.

Daiyu lifted her strict gaze and *projected* her powerful aura in an expanding sphere high above the rooftops. The monster had already proven capable of tracking vampires, but she wanted to ensure it targeted her first by lighting a bonfire under its nose.

"I will show you true violence," she uttered in anger.

Hours passed. Daiyu may as well been a statue in the middle of the plaza, for she had not moved. She listened. Watched. Waited. She sensed Amoxtli and Emanuel in their hiding spots. She smelled Martha and the humans in the shadows, the scent of gun oil and sweat strong.

Daiyu's phone suddenly buzzed from a text. She finally moved to glance at the screen and saw Martha's message to the group: *Spy network in Oaxaca spotted the creature. Three minutes out.*

Three minutes for a human to see it, but Black Jade had already sighted the beast far in the distance. Not any beast, but a demon! The thing moved fast across the sky. Wings rose and fell in forceful strokes. The demon flew without precaution, uncaring about cover or being stealthy. Daiyu's anger intensified. Did arrogance drive the creature's nonchalant approach? Did it think itself so powerful that nothing could stop it?

Black Jade fixed a hateful stare on the monster and screamed in rage. The demon had already passed through the edge of her aura and more than likely detected her. However, she desired to spice up its hunt through a call of fury from its supposed victim.

The demon accepted the bait. Wings pressed against its body, the beast dove like a missile toward Daiyu. Gunfire exploded from an alley as the monster neared the plaza. Bright tracer rounds zipped toward the target and lit the sky. Several rounds missed, but the few that struck its thick flesh did not slow or deter the creature.

Daiyu set her feet and crouched in a defense, ready to leap or block. Two of the demon's six slanted eyes fixed onto her—the other four flicked in all directions, scanning. A bullet ricocheted off one of the sharp bones growing from its shoulder. Another pierced its muscled, gray flesh. A mouth in a nose-less face split to expose jagged teeth.

114

The demon spread its large wings and suddenly veered right. A powerful flap drove the creature toward the vampires hunkered in shadow across the street.

"Watch out!" Daiyu shouted.

The vampires scattered. Their undead bodies moved in a blur, but the demon easily matched their speed. The long-clawed monster caught Emanuel, the nearest. A swipe from the beast's strong arm tore the vampire's head off.

Daiyu's warning and subsequent charge arrived too late. Her speed practically teleported her to the creature, yet a powerful blow from its wing knocked her into the side of a building. She crashed through the wall and into an office. Rolling for several more feet, her body plowed a bookshelf and desk, the furniture bursting in sprays of wood and loose paper.

Black Jade stood and gaped in horror through the hole in the wall. The demon knelt next to Emanuel's headless body, claws slashing wildly at the corpse. It dug into the chest cavity and ripped out a blackened heart and dead organs. The frenzied monster then peered inside the gaping wound as if searching for something.

"Emanuel!" Daiyu uttered in anguish. Another of her kin lay dead. "What sick, demented creature is this?" she added in disgust.

A blur of color zipped down the street toward the demon—Amoxtli. The agile vampire dodged an arm swipe then delivered a thundering kick to the monster's face. The demon flipped backward and bounced across the concrete tile of the plaza.

No time to mourn, Daiyu sprinted through the broken wall to follow up Amoxtli's attack. The beast regained its footing, but she timed her approach and

115

buried a hard fist in the creature's midsection. Another punch rocketed upward and smashed beneath the demon's jaw, breaking it.

The monster recovered in a flash. Daiyu side-stepped a clawed foot as it swept past her head, but a large hand wrapped her neck in a steel grip. The demon's opposite fist smashed her face, returning a break as her nose shattered. Her black, lifeless blood spattered the monster as it stared.

"Madness," Daiyu whispered.

The brief lock of eyes revealed enough; this thing was far from normal. She had met hundreds of demons over the millennia. Many had been cruel and evil in their own way, but nothing compared to what stood before her now in the abandoned Zócalo. This demon's irrational behavior and empty, terrifying gaze surpassed normal malevolence. The raging beast lacked emotion, consciousness, and even basic intelligence.

An additional realization stunned her even more. Daiyu *recognized* the demon. She had met it before, imprisoned in the green eyes of Marcelo Abana Flores.

This fight in Mexico marked the second time the creature had broken her face. The first battle took place on Dead Horse Beach in Salem. After initiating her trial against Marcelo, the false vampire had lost control and allowed his demon spirit to come forth. She had witnessed the soul raging behind Marcelo's gaze when it briefly overpowered Daiyu to land a severe blow.

A terrible comprehension sprang forth as she struggled in the demon's grasp. The insane beast didn't randomly kill vampires without reason. It only hunted a *specific* vampire—Marcelo. The soul, and its physical body standing before her, wished to reunite. But the mindless monster lacked the understanding to discern one vampire from another. Daiyu saw what the monster did to Emanuel. The creature had ripped him open, desperately searching as if to pull out the actual soul and absorb it.

Searching for undead proved to be the berserk demon's only instinct. However, it did have some sort of mental compass to help achieve its goal. After studying the monster's pattern of travel across South America, Central America, and into Mexico, Daiyu grew certain that the soul somehow pulled the demon toward it. The beast had a path; it just didn't know who stood on it.

Over the last two-thousand years, Daiyu had forgotten what fear felt like. The sensation now pooled in her gut—cold, undesirable, and detested. The crazed demon must be destroyed at all cost. It had already slaughtered numerous vampires and would not stop until reunited with its soul.

A loud crack sounded as the monster's jaw repaired and snapped back into place. Daiyu's broken nose had also healed. Another pop erupted as a bullet slammed into the demon's head. Its grip loosened on Daiyu's throat, and she pulled free.

Bullets peppered the beast as Martha and the humans closed in. Automatic fire ripped through the air and shotgun blasts roared. The creature snarled and leapt high into the sky, then soared over the plaza in rapid circles.

"Martha, take everyone inside the cathedral and stay there," Daiyu ordered.

"Why—"

"Now!" Daiyu shouted.

117

"But Black Jade, strength in numbers," Amoxtli protested. "We shouldn't divide our forces."

"We are not dividing," she answered. "You will also join the humans inside. Emanuel has fallen, and I won't risk losing anyone else. I will fight this demon alone."

Her hard, ancient stare expressed volumes of her command. In deep silence, the vampires and humans marched into the cathedral. Daiyu looked up at the circling monster. She launched her aura again, taunting the creature.

"Face me!" she cried.

The demon swooped down but headed for the cathedral. Black Jade anticipated the move and burst into action. Her body zoomed across the plaza, and she vaulted off a wood vendor booth. Sailing upward, she extended a leg and plowed her foot into the beast's shoulder. The demon lost control of its flight and slammed headfirst into the side of an adjacent building. The cement wall cracked, and windows shattered as the creature fell in a shower of rubble.

Daiyu barely landed from her jump when the enemy recovered and charged. The combatants danced and struggled in an exchange of thunderous strikes. Punches cracked ribs and dented skulls. Kicks sent teeth flying and snapped bones. Claws and fingernails tore flesh and splashed blood. Back and forth wrestling smashed bodies into the ground and dislocated joints.

The brawl continued. Twice, the demon broke free and sped toward the cathedral. Daiyu rushed across the plaza and barely halted each effort. She strained to keep her enemy from the structure and protect her friends.

118

The fight dragged on. Neither opponent gained a significant advantage. How long would this continue? The demon was too strong. No…too *insane* to deal with. The rabid beast had an endless battery and an unstoppable, perverse will. Pain had no effect. Every attack or strategy became nulled. How much longer before sunrise? If this went on too long, Daiyu would have an even greater foe to handle.

Several minutes later, the monster broke contact and shuffled back. Its six eyes glanced between the cathedral and Daiyu. Its hands opened and closed, sharp claws clicking rapidly together in agitation. The gray, misshapen head tilted slightly to the side. The monster seemed to be making an assessment. In what could only be described as a fraction of thought, the demon finally reached a conclusion and leapt into the air. Strong wings beat against the night sky as the beast finally disappeared.

"North," Daiyu observed.

The creature was headed further along Mexico, toward the United States. Her premonition about the soul laying a path for the demon seemed true. In a matter of time, the thing would find Marcelo. But how many more vampires would be murdered along that path? Daiyu had to think of something. She couldn't stand the thought of her kin dying at the hands of this demented monster.

Gaping holes pocked most of the Zócalo square. Concrete tile lay shattered, pulverized by the battle. Pieces of vendor booths littered the area. Deep cuts bled from Daiyu's body, her black, cold blood staining the ground. Limping on her fractured femur, she stepped through the plaza mess and entered the cathedral.

Her friends ran to meet her in the foyer. Amoxtli wrapped an arm around Daiyu's waist and led her to a pew. Martha inspected Black Jade's body and pressed a cloth against the worst wound. Daiyu didn't feel any pain or weariness, and the blood loss posed no danger. Her body had already started to heal, and the more severe injuries would vanish after a good snooze. Her companions more than likely understood this, but she loved the warm gestures of care from the old Aztec and modern human.

Martha wiped a tear, her face raw from crying. "Oh Emanuel, I can't believe he's gone."

"Neither…neither can I," Amoxtli whispered, his expression distant. He appeared quite lost and even glanced around as if Emanuel might show up at any moment.

With the battle completed for now, the impact of Emanuel's death hit Daiyu hard. She winced, though not due to Martha's touch as the woman continued to clean black blood. The weight of losing a centuries-old friend crushed Black Jade's spirit. She desired to cry, scream, and punch holes in the cathedral walls. But with Amoxtli and Martha in their own dark places, losing control now would not help the situation.

"Martha, was anyone injured?" Daiyu asked in a strained voice.

"Carlos was burned by a shell casing and Steph received a shrapnel wound from exploding concrete," she answered. "It was nothing serious. I sent them home already."

"Good," Daiyu responded. "As for the demon, it fled north and won't be coming back."

"We need to follow," Martha said. "I'll notify my contacts. We can lay another trap in León or flush the monster toward San Luis Potosí."

Daiyu patted Martha's knee. "Thank you, but that won't be necessary. I realized we don't need to kill this thing. Chasing it from city to city in an endless battle is futile. Nothing can stop that creature. Insanity and rage are its weapons and armor. Desire to reclaim its true self fuels the beast. The only way to stop the demon is to give it what it wants."

"What do you mean?" Amoxtli inquired.

"Tonight, we will place Emanuel to rest," said Daiyu. "Tomorrow, you and I are flying over to Los Angeles. I'll explain everything on the way."

Chapter Nine

Council of Memories

With Amoxtli at her side, Daiyu walked past the long line of patrons waiting to enter Blood Rush, a ritzy blood studio in downtown Los Angeles. Muffled club music boomed from inside, the late-night attracting vampire and human alike. An impressive silver and black Bugatti Chiron drove past her and stopped at the studio entrance illuminated by neon lights. A uniformed valet welcomed the well-dressed passengers and took charge of the vehicle for parking.

Having no time to purchase her own Bugatti or other fancy automobile, an Uber had dropped Daiyu and Amoxtli off across the street. The tall, muscled human bouncer spotted her approach. His brown eyes widened, and he quickly opened the frosted glass door to allow the pair inside.

Another bouncer, this one an undead in an awful suit, greeted them. "Everyone is upstairs, Black Jade. Well, not everyone. Nathaniel did his best to summon those you had asked for, but on such short notice…" He appeared uncomfortable, glancing around the foyer and back at Daiyu.

"It's fine," she said. "I know the way."

122

"Of course," the bouncer responded, stepping aside.

Daiyu strolled past the long check-in counter and returned several greetings as people recognized her. And who wouldn't know her, for she was the owner of the damned place. She didn't operate the location as Nathaniel handled that aspect, which he was quite good at. She noticed nice upgrades to the sound system, a different paint scheme, and remodeling in the lobby since she had last visited. She liked the changes and would let Nathaniel know.

Blood Rush had become renowned ever since its doors first opened decades ago. Hollywood elites and famous sports athletes visited. Popular politicians, rich lawyers, and even foreign dignitaries stopped by. Daiyu had grown proud of the establishment, a place she always returned to no matter how far she traveled or how long she'd been away.

She passed through a second set of doors into the main club area, where the music intensified. An ocean of supernatural beings and humans packed the multilevel dance floors. Crowds surrounded the various bars spread throughout the establishment. Highlighting the principal feature of Blood Rush, long couches and private booths held humans willing to offer their blood to some thirsty vampires. Strict regulation governed the process. Security cameras ensured enforcement of law, while registered nurses supervised the transfer of blood. Beneath the strobe lights and tempo of great music, vampires received an essential meal and humans experienced a natural "high" to further enhance their evening.

Daiyu inhaled the rich scent of A-positive blood from Spanish male in a corner booth. B-negative tickled her nose, the source a Tongan female draped across a vampire's lap as he sipped from a tube connected to her arm. Daiyu glanced back at Amoxtli, his wide smile matching her thoughts—after the meeting, a nice drink.

But first, business. A grave issue needed to be addressed, something that may soon affect the vampires in Los Angeles and perhaps beyond.

Daiyu rode the glass elevator to the fourth floor, a much quieter area consisting of offices, a coffee bar, and storage. She moved down a hallway and into a large, carpeted meeting room. A computer workstation in the corner ran the projector and IT equipment for video teleconferences, a dry erase board on the opposite side. A room-length window displayed the bright city lights and nightlife.

In the center of the room, twenty leather chairs surrounded a giant oak table. However, only fourteen vampires occupied the plush seats. Conversation halted when the group spotted Daiyu. Dressed in a crisp, well-tailored suit, Nathaniel smiled and rose to greet them, then led Daiyu and Amoxtli to empty chairs at the head of the table.

"Black Jade, welcome back to Los Angeles," Nathaniel began, his light blue eyes displaying genuine pleasure at seeing her. "It's been some years, and much has happened lately. The supernatural world has been turned upside down. Sun and moon goddesses, witch uprisings, Umaq, demons…where does one even start? I assume that is why you brought us together?"

"It is," Daiyu confirmed. "But there's more. The situation has escalated into a direct threat to our kind."

Anxious murmurs and troubled glances flew across the table. Nathaniel held up a hand to silence the group, his disturbed expression corresponding to the newfound concern. "Most of those summoned by your message arrived as soon as possible, and the rest will show up tomorrow. How may we be of service, Black Jade? What do we know about this terrible threat?"

Daiyu stood and slowly paced in front of the assembly. She paused to study their uneasy postures, each vampire a good leader for the undead within their respective communities across southern California, Las Vegas, and Phoenix.

"I appreciate everyone's prompt arrival on such short notice," she said. "After a difficult journey, I've confirmed reports of vampire murders stretching across multiple cities and countries. Our brothers and sisters are being systematically murdered by a demon, one of Umaq's stock. I last fought the creature in Mexico, and it's headed this way."

A curly-haired female named Eloise cursed in French. She had been born in south France nearly two hundred years ago, her native accent heavy as she spoke in English after her foreign outburst. "I heard a rumor of sorts and am deeply ashamed to have not paid it much attention. How many have perished, Black Jade?"

Daiyu had tried to stop counting after the first few. Each death hammered a painful reminder into her skull of her complacency. "By the time I faced the beast, twenty-two of our kin had fallen... and one more a day ago."

Another loud murmur ran through the attendees. Arms waved in agitation to emphasize shouts. Some hands covered faces. Others looked down in grief or shock. A fist slammed the oak table. Side conversations erupted. It took Nathaniel several moments to calm everyone, although he had initially joined the ruckus as well.

"That magnitude of death in such a short time hasn't occurred in centuries," Maxwell stated, a bald and brown-eyed resident of Las Vegas. After eight-hundred years of walking the earth, he would know, having lived through the vampire hunts of old. "At least it's not humans doing the killing this time. Please tell us more about the demon and its purpose, Black Jade. Why did you say the creature is one of Umaq's stock? Word from Salem is that he had been killed by the witch, Sybil, and her companions."

Daiyu told the group everything she knew. Her story began with Umaq fusing a demon's soul to Marcelo and creating an unnatural version of a vampire. She explained how Umaq tried to compel Marcelo to convert Sybil into an undead, demon-possessed witch under his command. If successful, Umaq would have been able to create other demon-infused undead, a twisted version of vampire that did not belong in this world. This had led Daiyu to commence her trial of Marcelo, to judge if his abnormal existence posed a danger to society and her kind. She continued her account of seeing the demon in Marcelo's eyes, then later recognizing the same beast as the homicidal monster.

"This thing is coming home for its soul," Daiyu concluded. "Marcelo lives in San Luis Obispo north of here, and the demon will slaughter other vampires until reaching its destination."

"But how do we stop this mad monster?" Eloise asked. "Even you couldn't defeat it."

"We don't need to slaughter the demon," Daiyu answered. "Marcelo must die. He is our target."

"But if Marcelo is killed, won't the demon soul be free to return to its body?" Nathaniel asked.

"Yes, exactly," Daiyu replied. "The monster's soul will enter its natural host to reunify. Its sanity will return, and the beast's hunt of vampires will conclude. Afterwards, I could care less about what the demon does. The point is no more deaths of our kin."

"Marcelo is a tough nut to crack, and his friends are also powerful," Maxwell observed. "They defeated Umaq, rescued a sun god, and have the favor of other deities. Rumor has it Marcelo flies in moon chariots and travels across the planet in ley lines." He shook his bald head. "This is no easy task. Some vampires may die, which ironically is what we are trying to avoid." He spread his hands. "Out of the pot and into the fire."

Despite constant muffled beats from the club music below them, a thick silence coated the meeting room. No chair creaked or rustle of clothes sounded. Everyone seated at the table watched Daiyu. Worried expressions sank into her flesh and stirred her dead heart. Fear lingered in their eyes and woke painful memories of a darkened past in vampire history.

Daiyu had lived in ancient China during the time of Emperor Qin Shi Huang's construction of the Great Wall. Huang's rise had been born through the violent subjugating of various states to create the Qin Dynasty, a period of strict laws to establish control and eliminate any threats to his rule. Already a transition of chaos, Qin additionally ordered the incineration of all books containing topics he did not find useful, and allegedly buried hundreds of scholars alive.

The unstable era did not bode well for vampires like Daiyu. Supernatural entities had been thrust into the category of menace to the new emperor. Books were not the only thing destroyed by fire. Countless undead died screaming as they crumbled into ash. Vampire clans fled across towns and villages, but no refuge existed. Even hiding in the wilderness turned into foot chases and executions as riled mobs hunted everything devoid of a heartbeat.

But dead hearts did not mean a lack of feelings. Terror, tears, and panic fueled Daiyu's will to live and aid others. She had helped a family of vampires escape death in a small village. In another town, she directed the evacuation of three clans and led them to safety in the mountains through smoke, flames, and screams as houses burned.

When she fled her own destroyed home, other undead families followed. Her initial irritation later turned into compassion. The families' desolate faces and empty eyes matched her own sentiment of broken hope and bitter dread.

Word spread across the countryside of a young savior, a symbol of hope for the dying vampires. Her followers increased. Daiyu never understood why the undead flocked to her side, as if she embodied some powerful warrior or prodigious leader. Back then she possessed neither of those qualities. Everything terrified her. She mostly ran away from conflict. She never planned anything. Yet the local vampires continued to trust Black Jade, perhaps due to the realization they had nowhere else to go.

After the Qin Dynasty collapsed, China once again fell into war. Daiyu and her growing clan found some respite as the humans battled for control and supernatural beings had regressed into an afterthought. When the Han Dynasty emerged, the vampires' limited hiding places once again grew dangerous to inhabit.

To escape the carnage and hopefully discover a better sanctuary, Daiyu led an expedition into Europe—an even greater catastrophe for the undead. At first, the vampire clans prospered for several hundred years without significant risk. However, the chaotic Middle Ages proved to be full of ignorance, superstition, and social oppression that produced an even greater threat to the supernatural.

The hunting and slaughter recommenced. The uprooted vampires fled back into the wilderness. Once again, Daiyu shouldered the responsibility of saving her kin and finding them refuge across Europe. She fought, bled, and watched her people die. During this dark time, she met Maxwell, one of the few people seated at the table that truly understood the pain of losing family through violence.

The distraught faces that looked up to her now mirrored the expressions from centuries ago. Birthed by trauma and imminent danger, the same emotions from the past currently frightened the individuals in the conference room as they sat stiff and unblinking. The number of deaths caused by the demon paled in comparison to the Qin Dynasty and the Middle Ages, but that didn't mean the resulting grief impacted the modern-day vampires any less.

Whether Daiyu's undead family consisted of ancient refugees escaping throughout the continents or contemporary kin fighting in the streets, she would protect them at all costs. She swore no one else would be murdered by the demon. And if the situation called for it, she would gladly sacrifice herself to uphold that promise.

Out of the pot and into the fire, Maxwell had stated. Daiyu couldn't agree more, but not everyone had to get burned. She had started a trial for Marcelo, and it remained her duty to finish it. The demon's killing spree now provided the ultimate evidence of the false vampire's danger to their society. The gavel had fallen. Marcelo's trial just reached a critical stage and an immediate sentence handed down—execution.

"We have the advantage," she told everyone. "I saw Marcelo and his friends in Salem after their battle with Umaq. They are in no shape for a new war and are surely taking time to recover. Their guard is down."

She faced Maxwell. "Your team is with me. We'll go to Avila Beach and rush Marcelo in force, but I'll be the one to face him alone. The witch is sure to be by his side, yet there's no need to worry. She's grown old and weak after paying a heavy price to take down Umaq."

Daiyu nodded toward Eloise. "Your team's duty is to prepare for the demon's arrival. Network with your contacts throughout southern California for news of the monster's appearance. Be vigilant across San Diego, Carlsbad, Irvine…check them all. If I can slay Marcelo quickly enough, then no more vampires will die. But if I fail, our defenses across the cities must be maintained. Plan for evacuations, if necessary."

Evacuations. Hiding. Running. Dodging arrows, fire, and swords throughout multiple countries. Daiyu shuddered at the memories and horror. Would history repeat? Would this berserk demon scatter her kin across freeways, skyscrapers, and blood studios? Before he died, Umaq the demon master had orchestrated his most admirable work. If Sybil and her lucky friends hadn't defeated him, Daiyu would have torn his limbs off.

"Refresh yourselves downstairs, then gather in the lobby," Black Jade directed. She exchanged a glance with Amoxtli, then her hard gaze swept those gathered. "We leave tonight."

Chapter Ten

Only Dark Paths

Through the window of a Greyhound bus, Sybil stared at nothing. After excessive amounts of crying, her tank of emotional reserve had been emptied. The northern journey across California held no captivating scenery. Cites, houses, forests, and freeway passed by in bland repetition. Everything had lost meaning, and nothing stirred interest in her bare heart and soul.

The stops for food and bus changes occurred on autopilot, her body moving on instinct without thought. Flavorless meals and bland drinks failed to satiate her. People's faces blurred, their attempts at conversation dull or ignored.

She napped in nightmare and discomfort. Miles ticked by. The view outside the grimy window changed repeatedly. In Crescent City near the north border, she stepped off the bus and climbed into a taxi for the rest of the trip to Cave Junction in Oregon. She checked into the Holiday Motel, the same place she had stayed with Marcelo and Johann the last time they arrived here. She ate, stared at the TV, and slept.

The next morning, another vehicle took her to Illinois River Forks State Park, part of the massive Klamath Mountains and great national forest spanning across millions of acres between southern Oregon and northern California. She instructed the driver to head down a narrow service road and drop her off within a secluded area.

"Here? Are you sure?" the overweight man asked as Sybil climbed out. "There's nothing around for miles and you're alone."

She appreciated his concern, but *alone* is what she had to get used to from now on. Or at least for how little time she had left.

"I shall fare well, thank you," she responded before closing the door.

Sybil stepped off the worn road and into the surrounding conifers. She inhaled the rich odor of pine as her feet crunched over beds of fallen needles. Hundreds of cones lay scattered around the area. Squirrels darted along the ground and raced up tree trunks. The trees whispered, slept, or sang, their ancient spirits flowing across a massive network of root and branch. She had always enjoyed the peacetime and hospitable silence of forests. The sensation brought comfort, and she welcomed a short period of respite against the raging misery within.

She continued until the trees thinned to reveal a large thicket of shrubs that varied in height from three to six feet. She had first met Salix here in what seemed years ago, a much happier time when she had marveled at the dryad that lived among the species of Del Norte willow.

Salix didn't just dwell in this location; she *was* this place. Similar to the conifers, the dryad's life and spirit roamed among the thicket. Her consciousness thrived in every willow leaf, branch, and root. Her song

133

continued in nature. Her laughter endured on the wind. Grief tore Sybil's heart knowing that Salix's physical presence no longer existed, but the dryad would return in time. For the moment, all Sybil required was her friend's beloved soul.

Sybil listened to her surroundings: the scratch of a squirrel's claws on bark as it climbed, the buzz of an insect, the flap of a bird's wings, a whisper of leaf-covered branches in the breeze. Each sound carried a note of beautiful music. The notes combined into lovely measures, the tempo animated, the melody sweet. The spiritual composition flowed through the brush. The boom of bass wrapped branches and darted between the willows. Treble, light and airy, leapt among leaves and swirled overhead. The touching, omnipresent music conveyed the dryad's words.

Welcome, Spell Weaver. The wind spoke of your arrival, and the Earth Mother relayed all that occurred underground. Many things have changed, and your heart is heavy, your soul in pain. Illness plagues your aged body. You are free of the tunnels, yet you still wander, lost in the dark and deprived of hope. I am sad.

"Dear Salix," Sybil whispered, kneeling. A tear wet the soil as she bowed her head. "My heart hath missed you so much. You also suffered pain, and thus offered the ultimate sacrifice for the world's behoof."

Do not worry. Time and nature will restore me, but your condition will endure. The dark ailment inside you is not of this world. No natural or magical cure exists in our realm, and your age is another matter entirely. I am troubled.

The melody floating through the grove changed. Some notes twisted under strain, their sweet sound now distorted. The rapid tempo beat out of tune. Measures fractured and streams of music warred in conflict. The shattered composition now carried Salix's somber emotion. Each sour note represented her tears, every missed beat a cry of grief.

The last thing Sybil desired was for Salix to feel agony on her behalf. Offering a slim chance of hope, she told the dryad about Umaq's desperate promises before he disappeared into the netherworld.

I am deeply sorry for what you experienced, Spell Weaver. You also committed a sacrifice to rid the world of Umaq. As for the demon master, he spoke true; only he can provide a cure for the illness. Umaq also has the power to restore your youth. I am hopeful.

"Then I shall go forth to yonder demon realm and have a fair sight of Umaq," Sybil replied. "The ancient vampire, Daiyu, hath truly threatened Marcelo. Thereof I must strive to regain my strength, lest he remaineth in peril."

Daiyu is not the only danger to Marcelo. Nature has detected the birth of something evil, a corrupted entity whose disturbance I felt even here in the willow grove. The trees quake in fear. The waters rush and recede in anger. The meadows bend and weep in grief. A demon has awoken, but not just any monster. This animated corpse searches for its soul—the very one inside Marcelo. I am afraid.

Sybil froze in trepidation. A memory flashed and punched her in the gut. Machu Picchu...the demon she had seen! She had looked into that horrid creature's dead eyes and recognized something.

Ever since meeting Marcelo, she had noticed glimmers of the demon soul in his gaze, mostly in times of distress or anger. After witnessing the reanimated body, she had failed to make the connection, but it made sense now. The rabid creature hunted for its lost spirit. In defeat, Umaq must have risen the demon's corpse, the very one Marcelo fought against centuries ago.

Sybil's heart thundered in panic. What would happen to him if the monster reclaimed its soul? Marcelo existed as an undead, but he was not a true vampire. He died long ago, and the soul sustained him. Without it, would her greatest love perish and collapse in a pile of bones? Would he—

Sybil crushed the maddening thought. She took several calming breaths and could barely swallow, her throat dry. First Daiyu and now this beast. If she raced back to Marcelo's side, how useful could she be? She had no magic, no health. She would be in the way, if anything.

As if reading her angst, Salix provided a candid answer, exactly what Sybil had been searching for. *You are no good to anyone if dead, Spell Weaver. Journey into the netherworld to find Umaq. Restore your youth and eliminate the illness. In the meantime, place your trust in Marcelo. He has endured five hundred years of hardship and extraordinary challenge. His heart may not beat, but I have faith in its boundless passion for life. You are his strength and indomitable will. From you, Marcelo already has all the protection he needs. I am truthful.*

Sybil wiped her eyes and sighed. She grasped a branch of a Del Norte willow and caressed its leaves in a soft, loving gesture. "Forthwith I very much wish to embrace you, dear Salix. You speak true, and I shall trust Marcelo with all my heart. But wherefore I ought to trust Umaq? He prattled about reviving Inti. Yonder sun god's

136

light would restore balance to the world and thereof heal the Earth Mother. Of a truth, I owe her my life." She shook her head, dazed by the unexpected path she must take. "I must strive for faith in my worst enemy to uphold his sundry of promises."

And that may be your greatest battle. In his defeat, Umaq left behind chaos and destruction that require additional toil for the greater good. The war, unfortunately, must continue. However, no sword or spell will result in victory against him. Only hope remains, and you must wield it as a weapon. I am confident.

Sybil stared at her feeble, wrinkled hands. She imagined a tiny light—hope—resting on her palms. Marcelo's life pulsed in the glow. The Earth Mother's essence floated in the radiance. The world—restored and free of demons—bathed in the light. Sybil pressed her hands against her chest and buried the sensations deep inside. Her heart beat like a blacksmith's hammer, forging and strengthening that hope into her greatest weapon of all.

She exhaled a deep breath, then stood. Leaning forward, she kissed the willow branch and smiled at the surrounding grove of Del Norte willow. "I love you, Salix. My heart yearns to have a fair sight of you and hold you tight in my arms. Rest well, and grow strong beneath yonder sun and the nourishing rain."

The surrounding foliage and wildlife stirred. Delightful music drifted on the breeze. Rich notes and vibrant beats caressed Sybil's skin as she walked away. The pleasing melodies intertwined and danced among the willow, a sweet farewell.

Reaching the service road where the car had dropped her off, Sybil paused to think. How could she reach Machu Picchu and the portal to the nether realm as quickly as possible? Booking a slow, inconvenient flight was out of the question. She would also not summon Selene's team of horses as the moon deity had gifted use of the chariot to Marcelo. Sybil would not take the vehicle from her love, not even for a second; he may need it to escape the demon at any moment.

A ley line remained the only viable option; a revisit to her nightmare and replay of her trauma. Yet no fear overcame Sybil. Dread did not flood her veins, and no sorrow weakened her legs. Confidence replaced the negative emotions. Experience boosted her resolve. Sybil had discovered the secret of ley travel…at least what worked for her. Having already faced the terror of the underground and defeated it, a repeat encounter failed to discourage her.

She no longer felt afraid, but that didn't stop shame from wrapping her heart in ice. Back in Machu Picchu after Umaq disappeared, she had accepted her near-death condition and settled on the grass to die. Cowardice and self-pity had been her true ailment, not age and black illness. Countless problems existed in the world, so much larger than her own.

Sybil would not give up, nor lay down and fade away. Too much to work remained. A powerful, rabid demon threatened Marcelo's very existence. With Inti's death, the world still lay in unbalanced darkness. The natural, mystical energy across the planet and in-between realms had grown unstable. Umaq may be gone, but the portal in Machu Picchu still functioned. Powerful demons, new ones not under his control, could still emerge.

And the Earth Mother, the sole reason Sybil still breathed. The Mother's absolute love and persistent care had saved Sybil's life. She couldn't ignore that fact and allow the omnipotent earth spirit to suffer her own dark illness beneath the ground.

Sybil wrote her note to Marcelo as a final word, for she never expected to see him again. She had not given up, but the reality of her condition stood large and menacing. Older, weakened, and ill, her impossible journey into the demon realm to rescue a bitter enemy only reinforced that final word—her last sentiment of love for Marcelo captured on pen and paper.

Only dark paths lay ahead, but how would they end?

Chapter Eleven

The Hunt

The nameless demon flew through the night sky, searching. Thousands of lights glittered below. Organic lifeforms moved about the large city. Spirits drifted in-between the realms. Humans and supernatural entities mingled. Magical residue flowed inside homes, down streets. A world of life and energy thrived beneath the monster, but it only craved one thing.

Its prey.

Seen from high in the air, purple illuminations also traveled about the city or remained gathered in places. These particular lights called to the demon. The attractive glows birthed a ferocious addiction inside the creature. Its mouth salivated in hunger. A reanimated heart boomed in its chest. The beast's claws clicked together in anticipation. Absolute, uncontrolled desire fueled its rage as it dove toward a cluster of purple radiance on the corner of a busy intersection.

The demon swooped lower across many strange buildings. The city swallowed the beast as it landed on the street. Loud human noises, flashing machines, and the horrid stenches of society assaulted the monster. People walked about. Doors opened and closed. Smoke, bottles, and disgusting food. Nothing made sense here or in any of the places the beast hunted. Confusion rattled its nerves. Bedlam warped the demon's mind. Insatiable hunger tore its insides.

But the purple light, the irresistible force, stood nearby. The violet illumination surrounded the bodies of several undead beings. The aura promised salvation. Paradise awaited. The glow sang of a hidden secret trapped inside each body. All the monster had to do was rip it out.

The demon's clawed feet scraped on the asphalt as it sped forth and knocked away a rolling human machine. People screamed and ran—except the prey. The targets held their ground and engaged in battle. The beast tore the limbs off an undead, then slammed a hole through another's chest. Rib bones and vertebrae flew as the demon searched for the secret.

Nothing.

A barrage of kicks and punches rained on the monster. Bricks, long metal poles, and wood shards pounded. The beast turned and bit the head off another undead. Long claws ripped open the target's abdomen. Another fruitless search.

Gunfire tore chunks from the demon's flesh. It retaliated and broke an undead in half. No secret. More fighting and chaos. Store windows shattered and rolling machines flipped over in the wide street. Overhead lights broke and glass clattered on the ground. Beneath their glowing purple aura, two additional undead provided no answer as they lay in pieces.

Not here. Keep moving. Come to me.

The monster paused in alarm as a voice spoke inside its muddled head. The familiar words had called out before, several times in fact. The voice sounded so convincing and truthful, telling him the secret would not be found here. Time to search elsewhere.

With a rage-filled bellow, the monster launched into the air. It soared onward to the next shining city. The demon sensed an unexplainable tug, something drawing it ever closer to the secret.

Perhaps in this new place, its hunt would finally end.

Chapter Twelve

Verdict

Marcelo ripped open a vampire's chest cavity. Cold, black blood sprayed his clothes and face. His eager hand dove into the grotesque wound, searching. Nothing found. He cast the broken body aside. Bullets peppered Marcelo's body. Baseball bats hammered his shoulders and limbs. The damage barely slowed him. His flesh healed in moments.

He glanced around the chaotic, long city block. Mortals ran in fright. Vampires lay in shredded piles. Their severed arms and snapped bones littered the street. Marcelo screamed in horror. Blood soaked his hands. What had he done?

Not here. Keep moving. Come to me.

***

The familiar voice jolted Marcelo out from his nightmare. His eyes snapped open, and he stared at the bedroom ceiling. If he had been human, sweat would drench his skin and soak the sheets. Gasps would fill his lungs as he struggled for air, heart pounding. Those mortal traits didn't plague him, but the severe impact of

143

the dreadful and violent dream left him momentarily paralyzed.

His shocked mind tried to relax and process the lifelike imagery he had just witnessed. Not once in his centuries-old existence had he ever experienced such a realistic, powerful nightmare. He heard the screams and shouts. He *felt* the torn flesh and cracked bones in his hands. The crunch of glass beneath his shoes, the gum on the sidewalk, the smell of greasy burgers from the diner on the corner...it seemed like Marcelo had truly stood there.

And strangest of all, the voice that woke him belonged to the demon soul trapped in his body.

Nice work, Sherlock, the demon spirit suddenly said. *Glad you figured it all out.*

Flashes of the city street horror continued to plague Marcelo. Trying not to wake Sybil, he carefully rolled out of bed and stepped into the bathroom. He shut the door and snapped on the light. Placing his hands on either side of the sink, he leaned close to the mirror and stared into his green eyes.

"What in the hell are you even talking about?" he whispered to the beast inside him.

I wanted it to be a surprise, but there's no more use hiding the truth, the demon answered. *Our mutual friend, Umaq the Betrayer, resurrected my body. It's coming for you, Marcelo. I will finally unite with my flesh and be rid of your useless human shell!*

Marcelo backed away from the mirror as if it struck him. Fear and revulsion twisted his face. Dread pooled in his belly and froze his legs.

"That's not possible," he said in disbelief, but understood that Umaq had proven capable of anything.

144

"My dream…all of that really happened. You killed those vampires!"

He shook his head over the somber realization. Marcelo shared a cursed existence with the demon soul; knowing he had somehow peered through the creature's reanimated eyes didn't surprise him much. Sybil had described the end of Umaq, but the demented man's work continued to plague the world. Marcelo's initial shock melted into simmering anger. He clenched his fists and stepped close to the mirror.

"I'm going to stop this madness to prevent more death," he whispered to the malevolent spirit. "Your rotting carcass will return to the earth in pieces!"

The demon soul laughed. *Great plan! Going after my body will only expedite the union. So please, hurry along.*

Marcelo hesitated. The demon's taunt seemed to make sense. Would an attempt to seek the body only give the beast what it wanted?

Frustrated, Marcelo snapped off the light and reentered the bedroom. His preternatural vision saw clearly in the dark…and the empty bed where Sybil should have been. Had he woken her, and she slipped out to the kitchen for a snack or drink?

Unease chilled him as he stepped out into the hallway. No lights on in the house. Not a sound.

"Sybil?" he called into the dark.

He hurried into the living room, turning on lights. Panic began to surge when he didn't see her in the kitchen or study. He rushed into the dining room and stopped cold. Sybil's phone and a note lay on the table.

Before approaching, Marcelo already knew the meaning contained a terrible story. His body numb, he

145

neared the table. Hands trembled while picking up the sheet of paper.

He read. He cried.

Sybil's writing ripped an emotional hole in his chest. He swayed and gripped the back of a wooden chair. Marcelo cursed and shouted in despair. He read the note again, then raced to the bedroom and threw on clothes.

Self-disgust and anger boiled inside him. His guard had dropped upon hearing of Umaq's demise. He had grown careless after finding Sybil and returning her home. Meanwhile, his love continued to suffer, ill and aged after a horrible trauma he wished to erase. She had worked to comfort him while he acted too self-absorbed to realize the truth of her deep pain—it hadn't lessened but grown worse.

And now she had disappeared on him for the second time.

"Please forgive me, Sybil," he said, grabbing his wallet and phone. "You are never alone."

Her words from the letter stung. Each sentence bit his skin, every paragraph impaled his heart. His mind reeled as he flew out of the house and toward his car. Sybil's voice echoed as if she recited the message.

My dearest love, Marcelo,

Some things in life must be striven for on one's own. Hardships shall be endured lest we never conquer them. Nightmares shall be experienced to truly conceive their meaning. The darkness from yonder underground remaineth in my heart. My disquieted spirit lingers in the tunnel, lost and alone. Often, I wonder if I still dwell down yonder and standing hither is illusion wrapped in madness.

The intent of this bitter writing—'tis not to distress you, my dear love, but to make you conversant of the truth as lies carry greater pain. Time shall not provide remedy, I warrant. Thereof, I cannot smile and prattle that my heart fares well. Forthwith, I am unable to lay by your side and thus pretend fear does not incapacitate me.

Of a truth, I ought to journey forth alone, Marcelo. To have a fair sight of myself, I shall search outside my body and within my soul. If I do not find what I seek, then this is goodbye. Yet if I do find the answer to my behoof, it may still be farewell. Aforesaid, no easy path exists. Fog lies before me on yonder road. No signs shall guide the way home.

Be well, sweet Marcelo. Truly, you are the greatest thing that hath ever happened to me. I love you very much.

Yours forever,
Sybil

Marcelo dove behind the wheel of the Aston Martin and fired the engine. Where should he begin looking for Sybil? She couldn't have gotten far. Her words continued to haunt him, making it hard to think. What did she intend? Did she mean to go into the netherworld to search for Umaq? Was she headed back underground to face her personal demons? Had she embarked on a quest to find a cure to her illness?

Not having any idea what she planned, simply finding his true love remained the important task. The answers would arrive later. Marcelo sent a rapid text to

Johann and explained the situation, to keep an eye and ear out for any whisper of Sybil. Car revving, he raced out of the long, curving driveway and onto the street. He had a couple hours to search the night before sunrise caused him problems.

A thunderous force slammed the driver's side door. Through the windshield, the dark road and houses flipped over and over as the car rolled from the impact. Restrained by the seatbelt, Marcelo's arms and legs flailed helplessly. The crumpled vehicle finally stopped atop its roof on someone's lawn.

The strong odor of antifreeze and hot oil filled the warped interior. Smoke billowed from the sides of the dented hood. Covered in glass, Marcelo struggled out of the seatbelt and crawled through the shattered windshield to escape the wreckage.

He barely rose when a strong fist knocked him against the car. A kick from a second individual sent him to the ground. Marcelo scrambled to his feet, arms up to block. Two vampires faced him on the lawn. One more crouched above the roof of the house. A glance behind him revealed three more vampires standing in the street next to a black SUV, its front end smashed from where it struck the Aston Martin.

Marcelo sprinted away, but too many opponents made escape impossible. The vampires sped in blurs of color, darting back and forth in a game of cat and mouse. Hard shoves plowed Marcelo into the road. Feet tripped him into crashes on the sidewalk. Each attempt at flight only caused further injury and torn clothes. He finally gave up as the group surrounded him.

A blue sedan pulled up next to the damaged SUV, and a single undead emerged. "Maxwell, the witch is not in the residence," the driver announced to one of the vampires in the street. "We can't locate her anywhere."

Marcelo tensed, the fear and rage warring. His opponents also searched for Sybil! What did this group want? At least she remained out of sight, hopefully far from here.

"Forget about the witch, Amoxtli, we have what we need in front of us," the bald vampire named Maxwell replied. He stared at Marcelo, his brown eyes narrowed in anger as he pointed a trembling finger. "It's your fault our brothers and sisters are dying! I want to kill you myself, but it's not my place. Go back down the road to the beach. Black Jade is waiting for you."

Marcelo recalled his last encounter with Daiyu back in Salem. A similar situation had occurred when vampires forced him into a vehicle to meet Black Jade. There, his absurd trial began on Dead Horse Beach. He had a feeling it would end here on Avila Beach—and not in his favor.

Based on Maxwell's accusation, Daiyu and her clan knew about the approaching demon. As Marcelo had witnessed in his horrid vision of slaughter, the deranged beast must have caused havoc ever since its resurrection. It seemed Daiyu had been right; Marcelo's existence proved to be a danger to society. In a night packed with grief, frayed nerves, and wild surprises, he could almost laugh at the irony. Having no choice but to face the outcome of the trial, he turned and headed toward the nearby beach.

"I'll be with you soon, Sybil," he whispered.

That's all that mattered now. Facing Black Jade brought no fear, but losing the love of his life terrified him. His mind worked in overdrive. How could he get past Daiyu and her gang? Even if he did, would he be able to find Sybil?

This is why I can't wait to be rid of you, the demon soul remarked. *Weak. Moody. Too human for my taste.*

Despite the odds against surviving the night, an idea suddenly struck Marcelo, a crazy one with no time to plan. "If Daiyu kills me in the next few minutes, you get nothing," he replied, nearing the sandy strip a couple blocks from his house.

The demon returned a hard silence. In all its boasting and preparation, the evil spirit had overlooked a critical aspect of the situation.

"I saw through the eyes of your rotten body and learned something interesting," Marcelo continued. "If I die, the soul becomes free, but your physical form needs to be in proximity for the merger to succeed. That's why your animated carcass is tearing vampires apart. It's insane and doesn't know any better, but your body's instinct is spot on. Gotta be close or be nothing. Without a proper vessel, the spirit will fade away. It just might get lost between multiple realms or wander the netherworld forever. Who knows."

The demon soul growled in Marcelo's mind. *What…what do you propose, then? You wouldn't allow Daiyu to murder you just to spite me. You have Sybil to think of.*

"Of course, and I actually do have a proposal," Marcelo said. "Fight with me instead of against me like you have for the last five hundred years. Accept my body and utilize its strengths and weaknesses. In Salem, I allowed you to take full control and we achieved a moment of success against Daiyu. This time we'll work as one. Let's join forces, demon. This is your only chance for survival…and mine."

Another round of silence as Marcelo waited. He left the concrete and stepped onto the soft sand. The cold ocean water stretched across the dark horizon. White froths appeared at each wave break. Ahead, Daiyu stood barefoot on the shore just as she had waited for him on Dead Horse Beach. Déjà vu, except Marcelo might not walk away this time.

"Time up, demon," Marcelo uttered under his breath in desperation. "What's it going to be?"

A moment of quiet. Then…*Yes. But you're only delaying the inevitable. After Daiyu is dead, my corpse will arrive to tear you in half and claim the soul regardless. You're a fool, only buying yourself a few more minutes of life.*

"True," Marcelo responded. Having no real plan, he had nothing to hide or bargain with. This option represented the only way forward. For now, he could only live in the moment, one precious second at a time. "You let me worry about that."

I'm going to enjoy pulverizing Black Jade into dust! the demon roared.

Immense relief coursed through Marcelo as the monster expressed its enthusiasm to cooperate. His steps seemed lighter, the large weight on his shoulders reduced. A heavy cloud of worry dissipated from his mind. He had achieved a mental victory in one battle. Yet as he approached Black Jade, the greatest and most dangerous encounter may soon commence. He stopped several feet from her outside the range of her icy, crushing aura.

"Welcome, Marcelo," Daiyu began. "Your road has been long with much adversity. You've traveled the world and faced a multitude of challenges. In a short amount of time, you and Sybil have experienced an era of hardship and emotional distress. And to highlight this chapter, your trial has finally come to an end."

Irritated, Marcelo shook his head. "You just can't help it, can you? The grand speech and pomp, I mean. Your fellow vampires are being slaughtered, and yet you still waste time making a show of everything. Forcing me to walk to the shore, replicating the scene at Dead Horse Beach in Salem, and now a long-winded monologue."

She smiled and stroked the long black braid hanging in front of her shoulder. Despite the inevitable fight, the ancient undead still wore expensive jewelry around her neck and wrists. The silk designer blouse probably cost a fortune. It seemed even her appearance had become part of the overall spectacle.

"You are right, I can't help it," Daiyu admitted. "I've lived for over two-thousand years. With so much extra time on my hands, patience and savoring special moments like this are my nature." She offered a light shrug. "But your observation about wasting time is also correct, so I'm going to slaughter you in the next few moments."

"Then I suppose you found me guilty," Marcelo responded. "That crazy demon is murdering vampires because of me, I get it. I'm genuinely sorry for what is happening, Black Jade. But my long road and era with Sybil, as you described it, is not over. She's in trouble and needs my help, so shut up for once and let's end this."

Daiyu laughed as a wave broke on the sand. "I'm not laughing at your defiance and dismissal of my threat to kill you. I'm humored by your macho claim that Sybil needs your help." She folded her arms and clucked her tongue. "Sybil's condition shocked me when I saw her in Salem. I saw something in her eyes, Marcelo, something that—"

Daiyu stopped and waved a dismissive hand. "Here I am launching into pomp again at a time-critical juncture. Oh, but what a conversation we can have right now about Sybil! It's too bad our chat has ended. My gavel has fallen, Marcelo. You are hereby guilty of crimes against society and my vampire kind. Innocent blood stains your hands. Your sentence—death!"

Black Jade fell quiet, her hardened gaze on Marcelo. All humor and casual attitude vanished from her features. Her diminutive posture changed, no longer nonchalant, but tense and prepared for movement.

Showtime, human, the demon said to Marcelo. *After we rip her face off, just remember you couldn't have done this without me!*

On the beach in Salem, Marcelo had allowed the demon full control of his body. His strength had surged. Speed and agility boosted his movements. Marcelo "watched" the action and likened the situation to taking a back seat to his own body. He had released the steering wheel, removed a hand from the shifter, and let the demon soul drive the car. The beast had managed to smash Daiyu's nose and mouth, but in the end, Marcelo received a major beatdown in defeat.

This new agreement—a deal with the devil, as the saying went—changed everything. The genuine need to survive cemented the demon and Marcelo's collaboration, a shared interest for once in five hundred years. This time, Marcelo gripped the wheel next to the beast's clawed hands. The shifter slammed forward and back through the gears, powered by the combined strength and will of human body and demon soul. The vehicle roared, a thousand extra horsepower revving the engine.

Daiyu exploded forth, her small fist a missile aimed at Marcelo's jaw. He moved his head to the side. The force of Black Jade's missed blow caused her to stumble forward in surprise. She nearly fell on the sand, then turned around, bewildered. The old Marcelo would have been incapable of dodging or blocking the strike, the potential impact possibly tearing his head off.

He smiled and crossed his arms. "You've lost a step since we last met."

"Not at all," she replied, taking a cautious step forward and staring for a moment. "The demon soul lurks in your gaze, Marcelo. I see it, can almost hear it laughing. I haven't lost a thing, but you've gained an ally."

"Desperate times, as they say," he said with a shrug. "Now come at me, Judge Jade. Swing your little gavel and put me down!"

Seemingly unaccustomed to receiving taunts, Daiyu's face narrowed in fury. With a loud cry, she burst forth, her kicks and punches barraging Marcelo. Like an invisible shield, her thick and heavy aura threatened to weaken and slow him. However, his newfound strength and speed allowed him to maneuver in ease. He blocked her strikes, dodged, and toppled when a hard blow finally knocked him flat.

Daiyu threw herself on Marcelo, and the pair wrestled for control. Sand sprayed and clothes tore. Elbows found faces and knees exposed ribs in a furious exchange. Daiyu maneuvered on top, and her headbutt smashed Marcelo's nose into pulp. From his back, a returned fist cracked against her cheekbone and sent her rolling.

On their feet, they danced around in feints and strikes. Punches plowed into each other's guts and smashed mouths. Marcelo landed the more significant attacks, his blows snapping Daiyu's head back.

As the fight dragged on and intensified, Black Jade must have realized her inevitable defeat. The blazing light in her eyes diminished, her fierce mask replaced by apprehension. The cockiness dwindled as well as her strength. Overconfidence waned in sloppy punches and less agile maneuvers.

Marcelo didn't waste the advantage. He grabbed her wrist after a failed punch and twisted her arm until it snapped at the elbow. A sharp blow broke her jaw. His shoe bashed into her chest and sent her flying into the frothing salt water. Following, he splashed knee-deep into the ocean and dragged her writhing form out by the braid. Marcelo then swung her body and tossed her up the beach like a sack of grain.

Covered in sticky sand, Daiyu stood and failed to react to Marcelo's relentless charge. His forehead smashed into her nose and knocked her down, where she remained. He knew she didn't experience pain, feel winded, could lose consciousness, or die from blood loss. She simply lay there by choice. As he stood over his defeated opponent, her battered face expressed humiliation and shock.

To add insult to injury, Marcelo kicked a little sand over her. "I don't have to prove anything to you or anyone else," he growled. "No evidence required. I just beat the judge, jury, and prosecutor's ass. That's my testimony, Black Jade. Case closed."

Marcelo held out his fractured hand. Daiyu glanced up, then took hold of it. He pulled the ancient vampire to her feet, and his already snapped collarbone popped. A couple fractured ribs grated together from his movements. The black, lifeless blood on his face started to dry in dark granules.

A bone clicked loudly when Daiyu set her dislocated elbow. She gripped her jaw and corrected its alignment. Drying blood on her face also flaked. She then slapped away wet, caked sand from her clothes and brushed it out of her hair.

"Look who's showing off with pomp now," she said at last. "Not bad. I liked the 'case closed' finishing touch, although it sounded a bit cliché."

Let's finish her! the demon soul shouted. *Don't tell me your weak humanity will show mercy. You are a fool!*

"I don't have time for this," Marcelo responded, to both the demon soul and Black Jade. "I'm going to find Sybil now."

Then you don't need me anymore, the demon mocked. *You can have your useless body back while mine will soon arrive. All I have to do is wait.*

Marcelo sensed the demon spirit retreat deep into his subconscious where it normally dwelled. No longer powered by the beast, Marcelo turned to leave, but halted when Daiyu spoke.

156

"Sybil doesn't need you, you dolt. If the girl wanted a knight in shining armor, she would have stuck around. The witch has her own business to take care of."

Though burning to chase after Sybil, Marcelo hesitated. Each moment that ticked by meant his love slipping further away. However, Daiyu seemed so sure of herself, and he recalled something the old vampire had mentioned earlier.

"Before we fought, you said you saw something in Sybil's eyes," he said. "What did you mean by that?"

"I saw a woman beyond reach," Daiyu replied. "During atrocious historical events, I've seen that look on thousands of people over the centuries. Her stolen youth was obvious, and I could smell the black sickness inside her. Also, her eyes held a terrible suffering, one branded to her soul that requires a mental, spiritual, and physical journey to alleviate. Sybil must travel this road alone. No amount of coddling or home cooked dinners will erase her pain. Let her go, Marcelo. She must find her own way."

Marcelo felt as if a Daiyu-powered blow had crushed his heart. Her words hurt, the truth behind them cutting deep. Black Jade's comments sounded eerily similar to Sybil's note, a punishing tirade of emotional pain. His love's handwriting flashed in his mind:

Time shall not provide remedy, I warrant.

Thereof, I cannot smile and prattle that my heart fares well.

To have a fair sight of myself, I shall search outside my body and within my soul.

No signs shall guide the way home.

And the worst statement of all—*Of a truth, I ought to journey forth alone, Marcelo.*

He closed his eyes and placed a hand over his chest. The gesture failed to diminish the ache roiling inside. His other hand trembled in a tight fist.

"I…I can't let her go," he said softly.

"But you must," Daiyu insisted. "And there's more. I may act petty and sometimes cruel, but I've always been fair. You pummeled me and earned your freedom. However, that maniacal demon is still out there destroying my kin. The trial may be over, but you still bear some responsibility for these deaths. Can your noble heart ignore that? Will you just walk away?"

Marcelo could never walk away; it would be a run with no end. The demon soul continued to call for its body. The insane, animated being would never stop pursuing…and killing. Daiyu was right. Although not his fault, Marcelo did have some accountability for the situation. He did not ask for this; Umaq remained the true culprit. The demon master had started this entire affair centuries ago.

As for Sybil…

Marcelo gazed out over the ocean. Just as the waves beat the shore and clawed away at the sand, the determination to chase his beloved witch eroded. He would have to trust Sybil and recognize that she proved more than capable of defeating her personal, unseen foe. His feet no longer tread the same path as hers, but his heart forever followed.

"I'm not going anywhere," he finally said. He turned away from the water and faced Black Jade. "You called me a false undead, an outcast, and a cancer to vampire kind. But I'm going to stop this demon because it's the right thing to do. Besides, I also have a personal score to settle, not just you. This monster killed me five hundred years ago after Umaq summoned it through a portal in his hut. Umaq may be gone, but destroying this beast is my only vengeance."

A rush of air sounded, and a blur formed on Marcelo's right. Maxwell suddenly appeared gripping a smartphone, his face distraught. He glanced between Daiyu and Marcelo, his features turning to anger. He more than likely expected Marcelo to be dead by now. Perhaps he wondered why the combatants stood having a conversation.

"The monster is in Los Angeles, Black Jade," Maxwell said. "I just received the call and its already killed two of our kin! Eloise is frantic. No one expected the demon to circumvent several cities and arrive so quickly." He glared at Marcelo, then cast a heated, accusing look at Daiyu. "But now I realize why the creature is still on a rampage."

Marcelo witnessed expressions on Black Jade he never thought possible—vulnerability and guilt. For the first time since meeting her, he realized the tremendous weight pressing on Daiyu's shoulders. These vampires trusted her as their leader. Her kin expected her to remedy the situation, to stop the murders and eliminate their fear. Marcelo had not wanted to die because of the trial, but he at least acknowledged Black Jade's reason for it.

"Gather your companions and attend to their safety," Marcelo told Daiyu. "The demon seems to be taking a faster and more direct route the closer it gets. It will find me quickly, as I'll wait for it here. I'll bury this creature, or it will kill me and retrieve its soul. Either way, vampires will be safe and the dilemma over."

Daiyu hesitated for a long moment as though considering her next course of action. She then looked at Maxwell. "Take everyone back to the city and regroup with Eloise. Marcelo's method is correct. One way or another, this ends now."

After a final, hate-filled glance at Marcelo, Maxwell nodded to Daiyu and sped back to the others.

"Marcelo, you are no match for this demon," Daiyu observed, a hint of compassion in her tone.

"I'll find a way," he replied. "It's what I do." He offered Black Jade a respectful nod.

She returned the gesture, then looked to the sky. "Sybil will find a way, too. Hopefully that will bring you some comfort and strength in the end."

Marcelo also lifted his gaze to the star-speckled night. "Yes. As long as she is all right, I can rest easy."

Daiyu sprinted away and left him alone on the beach.

Sybil had chosen her own way. Marcelo now elected his, to stand his ground. After defeating Daiyu, she had proven true to her word and set him free. Ironically, that encouraged him to continue the fight and help the vampires. Many of them had died because of his existence. Marcelo would not run. He had a chance to prevent additional deaths of his supernatural comrades, even though many of them considered him an outcast.

And his reward for aiding the undead? Probably nothing. His death, in fact, would save all of them. The demon soul would reunite with its body and continue on its merry way.

Marcelo thought of the rewards in his bedroom he had collected over the years. Plaques and certificates decorated the walls, bestowed from mayors and other civil leaders in great appreciation for his many financial contributions to public work projects and for improving citizens' lives. No one would hand him a silver-plated award on this occasion. Actually, he might well receive a certificate—a death one.

The final lines from Sybil's letter entered his mind. He expressed the words back to her through his heart and envisioned her sweet face in the sky. *If I do not find what I seek, then this is goodbye. Yet if I do find the answer to my behoof, it may still be farewell.*

Chapter Thirteen

The Road Taken

About three hours from Cave Junction, the car dropped Sybil off at Watchman Peak Trailhead on the border of Crater Lake in Oregon. The last time she had been here, Marcelo had parked his Aston Martin Rapide in the underbrush on the side of the road.

Following the same path as her previous visit, Sybil carefully made her way down the long, sandy embankment that encircled the lake. Almost sundown, the area remained empty of lake tourists and trail hikers. She reached the edge of the crystal blue water and took a moment to marvel at the scenery.

She stood at the bottom of a giant bowl five miles wide, the crater left behind after the explosion of a volcano called Mount Mazama thousands of years ago. The sky glowed orange and red as the sun set just over the rocky, top edge of the crater. The water level changed throughout the seasons, drained by evaporation and filled by precipitation and snowfall.

Sybil remembered Johann inflating a raft they had brought as Salix looked on in curiosity. Marcelo had then rowed the group across Skell Channel to Wizard Island, the only landmass in the lake, less than a quarter mile away.

162

Having no raft or handsome escort to transport her to the small island, Sybil waded into the cold water. She had anticipated this ahead of time while planning to use the ley gate at Wizard Island, but the logistics of a hastened journey didn't involve niceties or concern for herself.

Set on her chosen road, saving her friends and loved ones powered her motivation. Their wellbeing remained Sybil's only concern. Between her old age and illness, she already had one foot in the grave, so her own health had dwindled to an afterthought. But instead of fear or weakness under the threat of death, strength and courage pumped through her frail body. Too much remained at stake for her to fail. She willingly risked her life—however much remained—to ensure success and the safety of her friends. Already dying, enduring cold water and wet clothes represented the first sacrifice of many to come. If a little shivering stopped her now, how could she possibly bear the danger and hardship of the netherworld?

Soon a dogpaddle brought Sybil to the shore of the island, a protrusion of land caused by secondary explosions after the initial eruption of Mount Mazama. Dripping, she stepped out of the water and paused to wring out her blouse and the cuffs of her jeans. She suffered a bout of hacking and spit out black phlegm. After wiping dark liquid from her nose, she glanced ahead at a small mountain centered on Wizard Island. The top of the elevation housed a volcanic hollow, Witches Cauldron. Most importantly, the area contained the gateway into a ley line.

She labored up the incline and reached the edge of the small crater. Panting, she winced and tried to suppress the dreadful memories. The Witches Cauldron mocked. The hidden gateway laughed as decades of terror played out in the underground. Sybil had just escaped the tunnels and lost most of her life in the process. Now she must return to the dark and journey the ley streams once again.

"Enough," she said to herself.

I am with you. My power, spirit, and blood of the earth runs in your veins.

Sybil's breath caught as the Earth Mother's voice spoke in her mind. The words calmed her and helped to renew the confidence she experienced when conversing with Salix. Anxiety over revisiting the tunnel diminished, yet grief persisted. Not for herself, but for the dear Earth Mother. The great spirit's voice sounded weak and strained as if communication took incredible effort.

"Truly, and I am with you, dear Mother," Sybil whispered. "I shall set things right again."

She carefully descended the rocky slope and stepped into the center of the Witches Cauldron. Scant bushes and trees dotted the bottom of the wide hollow. Gloom filled the area as the sun nearly finished its course. Overhead, the first stars began to twinkle in a clear sky.

Sybil stared at the ground and wondered how difficult it would be to open the ley gate. Her magic still hadn't returned, but she already considered a few alternate scenarios that just might work. Through sheer willpower and ritual dance, she could perhaps manifest a single spark of magic to trigger an effect. Or she might use natural methods; the sparse foliage, rocks, and soil would be arranged in symbols and patterns to access the underground. If those methods failed, then chanting or even prayer to a deity would be next.

Sybil sensed a familiar vibration in the soil, the potential ley essence waiting for release. Thinking of various incantations, she gasped as her hands began to glow. A bluish tint radiated from her fingers and palms, warm and soothing. She lifted her hands, turned them over, and opened and closed her fists. Her initial wonder vanished as realization struck.

"'Tis ley energy," she said in awe.

But how? Ley lines ran throughout the bowels of the earth, their rivers coursing like the lifeblood of the planet. For her to radiate such a natural force…

The Earth Mother had provided the answer—*My power, spirit, and blood of the earth runs in your veins.*

The great earth spirit had meant that literally. Underground, Sybil had received decades of ley energy treatment by the Earth Mother. Bathing in its healing properties fended off the black illness, revitalized her, and generated the mental medicine for Sybil to not submit to despair. She must have absorbed enough for the blue essence to thrive in her body. She didn't know if the effect would be permanent, but for the moment, the tremendous gift lightened her dark journey and provided a key to the underground.

The first time Sybil unlocked the ley gate, her spiritual power worked as a catalyst for the spell while Salix's twig served as a focal point. The dryad's wood boosted the magic and triggered the opening. However, Sybil had suffered through burning pain as her spirit burst from her flesh in smoky tendrils. In tears, she completed the ritual amid a thunderous clamor and a violent shaking of earth.

Powered by the ley essence in her blood, Sybil knew this attempt would be a far different experience. She held out her illuminated hands. The vibration from the ground traveled up her legs, through her torso, and toward her splayed fingers. She called out, her voice gentle and unlike the shouted plea during the first occasion.

"Humble I stand before the door, blessed ley streams flow forevermore. In desperate need my hour grows late, and I ask the earth to open the gate."

The ground shook in a mild, controlled event. In front of Sybil, a patch of soil split apart in an oval-shaped hole. Teal-colored light rose from the fissure in a beautiful column, its presence even more distinct as the sun disappeared and true night fell. The soft glow from her hands disappeared, and she pressed her palms together in a gesture of gratitude.

Ready to leap inside, she stepped forward but collapsed in sudden pain. She held her throbbing head and writhed on the ground until the agony subsided. Out of breath, she wiped both her ears and stared at the black nether essence glistening on her fingers. At this rate, would she even make it to the netherworld, let alone find Umaq in time?

Too weak to stand, Sybil crawled to the gate and rolled over the edge. Falling, she watched the ground seal above, closing her eyes in elation as her body landed softly on a ley stream. An invisible, omnipotent presence hovered nearby in greeting. A familiar touch caressed Sybil's back, combed through her hair, and gently brushed her cheek. Warmth covered her skin and eased all discomfort. Weariness dissipated and lifted her spirits.

The Earth Mother's loving embrace wrapped Sybil, the same gesture that had kept her alive for years in the dark.

No dread over being trapped inside the tunnels manifested. She had mastered opening the gate; leaving the underground would be no different. The ley energy pulsed inside Sybil and granted unexplored abilities. The sensation felt different than spell-casting potential, but all the same, it existed as a power to wield.

Sybil rose and stood firm on the fast-moving ley line, eyes closed and arms spread. The encompassing, suffocating darkness no longer represented loneliness and despair. She had lost a lifetime imprisoned in the tunnels, but breath filled her lungs, heart continued to beat, and her mind accepted the reality of her current situation—she lived. She still fought for loved ones and carried their spirit inside her. She would see this through until the end, regardless of what lay ahead.

Be not afraid of what is or what awaits, the Earth Mother's ethereal voice called. *You promised to set things right for the world, but my concern is to set things right within you. Heal your heart, dear one. Remedy your soul and cure your mind. Reunite the pieces inside and find peace. Go forth, my child!*

Sybil shouted, a sound of triumph. The echoing scream did not portray solitude or fear. The emotional cry depicted courage, relief, and adoration for everyone who had ever touched her heart.

The blue ley line turned, dove, and climbed at her command. A mental compass displayed behind her closed eyelids, her focus anchored to the destination of Machu Picchu. The ley essence bound to her flesh allowed her to know every field, city, mountain, and river that raced by aboveground. The terrain, climate, and population changed every so often, but her mastery of location and ability to travel freely did not waver.

Leaving California, she next journeyed beneath Mexico and skirted Central America while riding below the Pacific Ocean. She crossed under Ecuador and past the border beneath Peru, then continued to the cities of Trujillo, the capital Lima, Ayacucho, and finally into the mountainous area of Machu Picchu.

Approaching the ley gate at the stone altar of Intihuatana, the ley river rose in a column and propelled Sybil toward the surface. The ground opened in a low rumble. She passed through the gap and stepped into the derelict temple overlooking the ancient Inca city. She moved outside toward the altar in the courtyard, the night sky and dazzling stars offering a breathtaking view.

She had been a decrepit shell of herself the last time she stood here, a physical, emotional, and mental mess. Still far from healthy, she at least had her wits and the motivation to push onward.

Sybil left the quad and reached the bottom of the stairs in the Sacred Plaza. A few demons scampered about the grounds, the low-tier guards she had seen before. She crossed the area and stepped inside the darkened Temple of the Three Windows. It took a few moments for her eyes to adjust to the gloom. The starlight spilling through the doorway and windows provided just enough illumination to discern some details of her surroundings.

But Sybil hadn't come here to observe the temple. All she needed was for Uku-Pacha, the window and portal to the netherworld, to activate. Umaq had said the gateway still functioned. She had seen it work when a dark, terrifying force had gripped the man and yanked him through. Sybil shivered at the memory. She rubbed the goosebumps rising over her upper arms and couldn't imagine what terror lay in the realm of demons.

Time passed as she waited for the portal to open. She paced the stone floor, sat for a while, then climbed to her feet and stretched her tired arms and legs. When she nearly fell asleep, the window suddenly flashed. Within the stone frame, the outside view of Machu Picchu vanished. In its place, jagged mountains and an ugly purple sky appeared over a black, rocky landscape. A hot draft of air rolled into the temple. An unseen creature roared in the distance, its eerie cry lifted by the wind.

Not wanting to miss the opportunity to enter, Sybil still hesitated. She hugged her midsection and stared at the abnormal world a few feet away. The window flashed twice in a possible sign of closure. Heart hammering, she broke her stupor and ran to the portal. She climbed through the opening and stepped into the realm of nightmare and despair.

Chapter Fourteen

Departed Soul

It's almost here. I'm almost here! Time for you to die, human.

Marcelo ignored the demon soul. Its sardonic comments and taunts had only increased the closer its body neared. Daiyu and her squad had long since departed, leaving Marcelo pacing on the beach. He cast occasional glimpses at the starry sky or out toward the neighborhood street, waiting.

He wished his battered body could heal faster. Black Jade's fists and feet had left him a beaten mess. Beneath his hand, he felt the broken collarbone moving back into place, although slowly. His ribs also worked to stitch together. Marcelo needed his bones and flesh mended so he could take another pounding from the demon.

He smiled wryly at the thought and shook his head. He checked the sky again, but thankfully saw nothing. Dozens of battle plans raced through his mind. How strong and fast could this monster be? It had bested Black Jade and even made her retreat. Did he even stand a chance? Marcelo desperately surveyed the area and looked for advantageous spots to attack from or momentarily hide in. Hiding would buy him time to recover or reconsider strategy, but in the end, a bloody brawl to the finish awaited.

His life may soon end, yet his foremost thoughts dwelled on Sybil's wellbeing. Had she retreated to a safe place to ponder her ailing condition? Not likely. An idea formed of where she might have gone, and although the prospect alarmed him, it also made him proud. If Marcelo knew his greatest love, the brave witch had marched straight toward the lion's den to take matters into her own hands. No illness would stop her. Old age be damned. Sybil Radella Cotterill would blow apart the doors to the netherworld, traverse the dark realm, and drag Umaq by the collar.

A long, overhead roar shook the sky. A familiar demon circled high above, then swooped down to land on the sandy beach. The monster stood tall, gray, and muscular. The veiny wings flapped once, then folded against the creature's wide back. Insanity—tangible and terrifying—flashed in its six slanted eyes. A distorted, horned head that lacked a nose sat on wide shoulders. The demon clicked its razor-sharp claws, the very set that had killed Marcelo centuries ago.

A five-hundred-year-old memory froze him. As a young Conquistador, Marcelo lay in Umaq's hut, barely conscious. A demon, also scarcely alive, crawled out of the makeshift portal inside the fire pit. Umaq commanded the monster to attack Marcelo, and the two of them struggled on the dirt floor until death. Umaq then cast a spell and thrust the demon's departed soul at Marcelo's corpse, reviving him.

Heated fusion. Unbearable pain. Nightmare and screaming—the demon and human became one.

Commenting on the awful memory, the demon abruptly wrenched Marcelo back to the current danger. *Leave it to a feeble human to be so selfish. You think you're the only one who felt pain and lived through a nightmare? I suffered just as you did. That's my body in front of you, and I rightfully belong inside it. Save yourself additional torture and die quickly.*

"For once I agree with you. Umaq destroyed both of our lives," Marcelo replied. "But I also have a right to live. Two bodies and one soul. Let's finish this once and for all."

The demon laughed. *Such bravado. But it's only win-win for me. After my physical form destroys you, I will become whole again. On the other hand, if you destroy my body, I will continue to endure inside you. An unfavorable situation, but the point is my life will continue in either outcome. You, however, only have flesh and bone inside that skin bag. Your soul was obliterated the moment I bonded to you, and you are not a real vampire who can live without one. Without me sustaining you, you'll cease to exist once your body dies. Still confident?*

The demon spirit proclaimed the searing truth Marcelo had refused to think about for the last few centuries. He had always known about that dark reality; ignoring it most of his undead life didn't make it go away.

Referring to the demon's question, yes, Marcelo had always been confident enough to not worry about *ceasing to exist*. Since the sixteenth century, he had escaped many deadly situations, defeated opponents, and talked his way out of or even paid to avoid trouble. Even

Daiyu's trial hadn't unnerved him; the promise of her issuing a death sentence had only angered him.

The current situation had also failed to wither Marcelo's confidence. However, the buried truth had risen to the surface—a real threat of his demise loomed. His adventurous, frightening, wonderful, miserable, and joyful years would end forever. He may never see Sybil again. Fighting, running, or payoffs would not save him.

Apprehension teased the corners of his mind, but he shook it off as the monster sniffed the air, roared, and charged. Marcelo burst forward to meet the demon head-on, then threw himself on the ground a moment before a jarring impact. The speeding creature tripped over Marcelo's body and bounced hard across the sand for dozens of yards in a spray of grit.

The demon stood and Marcelo braced for attack. The beast charged again, its fast-moving form a blur across the beach. It suddenly stopped ten feet away and clapped together its large, leathery wings. A thunderous shockwave of air crashed into Marcelo and lifted him off his feet. He sailed a good distance and plummeted onto the shore.

The demon met Marcelo as he hurried to rise. Fierce punches to the monster's face and body had little effect. The creature repaid him in a crushing blow and cracked Marcelo's sternum. Clawed fingers wrapped around his throat and squeezed. As an undead, Marcelo didn't have to worry about not being able to breathe. The devastating fist to his face, however, posed a real problem. Teeth flew from his broken mouth. Another blow fractured the orbital bone next to his eye.

He hammered a double-fisted blow into the arm holding him by the neck. The grip loosened, and a hard kick to the monster's abdomen followed. The demon snarled and stumbled back. Marcelo launched forward and slammed his forehead into the creature's chest, knocking it flat.

A swipe from a long wing slapped Marcelo's legs from under him. Before he could recover, a cloven hoof smashed onto his chest and pinned him on the sand. The demon knelt and plunged its claws into the right side of Marcelo's chest. He cried out—not in pain but in shock—when the beast closed its fist and ripped out a massive chunk of flesh and bone.

Intense heat blazed from the wound as a strange light glowed within. Afraid for the first time, Marcelo struggled and failed to remove the demon from atop him. The light emerged from his torso and stretched toward the monster's open maw.

Goodbye, stupid human! the demon soul called. *It has not been fun.* The soft glow, the beast's spirit, wafted through the air in a return journey toward its reanimated corpse.

Marcelo lay near death. He couldn't even move anymore. The sound of the ocean faded. The stars in the night sky blurred. Sybil…would she even know what happened to him? So many things he could have done differently, always easy to look back on and regret. And as for Umaq, it seemed the demon master won this round after all.

Something huge bashed against the demon. The violent impact sent the crazy monster rolling toward the water. Having nowhere to go, the light reversed course and seeped back into the wound in Marcelo's chest.

NO! the demon soul screamed.

174

Marcelo understood the spirit required corporeal attachment before it vanished into…well, wherever demon souls ended up. His empty flesh presented a safe haven as the monster's body now battled its surprise attacker further down the beach.

Strength surged through Marcelo as his undead life returned, a contradiction and miracle of his flawed existence. His vision cleared, hearing improved, and other senses fired in supernatural potency. He leapt to his feet, reborn and shaken by his near passing. From dead to living in only a moment, the seesaw of emotion nearly made him cry.

"In your face," he quipped to the demon soul, trapped inside him once again. "Your rotting carcass might still kill me in the next minute, but for now, if feels great to rub it in." He turned his attention to the violent brawl as recognition stunned him. "Johann!"

Marcelo had never witnessed Johann fight at this peak level of raw, unchecked aggression. The werewolf spun, dodged, slashed, and bit in a hurricane of long claws and sharp teeth. He had caught the demon off guard, and it could only defend. Johann carved deep grooves into the monster's chest. Powerful bites tore chunks of the demon's flesh. A *snap* exploded as bone broke. He grabbed a leathery wing and tore it. After knocking the beast to the ground, the frenzied werewolf grabbed the demon's ankles and spun it around and around. A release sent the monster spinning far through the air until it splashed in the ocean.

The werewolf turned to Marcelo and charged. Not slowing, Johann scooped him up and threw him over a shoulder. Marcelo tightened his hold on the werewolf's fur as Johann sped off the beach and down the street in a flash.

At a pickup truck, Johann tossed Marcelo into the passenger seat. As he ran to the driver's side, the hairy werewolf transitioned into the human Johann, birthday suit and all. The naked man climbed behind the wheel, fired the engine, and screeched the tires as the vehicle raced away.

Johann wiped dripping sweat from his face, his long blond hair hanging in damp strands. His dark eyes appeared wide in a frantic face.

"Sorry for treating you like luggage, Marcelo," he panted. "Something tells me that demon won't be stopped for long. And after what I just saw…" He glanced at the wound in Marcelo's chest. "I know a soul when I see one. You almost died, you punk! We need to get as far away from here as possible."

"You saved my life," Marcelo replied, unnerved from the assault of emotions over the last two minutes. He glanced through the rear glass of the truck cab, then checked the side mirror for any sign of the demon.

"Johann, you really saved me," he emphasized again. "I truly thought it was the end. I owe you—"

"Enough," Johann cut in. "Buy me a cold beer, a burger, or whatever. It's what friends do."

"How did you know to come?" Marcelo asked.

Johann raced away from the residential area and maneuvered through the curves of Avila Beach Drive, out of town. "My little plant face told me all about that monster in a dream. Salix and I have always shared a close bond, but ever since I buried the catkin, she's been quite talkative in my sleep. I immediately left Nevada City. On the way over here, you also texted me about

Sybil leaving and I imagined the worst for each of you." He glanced at Marcelo. "You're a mess, and my dream would have turned into a nightmare if I'd gotten here a minute late."

"A real nightmare for the both of us," Marcelo responded. "Fine. I'll buy you a burger *and* a beer. But shouldn't you, uh, put some clothes on? Riding with a naked man in the dead of night is comical, but it would make one hell of a story if a cop pulls us over."

Johann grinned, then nodded at the gym bag between them on the seat. "My sweats and shoes are in there, but I can't put them on just yet. Sorry, but you're stuck with this nudist until it's safe. Just keep your hands off my shifter while I drive, and we'll be all right."

Marcelo laughed, a sensation he thought he'd never experience anymore after tonight's trauma. He placed his hands over the various broken bones and again wished for a faster recovery. The ugly, gaping wound on his torso proved to be the worst injury. The flesh had already started to regrow, but he needed rest more than anything. He checked the mirrors and rear window once more. Rest? Not likely any time soon.

But he allowed a moment—*needed* just a damn minute—to relax. Marcelo sank back into the seat and closed his eyes. Sybil would not leave his thoughts even as his own life remained in jeopardy. Johann had raced over three-hundred miles to rescue Marcelo, and now death threatened the werewolf as well. Salix, the sweet dryad, had also saved him. Twice, including her self-sacrifice in Athens,

When would this madness end? Umaq's defeat had only led to more disaster. Gods. Demons. Witches. Vampires. The battles had lined up and drained him. His

177

mind churned, lost and confused. A wrecking ball fractured his emotions, the pieces scattered to the wind. He opened his eyes and glanced at the time on the dashboard. The sun would be up soon, another enemy added to the long list of problems.

"What about asking Selene for her cool chariot again?" Johann asked, breaking the silence. "We can ditch this truck and fly the hell out of here."

"Normally that would be ideal, but I'm not trying to escape the demon. I want this thing to catch me." Alarmed, Johann shot him a befuddled glance.

"I know, it's crazy to mention," Marcelo added. "Long story, but innocent people will die if I keep running. It seems I'm the only one who can stop that monster. I just…need a little time to figure this out."

"Then I'll give you some time," Johann replied. "Take the wheel."

"What?"

"Hold the wheel still. I have the truck on cruise control, just need you to hold her steady while I put my clothes on."

Marcelo reached over and grasped the steering wheel, his eyes fixed on the highway. Johann scooted the driver's seat back and rummaged in the gym bag. With a gymnast's dexterity, the naked werewolf quickly slipped on his clothes and shoes, then regained control of the truck.

"Now I understand why you don't work at the DMV," Marcelo observed.

"Or drive for Uber," Johann remarked.

They left Avila Beach behind and continued south on Highway 101 toward Los Angeles. Buying Marcelo every minute he could, Johann worked the gears and accelerated around other cars. The vehicle flew past the cities of Pismo Beach, Arroyo Grande, and Nipomo. Marcelo sat tense while continuing his search for the demon. He wouldn't run far; his promise to fight and prevent more vampire deaths held firm. However, the additional time to heal would prove invaluable. At full strength and Johann by his side, his chances for survival didn't appear so dim.

Just outside of Santa Maria, he called out as the monster appeared in the sky to the right of the truck. The demon flew in an awkward motion, a broken wing hindering flight. It dropped altitude, then struggled to rise as its good wing provided most of the lift.

"It's drifting closer to us," Marcelo warned. The demon suddenly swooped over the vehicle. "Wait—damn, I lost sight of it!"

Johann searched on the left and peered through the windshield. Marcelo pivoted in his seat, glancing in all directions. As he looked through the rear glass, the passenger side window shattered. Sharp fragments flew inside the cab. Marcelo shouted as powerful claws sank into his shoulder and pulled. He struggled to remain in the truck as the demon's distorted face glared through the broken window.

The creature's cloven hooves touched down on the freeway as it *ran* beside the speeding vehicle. The beast kept pace while trying to yank Marcelo out. Johann jerked the wheel to the left. A nearby car honked and slammed its brakes. The demon growled as it tripped, but did not release its tight hold. The truck dragged the monster's body, the strain on Marcelo's shoulder increasing. He punched, elbowed, and even bit the arm holding him to no avail.

Johann floored the accelerator. The truck caught up to a big rig rumbling in the adjacent lane. Johann drifted right until the long trailer of the eighteen-wheeler hovered just above the skidding demon. He stomped the brakes, and the rear wheels of the big rig rolled over the monster in a jarring thud. The creature finally let go and tumbled away on the asphalt. Brakes howling, the startled semi-truck driver blew the horn and swerved onto the shoulder, then corrected the large vehicle's trajectory. Johann hit the gas and zoomed off, the reek of burnt rubber pungent.

"Nice work!" Marcelo exclaimed, then frowned at his dislocated shoulder when he attempted to move it. "Man, I can't catch a break. Or rather, I'm catching too many of them, quite literally."

"Well, at least your handsome face is intact," Johann said. His eyes flicked to the rearview mirror. "I'd wager we only bought ourselves a short amount of time again."

"Stop the truck," Marcelo said.

"What? Why? That thing nearly tore your arm off. You want it to finish the job before you're ready?"

"This mad situation will never end until I kill that monster," Marcelo answered. "The demon just took an eighteen-wheeler to the face. If we attack now, we have a better chance of defeating it."

Johann drove ahead in silence. He sighed and drummed his fingers on the steering wheel, frustration creasing his brow. "Fine. But we'll fight him close to a big city instead of out here in the open. There's not much along this stretch of the highway, which gives that creature the advantage. The streets and buildings of a city will provide some cover and more opportunity. I'll stop in Santa Barbara." He looked at Marcelo. "If things go really bad, I don't care what happens, I'm throwing you back in the truck and heading for Los Angeles to regroup. Deal?"

Marcelo nodded at his friend. "Deal. Just make sure you're fully clothed while driving."

They continued down Highway 101 and toward Santa Barbara. Marcelo checked for the monster…and for cops. After the road battle and maintaining speed at 90 miles per hour, he felt certain flashing red and blue lights would appear at any moment. Los Alamos, Buellton, and Naples came and went, smaller towns spaced along isolated parts of the highway. Signs of civilization increased around Goleta with Santa Barbara not far beyond.

"We're getting off the West Carrillo exit near downtown," Johann said. "I'll take that burger and beer while we wait. Hopefully the demon gives us the courtesy to do so."

"You'll have—"

A sudden horn from behind them interrupted the conversation. Marcelo looked back just as a Honda swerved around something and collided against an SUV. A moment later, the pickup truck lurched when the demon leapt into the bed. Dark blood leaked from the monster's fractured head. One of its arms hung warped and broken. Two eyes had been punctured, the sockets swollen. And still the beast had somehow caught up, its demented mind knowing only utter rage and hunger to reclaim its soul.

The demon scrambled over the top of Johann's truck and settled onto the hood. It drew back a fist and shattered the windshield in a roar of wind and flying debris.

"It's the damn Terminator!" Johann hollered.

Marcelo clobbered the beast with a hard right, then wrapped his hands around the creature's throat. The demon grabbed the steering wheel and yanked it. The truck jerked left and bashed into the center guardrail. A wild rebound sent the vehicle back into traffic. A car smashed into the side of the truck and spun it across the roadway until it flipped over.

For the second time that night, Marcelo found himself head over heels in a vehicle. Metal crunched and tore. Glass sprayed in all directions. Gasoline, antifreeze, and oil spilled onto the highway. Adjacent cars squealed tires and blared horns. Some vehicles collided or slid onto the shoulder.

"Johann!" Marcelo called.

Terrified for his friend's wellbeing, he looked around the smashed interior but didn't see Johann in the cab. Marcelo struggled through an opening and stood on the concrete amid a sea of wreckage. Relief flooded him when he spotted Johann in werewolf form a short distance away. He must have been ejected from the truck; the transformation into the strong and durable werewolf likely saved his life.

Marcelo ran to his companion while surveying the terrible scene. "We need to help these people—"

Johann shook his shaggy head and pointed a claw-tipped finger. Further down the road, the demon stepped around a crushed SUV and charged at Marcelo.

Chapter Fifteen

Far From Home

Sybil stumbled and dropped to her knees on the dark soil of the netherworld. A cold, biting wind swept around her. Wrapping arms around herself did nothing to block the frigid atmosphere. Her teeth chattered and body shivered. Breathing became difficult. Muscles numb, she fell over into a fetal position.

However, she did not despair as the blast of cold would soon dissipate. She had already experienced this paralyzing freeze three times now. A certain period of warmth would follow, then extreme heat, and back to the chill again. The abnormal weather posed a vicious cycle of anguish in this strange place.

Resembling a bruise, the purple, uninviting sky dimmed hope and pressed upon the spirit. Frightening beasts flew high, their dark and twisted shapes calling out in woeful drones. A dull sun, blurred and distant, offered no indication of invigorating light breaking through. The sparse landscape held an occasional tree devoid of leaves, or a dried shrub. The soil, stony and black, seemed to drain hope after each footfall.

The demon realm presented everything she had imagined it would be. Unbearable loneliness. Physical agony. Emotional suffering. The dismal environment

183

affected her thoughts. She questioned if she had done the right thing by coming out here. She doubted her mission, the absurdity of rescuing Umaq based on his desperate promise to cure her and revive Inti.

The cold passed and the temperature rose to a comfortable level. Sybil stood, wiped black dust from her clothes, and moved on. An hour later, a terrible wave of heat slammed her. She ran to a rotted tree stump and dropped behind it, the sliver of shade hardly making a difference. It seemed as if fire danced on her skin. Sweat poured down her face and soaked her clothes. Every breath burned like lava down to her lungs.

The boiling temperature receded into a tolerable zone again. Having about an hour until the next freeze, Sybil stood and pressed onward toward a mountain in the distance. The massive crags stretched from horizon to horizon. Having no way to go around, she figured she'd march straight over, if such a passage existed.

As for finding Umaq? She could see no signs of anything that passed for civilization. No dwellings, outposts, or other indications of something resembling society existed out here. Umaq could be buried a mile underground for all she knew. He could have been eaten by one of the flying beasts. Or perhaps he found a way to elude his captors and could be on the run.

Not much point in having negative thoughts about where he was or if he even lived. She had made a decision and then committed to it. She just had to keep moving forward, searching. And if she ended up dying out here...well, not much she could do about that, either.

Sybil had not given up but merely pondered a fact. As long as one shoe kept stepping past the other, her focus remained on Marcelo and helping the outside world. The Earth Mother, Johann, Salix, Grace…each person motivated Sybil to trudge forward. She would surely fall again and get up. She was bound to get hurt and push onward. Nothing left to do except reach that mountain and see what craziness took place on the other side.

The dull and hazy sun, if it could even be called that, never moved in the violet sky. No indication of the light fading or brightening, of the hours even passing, occurred in the demon realm. Sybil had no idea how long she had walked. She wondered if a night and day cycle existed here.

After a few more battles against the temperature swings, she somehow reached the towering base of the mountain. And to her great surprise, a paved and well-constructed tunnel led inside.

Over the arched entrance of the passageway, a large sign had been carved into the stonework. Strange symbols created words and sentences, more than likely a demonic language unfamiliar to her. Along the high, curved ceiling, several magical lights encased in glass illuminated the tunnel as far as she could see.

Sybil stepped inside and began a new leg of her journey. She felt elated when the ferocious, changing climate outside did not occur within the mountain. Cool air brushed her skin and an occasional, mysterious draft through the tunnel fluttered her hair. She also realized something quite significant, a detail she hadn't noticed while shivering in the cold or being roasted by the heat.

Her sickness hadn't manifested since arriving in the netherworld. No sneezes, violent coughs, or bouts of vomiting black gunk. She seemed fine, at least in the sense of not being deathly ill since her aged body still plagued her. Before reaching the mountain, she had rested for long periods and at times barely had the strength to move. However, the calm, inviting tunnel provided a second wind. Sybil walked in confidence, although weakness continued to weigh down her limbs.

The long passageway curved, dipped, or rose in random spots. The rock floor and walls had been carved to a smooth finish. Supporting archways of cut stone appeared every fifty paces or so. Occasional sets of symbols like the language over the entrance decorated the walls in many swirls and sharp angles, a foreign yet beautiful script.

Had Sybil even reached the halfway point? She sat down and rested, wondering where all the demons were. Besides the scary beasts flying high in the sky, she hadn't seen any other creatures in the wasteland where she had first entered. Even the strange tunnel remained empty. Relief at not having to confront some raging demons pleased her; however, she anticipated an encounter sooner or later.

After a good rest, she continued until the pass through the mountain finally ended. She stood in the archway, staring in shock at what lay before her—soft green grass and tall, leafy trees where shiny fruit hung. A lake sparkled in the distance. Strange-looking, furry animals roamed about a distant field in a giant herd. The purple skyline and the dull sun represented the only familiar traits from the other side of the mountain.

It seemed she had stepped into a different realm. How could this lush paradise be part of the netherworld where horrific demons dwelled? Was it illusion...or perhaps Sybil had died in the tunnel and entered the afterlife?

She walked into the inviting atmosphere and gazed at the odd fruit decorating the branches. Some plump, bluish-green pieces had fallen on the ground. Sybil's stomach growled. She swallowed against her dry throat. She needed sustenance but wouldn't dare eat something from this place.

Trying to ignore her hunger, she walked faster and soon spotted buildings ahead. She hid behind a trunk and observed what appeared to be a small town. Demons moved along streets and between structures. They spoke in small groups or wandered in singles and pairs, some carrying objects. Sybil stared in wonder. Of all things to see in this monstrous realm, an actual community stretched before her. Should she go around and stay hidden? What if Umaq had been taken there?

A juicy crunch sounded from behind, the noise of someone biting an apple. Sybil whirled and faced a smiling demon. The creature stood tall and slender, the scales on its reptile skin gleaming. A small, single horn protruded from the top of its head. A clump of colorful feathers sprouted from the ends of twin tails. Long, claw-tipped fingers held a piece of fruit from one of the trees. The demon took another bite, its slanted orange eyes never leaving Sybil.

She stood frozen, thinking. Fight or flight? Age, exhaustion, and a lack of her magic wouldn't make for much of a brawl. Those same conditions wouldn't make for much of a sprint, either.

The demon finished the fruit and tossed the core onto the grass. "Do the denizens of your realm speak, outsider?" the creature asked in Sybil's tongue.

"Y-yes, of course," she replied. "My name is Sybil."

"Ah, so you're the girl everyone's talking about. You won't be able to pronounce my name, so just call me Vaz." The demon eyed Sybil in confusion. "I didn't expect you to be so old, however."

Still wary, Sybil cleared her throat and shifted her feet. Was this conversation the equivalent of a cat toying with prey before the fatal attack? "My age...'tis a very long story, I warrant. Wherefore am I the girl everyone speaks of?"

"Sybil the girl...old woman...whatever, the one who defeated Umaq," Vaz stated. "That man's name is a curse word around here. He opened a portal between our worlds and promised demonkind the freedom to conquer a new domain. But as you saw, his promise turned into a lie. He dared to enslave demons and sent our brothers and sisters into slaughter for his cause. You bested Umaq and allowed the dark gods to capture the traitor." Vaz smiled, but the expression held cruelty instead of joy. "I can't imagine the pain he's going through right now."

Umaq was alive! At least Sybil had learned something helpful. Now having a source to ask more questions, she had to speak carefully to avoid suspicion of her intention to set him free. "How did yonder news of me reach hither? Did Umaq mention a sundry of events from my world to make you conversant?"

"Not him, but the returning demons had much to say," Vaz answered. "After his downfall, the enslaving spell shattered, and the demons became free. Some stayed in your realm while others returned to tell the tale. That's how you became somewhat of a celebrity."

Sybil shook her head in disbelief. Upon entering the netherworld, she had expected to last all of five minutes after violent beasts or illness dropped her fast.

But here she stood, surrounded by a lavish wood and nearby town, having a normal conversation with a local.

Vaz draped an arm around Sybil's shoulders, and she cringed in surprise.

"No need to be so skittish," Vaz said, laughing. "Let's go hit the streets. Everyone would love to meet you."

The demon guided Sybil toward the town. She left the grass and stepped onto hardpacked dirt roads weaving around many enormous, odd-shaped structures crafted from wood and stone. The large doors and high ceilings proved necessary to accommodate a variety of residents while the creatures walked about. Short, tall, massive, multi-legged, slithering, leaping…the peculiar assortment of denizens amazed Sybil.

How the demons interacted astonished her even more. They shopped. They sat in groups and snacked. Several of them played some sort of rough game in an empty lot between two buildings. A full-blown society stood before Sybil, a grand community of monsters not behaving like monsters.

With a smirk, Vaz must have read Sybil's wide-eyed expression. "Not what you expected, outsider?"

"Truly…no," she admitted. "Hitherto, I have only met demons who strived to kill me."

"I don't blame you for being surprised by what you see," said Vaz. "However, many demons really are dangerous beasts. Those animals don't need to be mind-controlled to cause havoc—they relish it."

The pair moved further into town. Upon closer inspection of the buildings, Sybil noticed the crude yet effective architecture. Hewn from stone, some of the lopsided structures rose to five stories and served as food

189

or shopping establishments. Rough cut logs and haphazard pieces of wood created large dwellings. A large, muddy pond near the center plaza served as a bath where many creatures lounged.

All around, several demons stopped and stared at Sybil. She remained beneath her escort's arm, now grateful for the perceived protection it brought. She then grew alarmed as Vaz's raised voice suddenly made an announcement.

"Look everyone, this is Sybil, the vanquisher of Umaq! The traitor's lies and deceit finally came to an end, and many of our comrades returned home. May the dark gods punish Umaq forever!"

A loud cheer rose from the gathered residents. Many of them inclined their heads toward Sybil. Others reached out to grasp her hand. Her cheeks burned and heart fluttered from the attention. Still in shock over experiencing demons in this new light, she smiled shyly and returned a slight bow.

Her smile vanished the instant she spotted a certain demon standing behind the large crowd. A dark figure, taller than Vaz, stared through one yellow eye. Tentacles squirmed on its face. A spike sat on the end of its tongue when it opened its mouth. Jagged teeth grated and clicked together in a hard bite, an aggressive gesture directed at Sybil. Its horrid expression shivered her spine and froze her insides. This vile thing did not appreciate her visit. The demon would not celebrate and give thanks. Vaz had just spoken about this other kind of monster, ones who delighted in chaos and death.

"You must be rather hungry," Vaz said as the crowd dispersed.

Unnerved due to the one-eyed monster's stare, Sybil jumped when a hand touched her shoulder.

The demon laughed. "You still edgy, outsider? Come. Let's grab a tasty meal."

They approached a wooden booth covered in a rooftop of dry, woven grass. "Two plates of your best!" Vaz said to a portly, four-armed demon.

Sybil's mouth watered over the rich smell of spiced meat. A huge chunk of *something* turned slowly over a fire. Juice dripped and hissed in the blaze. The overweight demon hacked off several pieces into bowels and covered the food in a red sauce. With a nonchalant grunt, the cook set the bowls on the counter while Vaz laid out a gem as payment.

Sybil's stomach growled. Her mouth salivated. Not having eaten in quite some time, she realized just how faint she had been. She no longer cared about what the food here might do to her. Trembling fingers dove into the meat and shoved it between her teeth. She barely chewed, her body screaming for sustenance as she swallowed bite after bite. A large cup of juice appeared on the counter. She drank half of it in one breath. Pausing for air, she brought the drink to her lips and finished it.

Vaz smiled and purchased another bowl for Sybil. She nodded in gratitude and devoured the food, although more slowly. This time, she enjoyed the soft texture of the meat and delicious taste of the red sauce. Bowl empty, she licked her fingers and leaned against the counter in satisfaction.

"Thank you, forthwith I am in your debt," she commented. "I warrant 'tis the greatest food I have eaten hitherto."

"My pleasure," the demon replied, finishing its own meal. "It's funny how your kind eats so very little. These bowls are nothing more than a morsel for most of us here."

"Do other towns lie yonder?" Sybil asked.

"We have several towns and large cities," Vaz answered. "Some are pig sties, to put it in human terms, while other towns are quite pleasant. A few places are extremely dangerous as opposing clans or demons from different tiers battle over turf. You're lucky this town is the first one past the tunnel."

"Curiosity overcomes me about the tunnel and area on the other side of yonder mountain," said Sybil. "I wish to be conversant about them."

"The zone where Umaq's portal appeared is just your basic wasteland," Vaz began. "Only lower tier demons roam the fire and freeze. They either like it out there or are too dumb to know the difference. The tunnel is ancient, even I don't know its history. The writing you more than likely saw is from an older dialect. I can only make out a few words, but I'm glad for that. Very bad stuff. Things like omens and scary prophesies…I'd rather not know."

"Thereof, I too would rather not conceive of it forthwith," Sybil commented. "However, I fancy news of Umaq. Might he dwell in one of those dangerous places aforesaid?" After not ending up on someone's menu, she felt more relaxed and decided to ask about her mission.

Vaz shuddered and appeared afraid. "The unsafe cities are paradises compared to where Umaq is. The traitor was taken to the temple where the dark gods reside." The demon nodded toward another mountain in the distance. "On the peak of the highest crag sits a place where most of us dare not go. From here, the town residents say you can hear Umaq's screams—that is, if you *want* to listen."

Vaz studied Sybil, big orange eyes piercing and unreadable. "Now that you have settled down a bit, I finally want to ask why you came. When Umaq's portal had first opened, several demons rushed toward it in excitement over invading your distant world. But not surprisingly, no humans came this way. So outsider, vanquisher of Umaq, why are you here?"

Sybil had expected an inquiry ever since she stepped through the unstable portal. Thankfully, the interrogation did not occur as she lay bleeding in chains or roasting over a fire. While crossing the wasteland, she had plenty of time to think of a proper response. In the end, the truth would provide the best cover story.

"Some time agone, Umaq called forth a large amount of dark power from hither," Sybil began. "He—"

"Yes, one of his many other grave crimes," Vaz interrupted. "Stealing black energy from the dark gods in order to make himself their equal? How arrogant! He absorbed darkness through the portal and…eh, sorry. Please continue."

"Well, beforehand, he fashioned a dagger from aforesaid blackness and stabbed me," Sybil went on. "The dark blade hath poisoned me. Of a truth, only a short time remaineth before I die. No cure exists in my world yonder, thus I braved the portal and sought one in this realm. Yet strangely, the illness no longer ails me. That gives me some hope forthwith…and despair." She

193

offered a light shrug. "I must remaineth hither, trapped, lest I return home and die from sickness."

Appearing rather pensive, Vaz stared at the ground while chewing on the tip of a claw. "Hm, a conundrum indeed. Stay here and live or return home and die. Unfortunately, demons don't have much in the way of healers and medicines. Perhaps a natural remedy exists. Countless herbs, plants, and flowers grow in the wild. I'll ask about them in town."

Sybil smiled at the genuine concern from her new friend. "That would please me very much. Truly, my heart is grateful for your help and hospitality. Upon stepping through yonder portal, great fear unsettled me. However, being conversant of you and this town hath calmed me forthwith."

Vaz grinned, a sharp-toothed expression below fierce eyes that would have frightened any human unacquainted with the demon. "My pleasure. It's not every day I get to meet such an interesting outsider. Or any outsider, for that matter."

Sybil realized she needed something more. She disliked taking advantage of her host, but a long and extremely dangerous road still lay ahead. She required basic necessities and couldn't pass up the opportunity to acquire them so easily.

"Vaz, may you please give forth more food and drink to consume later?" she asked. "As a witch, I am conversant of natural remedies. While you inquire in town forthwith, I shall strive in yonder surrounding fields to experiment and record observations. I shall repay you for the sustenance through toil or any other method."

194

Vaz waved a dismissive hand. "Unnecessary to repay, outsider. You're a prisoner here and the situation unfair."

Two more gems clattered on the counter. The cook prepared additional food and placed it in a sack. The large demon also poured juice into a flask and set everything before Sybil. She took the delicious items and inclined her head in appreciation.

"I shall travel forth to begin," said Sybil. "I am grateful to you, Vaz, for everything hitherto."

"Don't stray too far away," the demon warned. "Hostile animals and other vermin roam the forest and plains. The wrong bite from something and you'll have more to worry about than the black poison inside you."

Sybil nodded. "I shall be careful. See you soon." An emotional pain touched her heart. Whether she died in the next hour trying to save Umaq or somehow managed to escape with him, she may never see Vaz again.

Not all of these demons represented the stuff of nightmares. This community had shocked Sybil in its similarity to her own decent neighborhood. Based on her limited demon experience, she had thought this realm would be full of snarling, evil beasts at every turn. That kind did exist, monsters like Zelaenah who displayed malevolence and enjoyment of any carnage irrelevant to being under Umaq's control. But overall, this realm turned out to be far different than what Sybil had anticipated. Ironically, she thought of her world, where many humans proved to be just as cruel and fearsome as some demons.

Her supplies in hand, Sybil left the comfort of town and walked between the scattered trees of the surrounding woods. The familiar, shiny fruit hung from branches or lay on the ground. A hairless animal the size of a racoon sprang from a hole. It raced across the leaf-strewn turf and snatched a berry in its mouth, then turned and plunged back into its home. The eerie call of a strange, four-winged bird pierced the air. The creature landed on a high branch and stared down its long beak at Sybil.

Peaking over the treetops, the distant mountain Vaz had mentioned loomed on the purple horizon. The disk of bleary sun, a cold orange smudge of desolation, remained in its perpetual state. No day and no night. Strange animals, unpredictable demons, weird sights, smells, and sounds—a deep loneliness crept beneath Sybil's skin and worked its way to her core.

She had already faced the worst solitude of her life in the ley tunnels. She defeated that soul-crushing isolation and had emerged damaged, yet victorious. The demon realm should not have presented an additional challenge of loneliness, nothing she hadn't handled before. Yet the further Sybil walked, the heavier that negative feeling pressed.

Everything felt bizarre in this odd environment. Nothing seemed right. The violet sky mocked. The dark mountain laughed loud. The four-winged bird cursed at Sybil. Vaz's friendship and the welcoming community appeared as though a dream.

Humans did not belong here at all. Their fragile minds and bodies would implode from confusion and despair. Just walking through the woods brought agony, fear, and self-doubt. Sybil wouldn't dare imagine what the so-called dark gods had unleashed on Umaq. Vaz's words haunted her: *From here, the town residents say you can hear Umaq's screams—that is, if you* want *to listen.*

Did Sybil just hear something upon the foul breeze? A voice, far and all too human. A distant wail, a cry out for help. No, it couldn't be. Vaz had implied a silly rumor, just some street gossip to frighten the demons of that town.

"Continue on," she said, surprised by the sudden command to herself. At some point in her fearful musing, she had stopped moving. Had she been so unconsciously afraid that her feet rooted to the ground?

"No turning back forthwith lest there is no place to go," she finished. Her little, half-hearted pep talk functioned well enough to start walking again.

The woods ended and an ugly wasteland like the one near the portal commenced. Dry, cracked ground containing sparse vegetation stretched to the base of the mountain. Packs of four-legged demons sprinted about raising clouds of dust. Sybil recognized these lower tier creatures, the same kind Umaq had used as guards and for labor in Machu Picchu.

After Umaq vanished through the portal, she recalled how one of those demons had inspected her in the grassy Central Plaza, then left in apparent lack of interest. Based on that experience, Sybil didn't grow concerned as a group of five demons approached in cautious gaits. Sleek gray skin stretched over skeletal frames. Some rugged horns dotted their curved backs. Misshapen teeth crammed jaws and forked tongues drooled. They sniffed and circled around her, multiple slanted eyes probing. One of the monsters cried out and the pack bolted off.

197

Sybil continued her trek until she reached the base of the mountain. She squeezed between a pair of boulders and collapsed in exhaustion. Too tired to care about hungry beasts or poisonous bugs, she quickly fell into a restless sleep. Sometime later, she awoke to the purple sky and a faded sun. She ate some of the "to go" food from the sack tied to a belt loop and drank juice from the flask.

After a series of stretches, she continued along the foothills and didn't have to worry about getting lost. In the far distance, several ascending lights dotted the mountainside and served as her guide. She passed huge boulders, a few spooky cave entrances, and knots of foul-smelling weeds. Nearing the first set of glows, she discerned a clear, upward path carved into the rock.

Magical lights inside glass, the same kind as in the wasteland tunnel, sat atop dark iron posts lining a stone road. Thin branches of iron had been twisted and hammered into beautiful leaves and black roses. Sybil admired the craftsmanship of each paved stone, smooth and cut in attractive geometric patterns. The demonic language, gorgeous in flowing loops and hard slants, had been etched into low brick walls on either side of the path. Wonderful architecture, but no one except an "outsider" to admire it as she stood alone.

Sybil speculated that not many visitors—demon or otherwise—climbed this trail to the temple on the mountain. Vaz appeared terrified just mentioning the place. The dark gods dwelled up there. What sort of horrifying and powerful beings awaited?

She began her endless ascent, legs burning from an incline that a young person would tolerate much better. Sips of juice accompanied continual rests and a shrinking view of the wasteland. Beyond the harsh and arid turf below, she could see the lush forest and Vaz's town far away.

At some point among the twists and turns up the mountain, Sybil spotted a cluster of shadowed towers on a high precipice. Not much detail could be discerned as she still had aways to go. More climbing, resting, and she eventually reached a stone bridge. On the other side of a huge chasm, a black, ominous temple sat.

Unlike the decorative work of the paved road, the dark ramparts appeared anything but inviting. Drab blocks of ash-colored stone had been carelessly stacked into walls, walkways, and towers. Ugly weeds grew from several cracks throughout the construction. No fine writing decorated the rock or any feature meant to please a guest.

Something else appeared to be missing here; no guards stood before her. No army of monsters patrolled the area or peeked out from battlements. Perhaps a need to defend the temple had proven unnecessary, for who would dare approach the dark gods?

Apparently, a battered, exhausted old woman named Sybil.

She stepped onto the long stone bridge and her shoes crunched over grit. No other sounds occurred. After a moment, she suddenly halted, trembling. Sybil gripped the waist-high partition edging the bridge and stared over the huge black abyss below. This was foolishness! Did she truly believe she would stroll into the temple, wave to the dark gods, then waltz out with Umaq like nothing happened?

Back in the forest, she convinced herself to keep moving. She had nowhere else to go. Well, that notion didn't entirely hold truth. She could become a resident of Vaz's town and somehow work to earn a living. After learning to adapt in the demon realm, her life would be extended absent the sickness. Climbing back through the portal to be with Marcelo presented another option. In that scenario, she would accept her fate and, in a few months, die in his arms on her own terms.

"Or forthwith I could leap off this bridge, thus be done with everything," she muttered.

At that, intense disgrace blasted her heart. An avalanche of guilt crushed her spirit. In desperation, Sybil had reached for excuses to run away or end it all. She allowed fear and lost hope to dictate the situation and her emotions. Hiding would not save Marcelo from that raging demon nor free the Earth Mother from her suffering. And certainly, a leap off the bridge would not provide a cure to Sybil's illness.

Her vision blurred and she wiped away warm tears. After a deep breath, she turned to complete the trek across the bridge, but stopped when an agonized howl—human—echoed between the high rocky peaks. Troubled by the disturbing cry, Sybil clenched her fists, her heart pounding.

"'Tis my imagination, nothing more. It ought to be the wind."

Moving onward in a cautions gait, she entered a barren courtyard paved with uneven rock. Layers of wind-blown sand covered parts of the area. Dry, thorny weeds sprouted in various cracks. She gazed up to the high towers and thick walls. Many darkened windows appeared devoid of life. Still no sign of guards…or gods.

Sybil crossed the silent quad and approached a gigantic entrance. A pair of open iron doors sagged on bent hinges, perhaps due to forced entry or simply age. From inside the temple, the tormented howl sounded once more, louder.

She now recognized Umaq's voice.

No longer a rumor or story to frighten wary demons, Umaq truly cried out from somewhere within. His pained yell echoed over the demon realm in all directions. The dark gods had more than likely arranged this as a harsh warning, their twisted way of keeping traitors—of any species—in hard check. Sybil again wondered what sort of deities ruled here, ones even some demons feared. Perhaps she would find out just before her voice joined Umaq's in a duet of death.

Stepping past the doors, she entered a cavernous stone foyer lit by the familiar magical lights secured to the walls and ceiling. Various stairs, long halls, and arched doorways cautioned against the foolish explorer getting lost inside. However, she only had to follow the sound of Umaq's call.

Still no demons or deities lurked anywhere. The shadow-draped loneliness weighed heavy, unpleasant on Sybil's mind. The isolation and mystery of such a dreary, senseless place had drained her emotions. She trudged up flights of stairs and shuffled down broad, tiled hallways. Weariness chained her feet. Depression sapped her strength and will. The ricocheting voice among the endless stonework and iron made it difficult to follow, but she eventually reached the source in a circular room at the top of a spiral set of steps.

Sybil stared through the open doorway and gasped in horror. Multiple dead bodies covered the floor. Pools of blood glistened on the tile and splatters stained the curved walls. Some heads had been crushed into pulp. Limbs lay torn and scattered. Other charred bodies littered the area, black and unrecognizable. Several victims had suffered deep cuts, whip marks, or massive bruises from severe beatings. Rope burns around necks, smashed bones, iron brands…the terrible causes of death went on.

Sybil ducked behind the entry wall and fell to her knees in a dazed, quiet sob. Umaq cried out again from inside the room. He might die soon, judging by how all the other people had suffered. But who were they? Had they also been kidnapped from the human realm?

She swallowed in fright and peered through the doorway. The initial shock of seeing the bodies had riveted her; however, she now spotted a vicious-looking demon on the far end of the room. The sweaty, cloven-footed monster rummaged on a bloody table packed with disturbing weapons and metal instruments. On a low platform, Umaq bled and panted, his wrists tied to a stone block. Near him on an iron pedestal, a strange object glowed bright white.

Sybil dove back behind the wall and quickly tallied her few options. Maybe wait until the demon's attention fixed on Umaq, then sneak in and grab a weapon off the table? Perhaps she could cause some commotion from downstairs, then slip past the monster when it left the room. Then what?

Sybil grunted and pulled her messy gray hair in desperation. She glanced back inside to better reassess details of the room, then froze as a sickening realization blanched her face.

The bodies…all of them were Umaq!

Many of the figures had been unrecognizable due to the extent of damage, but the others resembled her old arch enemy. She examined the dead once more and noticed features that left no doubt. Sure enough, the corpses belonged to Umaq.

An additional slow realization appalled her. The terrible comprehension of what lay before her proved unbearable. She peered at the beaten, living Umaq and a sudden crush of empathy squeezed her heart. Torture until death. A body then tossed to the side. Somehow a resurrection, followed by another round of punishment. Repeated until…when? How long would this go on?

Sybil lifted trembling fists. It would end now as this is what she had journeyed for. Several reasons had brought her to this very moment, but she gladly added another—Umaq did not deserve this. She had always envisioned a form of justice against the evil man who murdered dear Constance and placed Sybil in a three-hundred-year coma. However, the unspeakable horror in the room did not represent her intention. And if she had previously wished for bloody vengeance, then it had just played out dozens of times.

Umaq, restrained and sweaty, glanced up and locked eyes with Sybil. Through a mask of blood and exhaustion, he appeared just as shocked to see her as she felt. He looked at the demon's back as it continued to sift through the weapons, then gazed back at her. Rooted in the doorway, her mouth dropped open when he gestured for her to *stay put*. She shook her head. He repeated the gesture—*wait*.

The demon turned around. A long, spiked chain dangled from a clawed hand as it finally selected a weapon. Sybil ducked behind the doorway as much as possible while still being able to see. The beast stepped toward Umaq, and he spit a bloody wad at the creature.

The demon raised the chain and raked it across Umaq's chest in a powerful sweep. He shouted and fell against the stone block.

Sybil clamped a cold hand over her mouth and screamed against her palm. Tears welled as the monster whipped Umaq several times. She shook her head in disgust and thumped the wall in frustration.

Just as she had heard outside, Umaq's mournful wails and cries of pain commenced. His voice rose in pitch or boomed deep. His throat worked in short bursts of noise or long notes, syllables of torment and misery. Yet…could it be? After several moments, it sounded like intentional wording in a bizarre language. Sybil imagined he sang of death and desperate relief, of help and lost hope. She covered her ears and wished for everything to stop.

After a few terrifying minutes, Umaq slumped over in certain death. The demon dropped the chain and unbuckled the leather strap around the man's wrists. The creature picked up the body and cast it toward the other corpses across the room.

The odd white light on the iron pedestal flashed brighter. The illumination grew until Sybil had to turn away. After a few moments, the glow subsided and an unblemished Umaq suddenly appeared on the platform. Terror filled his face, his eyes wide. The large demon grabbed Umaq and tied his wrists in the strap again. The beast then shuffled toward the table and sifted through the weapons once more.

Sybil stared in fascination…and revulsion. From one perspective, Umaq appeared physically strong and healthy. He stood straight, the blood, exhaustion, and sweat gone. On the other hand, she understood the demon wanted its victim fresh and untainted—to bleed and mutilate over and over.

She met Umaq's frantic gaze. *Now*, he mouthed. Of course. He had wanted her to wait until a restored version of himself appeared. No use rescuing a beaten husk of a man that would die halfway down the stairs.

No time to think anymore. Sybil slipped into the large chamber and tiptoed around the scattered dead. Hurrying to Umaq, she unbuckled his arms and he grabbed the discarded chain the demon had used to strike him. Placing a finger against his lips, he nodded toward a pile of battered corpses a few feet away from the platform. Understanding, Sybil moved behind the bodies and ducked out of sight.

"Hey!" Umaq yelled at the demon. "You hit like a baby wearing mittens."

The creature grunted and whirled in surprise. Heavy cloven hooves pounded the stone tile when the demon charged at Umaq.

Seeing her opening, Sybil ran to the table and grabbed a long pike. Umaq dodged around the platform and swung the spiked chain to distract the monster. Sybil sprinted over and plunged the weapon into the demon's wide back, then yanked the sharp end free. The beast roared in pain and faced her, its teeth gnashed in rage.

Umaq hopped onto the platform and spun the chain like a lariat. He shouted in fury and smacked the monster on the side of the head. The demon tottered sideways with black blood gushing over its face. Sybil charged and rammed the pike into the creature's throat. It fell next to the other corpses and lay still in a pool of blood.

"Wish I could bring that thing back to life and kill it again," Umaq panted. "See how he likes it." He gestured toward the white light upon the iron pedestal. "Grab that and let's get the hell out of here."

Sybil released her weapon and hurried over to the glowing object. She grasped a gold-plated feather, the light emanating from it warm and revitalizing in her hands.

"It's an ornamental feather from Inti's golden headdress that contains the solar deity's spirit," Umaq explained. "When I sacrificed Inti on top of his own altar using nether energy, the dark gods took his spirit into the demonic realm as a prize. I wasn't lying to you in Machu Picchu. Bring that to Intihuatana, and the deity can be restored."

Sybil's eyes widened. She opened her mouth to speak, but Umaq gestured for silence.

"We have a million questions for each other, but no time to dawdle," he said. "Just know that the dark gods used Inti's power in the feather to resurrect me after every death. A cruel irony, since I'm the one that destroyed Inti." He shrugged "Let's go."

Sybil placed the gold-plated feather in a pocket for safeguarding and to obscure the glow. She followed Umaq out of the chamber and down the spiral steps. Everything seemed to be happening at warp speed. She couldn't believe Umaq walked free, and she had just killed a demon! Adrenaline hammered her heart. She perspired like crazy. The million questions would be answered eventually, but she couldn't help asking one now.

"What of yonder dark gods?" she whispered. "Where do they dwell?"

"I haven't seen them since they dragged me through the portal," Umaq answered in a hush. He also sweated and nervously glanced about as they descended the steps. "They threw me in that room at the top and vanished. Don't want to get their hands dirty, I suppose. Well lucky for us, it's the weaker and less intelligent monsters that stay behind for the torture."

Could they really escape so easy? Fear numbed Sybil's legs, and she nearly stumbled. Cold wrapped her trembling hands. Reaching the bottom of the tower, the pair hurried down empty corridors, crossed through large rooms, and soon entered the grand foyer.

The severe cold traveled from Sybil's hands and up both her arms. More than just a result of fear, a new freezing sensation pained her shoulders, squeezed her chest, and slowed her travel until she couldn't move.

Alongside her, Umaq also struggled to advance. Frosted breath jetted from his mouth and nose. He glanced at Sybil in panic, eyes wide in terror.

"The dark gods are here!" he uttered through chattering teeth. "I'm so sorry, Sybil. I honestly thought we'd make it out. I had every intention of keeping my promises to you."

Something tall and black shimmered before the large doorway. The strange, darkened mass solidified, turned nebulous, dripped like water, then hardened into gel, its presence an endless and irrational shift. Sybil couldn't discern if a single being or a dozen stood there. Her forehead pounded in confusion and dismay. She shivered before the black silhouette—its form literally nothing—yet somehow a dreadful *thing* that defied imagination and shattered her courage. A single voice spoke…no, many. A raspy chorus, jagged fingernails inside Sybil's skull.

"Umaq!" the dark god howled.

"P-piss off!" he stammered, chilled due to the unseen force.

A hazy fragment of dark energy lashed out from the god and struck Umaq in the chest. He shouted in pain and flew several yards before crashing on the stone floor. His body rolled and thumped against the far wall.

The towering form approached Sybil, its shape translucent, then opaque. She struggled to move as frost caked her feet and stuck them to the ground. The god's dark energy exploded forth. A shockwave slammed her, yet nothing happened.

Relieved, Sybil glanced down at a familiar glow surrounding her. The soft bluish light—ley energy—had absorbed the blow just before impact.

"You reek of the Earth Mother!" the dark god hissed. "How can that ethereal hag's presence be in my realm?"

"Dear, sweet Earth Mother!" Sybil whispered in utter joy.

The great spirit had saved Sybil's life again. The ley essence she had absorbed for decades lingered in her body. Just as it helped her ride the ley rivers, the Earth Mother's gift had also negated the dark god's attack. The sheer magnitude of how much the earth spirit had provided for Sybil brought her to tears.

"You mock me in your delight!" the dark god yelled in rage.

The deity unleashed a furious attack of nether energy. Dark lightning, shooting spheres, and black flames lashed out in earsplitting roars. Surrounded by the ley glow, Sybil wiped her eyes and stood, confident no harm would befall her.

The enraged mass of darkness pulled back. The phenomenon shrank and hardened, the dark power molding into a new shape. A humanoid figure suddenly stood before Sybil. A genderless being stared, thin and shiny black from head to toe. It lacked facial features; only darkness resided there, hollow and terrifying as if Sybil might fall inside forever.

A black splinter grew from the god's hand and a huge sword took shape. The being raised its arm, then struck the stone tile in a thunderous boom. The floor cracked, and the long blade sang in vibration. The dark god lunged and swung its weapon. Something hit Sybil and knocked her flat. Instead of cold metal through her chest, a gasping Umaq rested on top of her following a hard tackle.

"That dark sword will slice you in half," he said, quickly yanking her up. "I've worked enough nether essence to know ley energy won't block that weapon."

"I am unable to cast spells, I warrant," she told him, catching her breath after the collision. Her eyes fixed on the dark god as it stepped forward to renew its attack. "I fear nothing remaineth to fight with."

Umaq grabbed Sybil by the shoulders. Sweat moistened his withered face. Pain shortened his breath. Several emotions appeared in his gaze: panic, despair, anger, and deep sorrow.

"I will stay behind and fight on," he said softly. "You run, Sybil. Run as far and fast as you can."

Sybil looked in a mirror. Umaq's raw feelings, the ones choked by loneliness and depression, matched her own. They had both suffered inexplicable torment.

Each heart and soul struggled to hope, had broken, and longed for a release. He understood her anguish. And underneath his roiled emotions, she recognized her weakness at the bridge, her thoughts of plummeting to freedom as she stared into the deep chasm. Was this Umaq's own bridge moment? Had he given up and only wished to end his suffering?

"I shall remaineth hither by your side, Umaq. Together we—"

"Save yourself," he commanded, then pushed her away. "No time to argue. Now leave!"

Chapter Sixteen

Enemy of my Enemy

Grace walked the streets of Salem, her jaw set in anger. She found no pleasure beneath a warm sun and clear day. The relative quiet defied the recent battles across the city. Not long ago, she had tried to retake Salem from Cessani in a violent coup. Grace and her small coven had raced from block to block to fight Cessani's red-robed witches and their zombie pets. At the end of that long, terrible night, her desperate quest concluded in failure as swarms of supernatural beings and the Maiden moon goddess appeared in front of the converted Witch Museum.

On this business-as-usual day, it really seemed Grace's effort and imprisonment had been for nothing. Aside from grumbling about the witch tax, most of Salem had acquiesced to Cessani's new leadership. The police and other officials only desired calm and a return to normalcy. To avoid more bloodshed, Mayor Deque and the city council had reached an agreement with Cessani. A cleaning effort and repairs—most of the damage had been caused by Grace and her coven—had taken place throughout the area. Shops reopened and people emerged from previously shuttered homes to work, mingle, and purchase goods.

211

Grace had no fight remaining in her, either. Half-heartedly, she had joined some active members of the community to hold up a sign and picket against the ongoing monster activity. She hoped the continued supernatural presence would not spark more citizens to rebel. Salem had been through enough. She didn't want to see her friends and neighbors swept into a dangerous uprising against powerful witches. Following a copious amount of thinking over hot tea and bourbon, Grace decided it remained best for Mayor Deque to continue confronting Cessani about the monster problem.

Reaching her final destination for the day, Grace strolled into the Crow Haven Corner witchcraft shop. The shelves and display tables stood half empty as a pair of customers browsed the remnants of ingredients for spell casting. Toward the back of the store, Grace found the manager, Lily, squatting next to a crate of magical goods.

"Busy as always," Grace observed.

"Oh, hey you!" Lily replied, smiling. Beneath low-cut dark hair, her green eyes lit in pleasure. She stood and squeezed Grace in a warm hug. "How has my best customer been? I still can't believe Cessani held you against your will."

"Based on the history I've had with her, I can totally believe it," Grace remarked. "It wasn't exactly Alcatraz, and honestly, I've moved on. The moment I saw Sybil and Marcelo had returned safely from Athens after defeating Umaq, nothing else mattered."

"How are those two faring?" Lily asked. "What a horrible experience they must have gone through. With so many witches and supernatural entities around Salem, one can't help hearing a rumor or two. Seems like there's been trouble in California. I hope Sybil and Marcelo are safe."

"I know what you're referring to," Grace replied in a dejected tone. "Vampire and demon trouble. I haven't heard from those two at all, and that's very unusual. I'm worried sick, especially after seeing Sybil in her condition. I haven't been much help, either. A solution to her illness and aging has eluded me."

"My researching and field contacts also haven't produced an answer," said Lily. "As a main dealer in witchcraft items, you'd think we could've dredge up a sliver of knowledge." She shook her head. "But there's nothing."

"I really appreciate all you do." Grace sighed, then nodded toward the crate on the floor. "Speaking of witchcraft items, it appears supply still can't keep up with demand."

"Not even close." Lily dug into the container and placed a large jar of yellowish powder onto a shelf. "Unfortunately, the seeds you ordered didn't make it this round. Hopefully end of next week. Overall, I can't complain about the booming business. However, on the downside, every sale I make reminds me of Cessani's takeover and the monsters roaming about. People just want to protect themselves."

"I wish I could do more," Grace said.

"You've done more than enough, my friend." Lily placed another item on the shelf. "You need to rest, Grace. I didn't want to say anything earlier, but you look like hell. It's time to be selfish and take a load off."

Grace offered a weary smile. No surprise she looked exhausted, and she truly felt it. A combination of physical altercations and elevated, continued stress had wrecked her body and mind. A load off sounded wonderful but didn't seem likely without knowing if Sybil and Marcelo were all right.

"Thank you, Lily, for your concern. I might try to take a nap after some tea and bourbon."

Lily set the final item in its proper place and picked up the empty box. "Sorry you came out here for nothing. I should have called you about the order."

Grace shook her head. "No problem at all. It's always nice to see you. Stay safe and don't work too hard."

After a farewell embrace, Grace left the store and returned to her car down the street. She drove home and pulled a pile of letters from the mailbox. Walking inside the house, she dropped the mail on the kitchen table and prepared her tea. A good nap did sound nice. Perhaps she would attempt one after a good drink.

Sipping on her favorite concoction, she browsed through the letters and nearly choked when Sybil's name appeared on the corner of an envelope. Grace set the tea down too quickly and some sloshed onto the table. The drink ignored, she tore open the letter and sat stunned by the note inside.

Her shock melted into tears as she read Sybil's message two times. The initial reading had triggered disbelief and fright. The second pass—after Grace took a few deep breaths—resulted in helplessness and grief.

"Oh Sybil, my sweet brave child," she cried. She rose and walked to the living room, only to pace the carpet as tight fingers gripped the paper.

Why didn't Sybil reach out any sooner? Grace would have flown to California in an instant. Yet after scanning the letter for a third time, she realized an

214

incredible amount of pain and confusion had sent the young—or old—witch into a dark and lonely mindset where no one could help except herself.

In the end, Sybil had traveled to Machu Picchu alone to rescue Umaq from…from the demon realm! Grace still had trouble believing it. She shuddered and slipped on a shawl that had been draped over the back of the sofa. Nothing could be done to assist Sybil now. However, the clever girl had left Grace instructions and finished the letter in a disturbing message of…*if I survive and return through yonder portal with Umaq.*

If I survive.

Fresh tears fell. Grace wiped them away and blew her nose. She finally collapsed on the love seat and attempted to settle her thumping heart and whirling mind. "Of course you'll survive, silly thing." She nodded and set the tissue box aside. "And that's why I'll ensure your directions are followed."

But how to do it? The task equated to moving a mountain. It required walking through fire and facing an adversary that Grace didn't want anything to do with. Worst of all, the assignment would necessitate swallowing pride and possibly begging, actions that made her cringe.

She stood from the sofa and looked out the front window. Plenty of daylight left, so no excuses. No time to waste. If Sybil had traversed realms to face demons in the dark netherworld, then Grace could muster the willpower to drive over to the Witch Museum and meet Cessani.

Armed with Sybil's letter, she got back in her car and drove across town to the witch headquarters near the grassy park of Salem Common. She climbed out of the vehicle and marched to the door where a red-robed witch guarding the entrance scowled.

"Never thought I'd see you here again," the man said. "Did you miss your prison cell that much?"

"Zip it," Grace retorted. "I have critical news about Umaq and need to speak with Cessani."

"Umaq is dead," he replied.

"I can see why you were assigned guard duty," Grace began. "It's the only task your puny brain is capable of handling. Umaq may well be alive. Do you want him showing up like I did on your watch? Now let me in."

The man's scowl grew more pronounced. "Fine, but you won't make it past the front desk without an appointment." He moved aside.

Grace strode past him and entered the building. The former museum had been converted into offices and meeting rooms, a place to conduct a business and apparently hold prisoners. Her cell had been an office room, not concrete and iron, but the experience proved unpleasant to say the least.

"Uh-uh!" a voice yelled as Grace crossed the tiled lobby. "No walk-ins. You need an appointment."

Grace turned and approached the large desk where an assistant stood. The young witch's face held a mask of irritation. She adjusted her glasses and glared over the top of the lenses. It seemed Grace's presence had a way of unsettling the entire facility.

"I have an appointment slip," said Grace. "I'll show you." She dug into a pocket, then pulled out her empty hand.

The puzzled assistant stared, then opened her mouth to speak. Grace snapped her fingers. The young girl fell back into her chair, asleep from an easy spell.

"Don't bother escorting me, I know the way," Grace said as she stepped away and moved down a hall.

She strode toward Cessani's office and didn't allow the closed door to stop her. She barged inside and found Cessani using chopsticks to eat noodles from a hot Styrofoam bowl. Mouth full, the old witch's eyes widened, then narrowed in anger. She stood, chewing, and wagged her index finger in a 'no-no' gesture. She swallowed and wiped her chin on a napkin, then finally spoke.

"What good is having an assistant if they're going to let anyone bull their way into my office?" she asked in frustration. "What do you want? Can't I even eat in peace?"

"I need your help," Grace responded.

She hated just uttering those words. Asking Cessani for assistance after their decades-long rivalry was a hard pill to swallow. Years ago, their problems had begun with petty arguments over starting a coven together, sharing magical ingredients, and which deities to invoke during spell casting. The many complications worsened after Cessani started up her own group. A competition formed, and their relationship deteriorated. The verbal attacks grew more personal. Intense dislike turned into hatred, and all this occurred even before Umaq showed up.

The wicked man's presence had elevated their conflict to unimaginable heights. Battles for survival, the darkest of magics, a god's death, and most recently kidnapping ending with Grace a prisoner.

"Help?" Cessani asked in total surprise. In the awkward silence, steam drifted from the red bowl of noodles on the desk. It seemed Grace's request had stunned her old rival. "What do you mean?"

Desiring brevity and minimal interaction, Grace took Sybil's letter from a back pocket and placed it atop scattered pieces of paper on the desk. Cessani picked up the message and read. Her face underwent a series of expressions, eyes and mouth reacting in astonishment, dismay, and fear.

"Umaq, that devil," Cessani said at last. "He just won't go away, will he?" She glared over the top of the letter. "You truly believe he's alive and that Sybil can rescue him in her condition?"

Grace nodded. "Whatever happens, I believe in Sybil."

Cessani's eyes fell back to the note. "So belief is supposed to convince me to travel to Machu Picchu, wait for Sybil and Umaq to emerge from the demon realm, ensure his capture, then seal the portal in the Uku-Pacha window. And all of this according to Sybil's directions?"

"Exactly," Grace answered. Based on Cessani's skeptical tone, Grace would have to resort to what she had dreaded—groveling. Asking for her assistance had been difficult enough, but now came the most appalling stage of all.

Cessani stepped out from behind the desk and moved slowly around the office. "Perhaps if we…," she began, then trailed off. She mumbled to herself in half sentences and broken thoughts. It seemed Grace had all but vanished from the room.

"But what if…," the old witch continued.

Grace tapped a foot. "Cessani, time is short—"

"It always is," the older witch responded, her attention back to the present. "I'll do it. I'll help you."

"Well, that was easier than I imagined," Grace uttered in surprise. "Why the eagerness to assist after all that's transpired between us, and between you and Sybil?"

Cessani sighed and returned to the desk. She plopped down and motioned for Grace to sit in the chair on the opposite side.

"Listen, I'm the one who ratted out Umaq," Cessani explained. "I told Sybil all about his plan for Athens. The Maiden even supplied her with magical objects to help her friends. I rooted for Sybil's success, knowing Umaq is not someone you betray. The young witch's failure would have led to my death and an apocalypse for the world. If Sybil rescues the demon master and returns him to our world, then yes, I'll do everything I can to guarantee his capture and seal the portal."

"It's wonderful to know you're looking out for yourself, as usual," Grace noted. "But what about your new empire and witch rule? All that may disappear if Umaq is true to his word and revives Inti, the sun god. The mystical balance would be restored and your power and influence lessened. You've worked hard to achieve your goal. Are you prepared to give all that up? Not that I'm concerned with your aspirations being dashed. I just need to ensure your effort here is genuine."

Cessani rose from the squeaky chair again to stroll around the office. Agitation furrowed her brow. Frustration set her jaw and ignited a fierce gaze. In the end, grief smoothed her features as she stopped and folded her arms.

"I am prepared," she replied softly. "I'm also weak, and a flake. You are correct, Grace. I planned, fought, and literally bled for my dream of witch rule. Now that I have it, it's driving me insane, and I'm losing control. Supernatural entities are growing more dangerous. The Maiden is sure to leave, covens are unraveling, I don't have enough help…" She trailed off and wiped her teary eyes. "Long story, but I've been looking for an escape and here it is. Restoring Inti's light and the mystical balance would erase all that I've achieved. But in the end, returning our world to what nature intended is best for everyone."

Grace studied Cessani's aged and exhausted features. The woman's narrow shoulders sagged. She had paced the floor as if her feet weighed a ton. Her white-streaked, long black hair dangled in a mess. A disheveled, dirty robe clung to her thin body. It was obvious the older witch spoke true; her words did not conceal a ruse or threat.

"Fine, then we are in agreement and can work together," Grace remarked. "We should head out for Machu Picchu at once. But I haven't figured out how to make it past Umaq's magical defenses and remaining demons. Since the beginning, all those troops from different countries haven't been able to make a dent."

"I think I have an idea," Cessani offered. "You remember the portal Umaq created in my house when he first transported all the demons to Machu Picchu? I'll need your help to reactivate it. It won't be easy and may take hours, but that may be our only way in. We'll end up in the Temple of the Three Windows and can wait for Sybil there. However, I believe the demons are no longer under Umaq's direct control and may be a problem."

"That's not everything," Grace added. "What about overpowering Umaq and sealing the portal to the netherworld? He may have struck a deal with Sybil, but the man cannot be trusted and won't go down easily. I doubt the two of us can detain him, even with Sybil's help."

"We can't alone, but I know plenty of *brujas* and *chamáns* from my Peruvian coven that can assist," Cessani replied.

Who would have dreamed Grace would team up with Cessani? However, they were only partnered for a similar and temporary cause. No friendship existed. A business arrangement, nothing more. The shared quest for the greater good represented a feeble glue that held the women together. But for Sybil's sake, Grace would have endured much worse.

She stood from the chair, determined and more than prepared. "Ready when you are."

Chapter Seventeen

Demonic Revolution

"Go!" Umaq shouted at Sybil.

He watched the old witch run across the stone foyer of the temple in awkward, exhausted strides. The dark god turned to pursue her. Umaq, still in pain after being struck by the deity's nether energy, motioned feebly toward the far wall. One of the magical lights moved in its sconce, but only a little.

"Come on!" he growled at the failed levitation spell.

Upon arriving in this lonely, dreadful world, the demons had siphoned out every black drop of nether essence from his body. His dark power, the force that nearly made him a god in the human world, vanished. Worse, he quickly discovered normal witchcraft didn't have much use here, the spells weak and inefficient. The demon abductors had overpowered him, and he proved unable to escape the nightmare room of torture.

Until Sybil came.

He still couldn't believe it. The brave girl had her reasons—none out of compassion for him, of course—but she had arrived, nonetheless. If Umaq had remained a prisoner, he would have been skinned by now, doused in oil and lit on fire, or beaten into jelly. Suffering and death, then repeated as he lay broken, bleeding, and sweating the life out of his body. A living nightmare. How many vocal cords had he ruptured screaming in agony? Crying, shivering, wailing, he had wished for death…only to receive it and then return to life for another round of anguish.

Umaq lifted both arms and faced the wall. In a renewed attempt, a loud grunt accompanied the spell aimed at the magical light. The glass case shook, lifted from the sconce, and sailed toward the dark god.

The clear glass shattered against the back of the deity's head. The black, humanoid form that resembled nothing more than hardened shadow stopped its pursuit of Sybil. The faceless god turned around and stared.

"Hey, your beef is with me, remember?" Umaq called. He dug deep into his spell casting reserves and scraped out a bit of fire that danced on his palm. Flicking his wrist, a jet of flame exploded from his hand and sprayed across the dark god's chest.

The deity walked through the blaze, the black sword raised to strike. "I will destroy you, human, then send you back to the tower for a hundred more deaths!"

Umaq suppressed a relieved smile. The demon god failed to notice Sybil had escaped carrying Inti's gold-plated feather stashed in her pocket. No more resurrections! Hopefully by the time someone dragged his body up the stairs and back to the tower, the witch would be long gone.

And he would be at peace.

Severely traumatized and broken by his horrid experience in the tower, Umaq didn't care if the deity struck him down in the foyer of this cursed temple. It would be a welcomed death—a final one. But first, he

223

would fight back as much as possible if only to allow Sybil more time to distance herself and find safety, if such a thing existed here.

Before Sybil appeared, all hope relied on the spell he had cast as he lay tied to the stone block. Despite his weak magic, the constant adrenaline and pain from torture had powered one final attempt. Bruised and bleeding, the agony boosted his resolve into screaming the words of a chant. The spell took multiple attempts as each death interrupted the cast. How many lives had he needed to finish?

The dark gods had amplified his screams and shouts of pain in a further sign of humiliation and defeat. In defiance, Umaq used the augmentation to carry his desperate, shouted spell to any monster that cared to listen. His words had been a desperate plea to a malevolent mob of demons that surely enjoyed his imprisonment. After the way he had treated their kind, why would those creatures pay any attention?

Hear me, demons of the nether, his chant had begun. For thousands of years, you desired to invade the mortal plane, yet did nothing. I alone established the portal between our realms to provide you the opportunity.

Yes, I manipulated some of your brethren. But why did I have to? You should have invaded my world on your own. I held the door, and you ignored it. Your weakness forced me to induce trickery—can you truly blame me? I stole your deities' power and performed deeds that your divine ones could never achieve. What shame that a lowly human defied the dark gods while you cowered in the shadows.

224

Even though I failed to merge our two worlds, the fight continues! Here. Now. In your gods' temple I bleed and cry my insolence to their faces. Come and join me, demons. Tear down these walls…or should a human act for you again? Together, we can bring down these useless gods and rip the portal wide. No more deceit. Wield your freedom and destroy the mortal plane, then rule a new empire grown from its ashes!

Blah, blah, his words had been. As Umaq faced the shadow deity in the foyer, none of his stupid spell mattered. The effort had proven futile. Not one monster had come. The demons probably laughed at the speech and relished his anguish. Umaq's voice had traveled from the temple and echoed across the realm, nothing more than useless, crazed prattle driven by blood-soaked madness.

The dark god thrust its sword in a killing blow. Umaq stomped his right foot and hollered a one-word command. A stone tile broke from the ground and rose to intercept the weapon. The black sword pierced the tile in a shower of dust and debris. The impact shifted the blade's course, and it grazed Umaq's side instead of cleaving his heart.

He fell onto the hard floor, laughing, even as blood dripped. After suffering indescribable pain and atrocious methods of death, the sword bite felt like a tickle. He stood in a wobble, drained of already feeble magic. Unable to buy Sybil more time, he smiled at the shadow deity and awaited the end for good.

A low rumble vibrated the floor. Past the entry doors, a dull roar sounded in the courtyard. The dark god paused, its head cocked in confusion.

Umaq also froze, but not from bewilderment. He grinned as disbelief at what he heard changed into amusement. Pressing a bloody hand over the wound, he slunk into a far corner to wait.

The rumbling grew closer, the shaking ground more pronounced. Dust rained from the ceiling. The enchanted lights on the walls and ceiling flickered. The shadow deity ignored Umaq and turned its full attention to the doorway. Tense, the god raised the sword, its dark feet planted in a battle stance.

"I win, jerk face," Umaq whispered.

A horde of snarling demons exploded through the doors and spilled into the foyer. The organized mob launched a frenzied attack on the dark god. Hairy, scaled, bony, and flesh-covered monstrosities roared in fury. Claws slashed, hooves kicked, and horns flailed. Disgusting welts oozed on a knot of yellow demons standing behind the throng. Chanting in unison, they launched spears crafted from fire, lightning, and nether energy.

Although the demon god lacked a true face in its shadowy visage, its body language signified complete surprise. Back peddling, the deity whirled its large black sword in defense against the onslaught.

Umaq howled with laughter. His pathetic 'join-me-in-a-coup' speech had worked. Did the magic fused to his words enchant the creatures? Or had he simply struck a nerve by highlighting the demons' cowardice while a human performed their dirty work? Either way, the enraged masses had taken the bait.

His humor ended the moment a second god appeared. The shadowy form materialized in the midst of battle, a huge mace tight in its grip. The fighting

226

intensified. Heart racing, Umaq stuck close to the walls and carefully worked his way to the doors. In a crouch, he waited for an opening through the chaos. Bodies and limbs fell. Spells flashed and exploded. Grunts and roars echoed. A wave finally parted in the bedlam, and he darted outside into freedom.

Umaq struggled in a slow jog. Pain flared in his side from the cut, his hand doing little to stop the blood. He moved through the courtyard and stumbled over the protruding corner of a dusty stone paver. Cursing, he continued past dozens of demon footprints in the wind-blown sand coating the area. Patches of thorn-covered weeds had been crushed by the stampeding mob.

The noise of frenzied combat faded behind as he reached the stone bridge. He shuffled across the gulf and reached the smooth downward path carved into the side of the mountain. The iron lampposts guided his descent. The enchanted light fell upon the demonic language etched into the brick sidewalls. Delightful phrases, more than likely chosen by the dark gods, welcomed visitors: *Bend knee and serve. Your worth will be judged. Death to those who refuse the Shadow.*

After thousands of years under harsh rule, slogans like that didn't exactly portray trustworthy leadership and rouse morale across the demon realm. Umaq figured the demonic horde would make the deities eat their words. No way he'd wait around to find out what happened next. He had never intended to spearhead a revolt and take these insane creatures into his world. Worse than evil, this particular troop of violent demons—like Zelaenah—posed too much of a threat.

Not long ago, Umaq had led a demonic horde to conquer the human world under suffocating darkness.

However, prolonged torture and repeated deaths had shattered his soul. The horrific episodes had cleared his consciousness and gutted his insides until only regret lingered. Suffering in the tower forced him to question why he had done those terrible things. He did not feel sorry for himself while a knife removed his fingers or a whip tore skin from his back. Umaq only experienced genuine remorse for the agony and destruction he had inflicted on humankind.

And Sybil, dearest Sybil, his arch enemy turned rescuer. The moment he spotted her face in the doorway of the tower room, he realized a second chance had been gifted to him. While chanting the spell, doubt that he'd escape always saturated his heart. But the witch's sudden appearance had spurred renewed hope. As he moved down the long mountain road, he grasped the optimism and soaked in its radiance while hurrying away from the temple.

After several minutes, Umaq paused to catch his breath. Where had Sybil gone to? She couldn't have traveled far. He hovered a palm over the wound in his side and muttered an incantation, but the attempt to heal failed. Continuing on, a soft voice from the shadows halted him.

"Umaq…"

He whirled to his left and studied the craggy mountain wall bordering the trail. Stepping cautiously, he exhaled in relief when he discovered Sybil wedged between two large rocks. She must have hidden when the train of demons barreled up the footpath. The witch did not appear well. Besides age, her body language portrayed a bone-deep exhaustion. Pale features, fever-sweat over her skin, and the empty eyes of surrender plagued her.

"You look how I feel," he told her. He nodded toward the temple. "Whatever happens in the next few minutes, we don't want to be around and need to keep moving."

He reached into the crevice to help her emerge. Sybil all but collapsed into his weak arms. The heat emanating from her body signified illness. He lifted one of her arms over his shoulders, then held her by the waist in support.

"Hitherto, I am sorry for being a burden," she mumbled. "The black sickness ails me not in this world. However, this new illness occurs thus of my age, plain and simple. I feel as though the last hour of exertion hath added another ten years forthwith. Not much time remaineth."

"We'll see about that," Umaq stated. "You are no burden, and I'm going to get you out of here."

He adjusted his grip on Sybil and took a deep breath. Together, the sick, beaten, and fatigued pair shuffled down the long stone walkway toward the dead fields at the base of the mountain.

The stone pathway ended. Umaq grunted, half-pulling, half-walking Sybil onto the dry, barren fields that stretched for miles. Cracks zigzagged the hard landscape. Ugly weeds and knots of bushes dotted the area. Overhead, the purple sky and fuzzy sun brought no comfort to his escape.

A loud cough exploded from his parched throat. He wheezed and gasped for air. Tired legs shook, and he almost collapsed. Sybil pulled free of his grasp and steadied him, her aged, frail body also trembling. She fumbled inside a satchel tied to her waist, then held out a flask and a bit of food.

Umaq shoved the strange meal into his mouth and moaned in delight, not caring what it consisted of. He also gulped down some of the drink. Wiping his chin, he smiled and blinked out a couple tears. As a prisoner, he thought he would never taste something so sweet again.

"My word," he breathed. "Thank you, Sybil. If I don't live another step, then that's the best meal I've ever had."

"Truly, my heart hopes you have more steps in you," she replied, putting the rest of the food and drink away. "The portal dwells far from hither, on the other side of yonder town and through a tunnel."

"Town?" Umaq scratched his cheek in thought, then gestured toward her satchel. "As in shops and places to eat?" Sybil nodded, and he chuckled. "This place gets even stranger by the minute. I was beaten unconscious when I first arrived, so didn't get to see much. Which way are we headed?"

Sybil glanced up at the violet sky. "Yonder sun never moves, so 'tis difficult to conceive a direction." She lifted an arm and pointed. "The town ought to lie that way, I warrant. Beyond it woods dwell, then a tunnel bored into a mountain. On the other side, we shall cross another wasteland before having a fair sight of the portal."

"The entire realm is in an uproar, or soon will be," he added. "We'll have to bypass the town to avoid attention. It's too bad. I could use more of that meat and drink. How much is left?"

"Not enough, truly," Sybil answered.

"I'm going to file a complaint with my travel agent after this vacation," said Umaq. He looked back toward the temple. "Let's get out of here."

"Wait." Sybil removed Inti's gold-plated feather from her pocket. She waved the object over the wound in his side.

Umaq studied her worn, wrinkled expression of concentration as she attempted to heal him. Nothing happened. She bent closer, her mouth moving in spell casting. The blood continued to ooze. Shaking her head, she turned the feather several different ways and tried again.

This girl's courage astonished him. How had she traversed this terrible realm and rescued him? Her unfathomable strength and determination stunned. As she worked to cure him, her honorable, shining spirit blinded him. Her giving heart thundered, deafening in its generous beat.

Umaq had really hurt this special girl. Their war started centuries ago as he preyed on the innocent and ushered in the dark. He had assaulted her mind and body in dozens of ways, cruel and relentless in his quest for world dominance. The demon gods had unleashed the same on him. The torture had destroyed his flesh and spirit. But worse, only through hard suffering and repeated death had he felt guilt for his actions.

Cheeks flushed, he looked away in disgrace as Sybil continued to try. He swallowed and fought back more tears, too ashamed to even apologize. Intense sorrow crushed his old heart. He couldn't even express regret in the simplest of words.

Umaq finally cleared his throat and laid a hand over Sybil's. "I appreciate the effort, but it's no use. Even

231

in death, that old Inca sun god wouldn't dare allow me some comfort."

"Thereof me neither," Sybil responded. "While hiding till the demon mob passed me on the road, I strove using the feather to make myself young."

Umaq looked at her in surprise. She shrugged and spread her hands as if to say, *why not try?* He suddenly laughed, and she joined him.

"Screw Inti," he announced. "After we're safely home, I'll make you young and healthy my way."

Arms locked at the elbow, the pair headed into the dusty wasteland. A sluggish pace resulted as they leaned upon each other for strength. Every step jolted Umaq's side in pain. It hurt just to breathe, let alone drag his feet across the turf. Sybil's breath grew ragged, her stumbles more frequent. After an hour, both of them appeared ready to collapse.

"Enough," Umaq gasped. He motioned toward a large crack in the ground. "Let's rest in there."

They shuffled inside the waist-high fissure and collapsed next to each other. Umaq's body hummed from exertion. His muscles throbbed and bones ached. Sybil appeared equally spent, her mouth open in heavy breathing. Occasional gusts of wind spilled grit and dead weeds over the edge and onto the pair. Umaq felt too tired to move or wipe dirt from his face. At some point he dropped into a feverish sleep.

He woke up later to find a dressing over his wound held in place by strips of cloth. Sitting up, he realized Sybil had torn pieces of her clothing to make the bandage while he slept. He studied her pained, restless features as she continued to doze after treating him.

Umaq stood and winced at every movement. His joints burned and spine ached. He stretched a bit, then started at the sound of a distant explosion.

High on the mountain, fire spewed from the location of the temple. Black smoke curled into the purple sky. A giant rumble echoed over the wasteland as another detonation shot fire and debris into the air. The brawl had turned into a war, and either winner meant disaster for him and Sybil.

He tried to awaken the witch, but she wouldn't stir. "Sybil, we need to go." He shook her shoulders again. "Sybil!"

Umaq dug his arms beneath her frail body and lifted her onto the turf. He climbed out, then picked her up again. Cradling the witch, he moved in the direction she had pointed. The rough, difficult journey consisted of frequent stops and terrified glances toward the temple. He shifted a limp Sybil from his arms to over his right shoulder in a fireman's grip, or across both shoulders in attempts to find some comfort and reduce episodes of rest. His heart hammered and sweat poured. Blood soaked the dressing and stinging blisters ruptured on his feet.

After an eternity, Umaq lowered Sybil to the ground and he collapsed, panting. The eerie sound of a demon howl on the wind couldn't even get him to move. Would the creature catch his scent, trot over, and rip out his throat? The horrible thought faded as utter exhaustion robbed him of consciousness.

He woke after some time as a flask touched his lips.

"Drink," Sybil's hoarse voice invited.

233

He swallowed two gulps, not daring to consume more out of fear they'd run out before reaching the end.

Eat," she whispered.

He ingested one bite and refused another.

"Worry not, have more forthwith," she insisted. "You shall have a feast once we reach yonder woods."

Feeling too weak to argue or ask questions, he ate more. The pair resumed their trek and soon Umaq discerned the outline of buildings in the distance. A wide mountain range loomed beyond the structures. He exchanged a glance with Sybil, and they headed toward the forest outside of town.

Umaq stepped between the first line of trees and couldn't believe his surroundings. Bright green patches of moss coated trunks. Gnarled branches crossed overhead, the leaves shiny red, yellow, blue, and green. Crisp, fresh grass cushioned his footfalls. Maroon and orange berries clung to thick bushes. Plump, fuzzy animals ran carrying twigs between their teeth or hung out in trees, chewing on nuts. The air smelled of clean moisture, hearty earth, and vibrant plant life. After miles of dead brown soil and the ugly, bruise-colored sky, the rich colors and inviting smells of the wood surprised and rejuvenated.

And Sybil hadn't lied about the feast. She tossed him a blue-green fruit that dangled from a low branch. Not bothering to ask details, Umaq dove into the meal. The tangy skin pleased his tongue, and the juicy pulp brought ecstasy between his teeth. Core after core littered the ground as he sat contented.

Sybil chewed at his side. Juice ran down her chin and she wiped it away. "We ought to be halfway to the portal, I warrant. With the demons in an uproar, my heart is distressed over the tunnel. Hitherto it might be guarded."

Umaq removed a thin stem from his mouth and flicked it onto the grass. "We'll find a way through no matter what. We are not dying in this cursed place."

"You speak true," Sybil replied wearily. Eyes half closed, she lay back and fell asleep surrounded by discarded fruit.

Should they keep hurrying on? Umaq debated waking Sybil up or carrying her again if necessary. However, fatigue also clouded his mind, and a nap welcomed a respite from the pain in his side. He lay down in the grass and joined her in a snooze. Sometime later, Sybil shook him awake.

"I hear voices in the wood," she whispered.

Umaq climbed to his feet and motioned for her to lead the way. Moving in a crouch, he followed her between bushes, pausing now and then behind wide trunks. He picked up distant voices in the demonic tongue and tapped Sybil on the shoulder to stop. She wouldn't understand the words, but he comprehended the entire conversation.

"Are you going to join the battle at the temple?"

"No way. The foul gods and crazy demons be dammed. My place is here."

"I heard Umaq escaped. He called for demons to revolt, but he's nowhere to be found."

"I don't believe in any wild rumors coming from that cursed mountain. Nothing can be confirmed until the fighting stops."

"Who do you want to prevail? This could be a new era for demons. Whether it's a good or bad thing remains to be seen."

"Oh, it will be bad either way. As long as our town is left alone, that's all I care about. Go on back and report. I already finished a sweep of the woods and there's nothing here."

Umaq waited until it seemed safe, then lightly nudged Sybil to continue. They crept away, cautious as if another voice might sound any minute. He glanced above the treetops and noted their position closer to the mountain.

Another hour passed and Sybil halted, out of breath. She pointed between the bushes. Umaq smiled at the dark opening cut into the side of the foothill, just past a cluster of trees.

"The tunnel!" he whispered in excitement, then squeezed her shoulder.

"I do not see anyone hither," she said, her voice low.

They stepped forward into the open, then froze as a tall demon emerged from the tunnel. The skinny reptilian creature folded its arms and stared at Umaq and Sybil, slanted orange eyes narrowed in anger. A sharp horn rose from its skull. Two tails swished in agitation, the bright feathers on each end rustling in the air.

"Vaz!" Sybil exclaimed. "I…do you fare well?"

Umaq gaped. Sybil knew this demon? Emotion roiled in his chest as he fought panic. The two appeared on speaking terms, but the monster's sharp gaze and aggressive body language did not signify friendship.

"Outsider," Vaz began in the human tongue. "I gave you food, drink, and pleasant conversation. But most importantly, I offered you my trust." The demon motioned toward Umaq. "And this is what I receive in return? You listened to me complain about this very man and how he deserved punishment, then you run off to help him escape?"

Umaq recognized the creature's voice. It had belonged to one of the demons conversing earlier, the one who supposedly performed a sweep of the woods with nothing to report. But how did the beast find them now? The demon hadn't been strolling in the tunnel by chance; Vaz had planned for this moment.

Sybil appeared shaken up. She wrung her hands, glanced at Umaq, then back to Vaz. "You speak true. I deceived you and I am sorry. My world yonder lies in turmoil. Thus, I need Umaq to restore the life of a sun god, I warrant."

"You also need him to heal you," Vaz observed. "You told me Umaq poisoned you with that dagger. I figure he is the only person capable of cleansing the blackness from your body."

"Thereof, yes," Sybil confirmed. "However, restoring the mystical balance in the human realm remaineth the greater importance."

The demon stepped forward and gripped Sybil's shoulders. Umaq tensed for a confrontation that may last only seconds, provided he could remain conscious that long. The tall demon's orange eyes glared down at the witch. Warring thoughts and emotions danced on the monster's reptilian features. Indecision displayed through gritted teeth, the upward curl of a lip, a twitch from a pointed ear, and the sharp swish of tails.

"I found you two sleeping under a tree, but I didn't say a word to the others," Vaz said. "I had to hear it for myself, outsider. Had to look in your eyes and judge your soul. I now understand you would die to save your realm. Nothing will stand in your way, not even the dark gods."

Vaz released Sybil and stepped back again. The demon flicked another glance at Umaq, then back to the witch. "Your sickness will return once you cross that portal. Even knowing that the traitor may leave you choking in the dust, you still braved the demon realm in order to save him."

The demon shook its head, clearly perplexed—and frustrated—over Sybil's tenacity. "You shook the earth in your realm and crossed impossible barriers to shatter mine. I have never met anyone like you whether demon, human, spirit, or powerful deity. You are an extraordinary creature, outsider."

The demon's narrow shoulders sagged, its fierce expressing melting into desolation. Vaz gazed toward the distant mountain where the temple sat. Black smoke continued to streak the purple sky. "Those dumb demons. They listened to Umaq's wailing blather while I chose not to, although I've learned enough since then."

Vaz faced Umaq and finally spoke to him. "You manipulated their pride, exposed their imprudence, and preyed on their lack of intelligence. You convinced my brethren to challenge the gods. Perhaps this had been brewing for millennia and you simply lit the match. Thanks to the both of you, this realm will never be the same, but that's a demon problem. My home is no place for a human, now or ever."

Sybil took a tentative step forward. "Vaz, please allow me to—"

"Go, outsider. That was your cue to leave. And take your baggage with you."

Umaq would live. He had expected the demon to slaughter him, and perhaps Sybil, for her treachery. It seemed Vaz had bigger fish to fry, as the saying went. Not one to waste opportunities, he took the witch by the elbow and pulled her toward the tunnel.

Sybil glanced back as they walked away. She cried in silence, tears moistening her face. Umaq could only guess at what had transpired between her and the demon. Had an odd friendship developed? Whatever the story, he knew the witch's big heart had contributed to the affiliation. Her grief exhibited deep remorse, the backward glances full of sorrow over a lost chance to rectify the situation.

For Umaq, he only desired to leave this hellhole. Supporting Sybil by the waist, the two continued down the endless tunnel. The enchanted lights illuminated the stone passageway as it bent in long curves, rose, or fell. They stopped more frequently than before, mostly because a fever gripped Umaq. The wound in his side had grown worse. Sybil removed the old, blood-soaked dressing and replaced it with torn cloth. Hot breath rushed from his lungs in labored gasps. Sweat dribbled down his face. Taking on the role of supporter, Sybil now held his waist and did her best to spur him onward.

Umaq at least felt safer. Vaz had caught them in the forest, but didn't sound the alert which meant no pursuers and no pressure to expend energy in haste. Sitting down once more, he enjoyed the cool air wafting through the tunnel as it caressed his warm, moist skin. He glanced at the fatigued witch. A profound, genuine pleasure from her being at his side welled in his chest, and not only because she had rescued him. Despite the insane circumstances, he enjoyed her company. Young or old, the girl's spirit shone in a way that made dark gods, rabid demons, and dreary purple skies a minor nuisance.

Umaq smiled at her. Sybil returned the gesture, her faded brown eyes shining bright in a worn face. He held out his hands and she took them. They helped each other to stand in a series of grunts and groans. Moving on, the unlikely pair soon reached the end of the tunnel.

Sybil explained the fearful workings of the next wasteland stretching before them. Just when Umaq thought the rest of the journey would be simple, he now had violent temperature swings to endure. Not far into their trek, a sudden blast of heat forced him to cringe and shout. Hearing about the hot and cold air didn't prepare him for the actual experience. His exposed skin seemed to melt. He had fallen into a boiling pot, tripped into a fire, and sat on a stove.

Following his hunched over companion, they found some cover in the shade of a large, protruding stone. Sweating, Umaq closed his eyes and tugged at his collar. He tried to fan his face, but the exertion produced more warmth.

"Forthwith be still and do not breathe too deep," Sybil advised through a sheen of sweat. "It shall be over soon. A bit of a respite shall follow, then the cold."

"Not looking forward to that either," he replied.

The inferno subsided. Sybil grabbed his wrist and they jogged as fast as their aching bones, screaming muscles, and empty lungs would allow. The worsening fever slowed Umaq down, the blood-loss and creeping infection threatening to topple him.

The comfortable atmosphere vanished, and a shattering cold slammed them. Frost chewed Umaq's exposed nose and ears. He trembled, teeth chattering. He dropped to his knees while unable to continue. Sybil embraced him, and the two fell on their sides.

"Noth-nothing we can do hither," she managed to say between shivers. "Thus, hold me tight for body warmth. Be not bashful."

Umaq nestled against Sybil and buried his face in her shoulder. She returned the favor, arms and legs wrapped around each other. Despite the frigid blanket surrounding them, he found relief in the witch's body heat. How in the world did Sybil make it through this wasteland on her own? The experience must have been terrifying. He couldn't ever imagine the loneliness and despair. She had confronted a dangerous, alien world by herself. No one had comforted the bold witch; she had survived on willpower and nerve alone.

The icy chill lifted. Umaq sighed in relief, then helped Sybil to her feet. The pair continued the journey. Their weakened bodies shuffled in haste during normal temperatures, dove for cover under scorching heat, and lay wrapped in each other's arms through the biting freeze.

After a few rounds of suffering under extreme climate shifts, the portal to their home world appeared off in the distance. Holding hands, Umaq and Sybil hobbled toward what should have been an improbable escape. They had battled dark gods, demon riots, injury, illness—an arduous quest in very hostile territory. Yet somehow...somehow the old and abused duo had found the exit.

Retaining the outline of the Uku-Pacha window, Umaq drew close to the trapezoid-shaped, illuminated gateway in the middle of the wasteland. He never imagined seeing the opposite side of his darkest magic.

241

At least the incantation still worked…sort of. The portal flashed on and off, stabilized for several seconds, then winked out. What if they'd succeeded this far only for the door to disappear?

"Let us hurry forth," Sybil urged, mirroring his frantic thoughts. Taking the lead, the witch waited for the doorway to activate, then pulled Umaq through the mystical rift...

…and into the Temple of the Three Windows in Machu Picchu. Starlight spilled through the night-darkened windows and single doorway. Umaq moved to where the electric lamps sat and snapped them on. In total disbelief, he gaped at the familiar surroundings in tears. He lowered to one knee and placed his palm on the cool stone floor. Full of magical relics and spell casting ingredients, his large wooden coffer sat against the wall. Tools lay scattered about. Closing his eyes, he inhaled the crisp, clean mountain air over the ancient Inca city, his beloved home.

Umaq opened his eyes, a wide smile on his face. "Sybil, we did it—"

The old witch collapsed. He rushed over and cradled her head. Dark nether essence oozed from her nose, ears, and mouth. Her breath sounded in struggled gasps. He placed an ear on her chest and listened to a feeble heartbeat; Sybil would die if he didn't act.

Now returned to his world, Umaq's magical abilities should function as normal. He pressed a hand to his side and cast a basic spell to heal injury. The laceration below his ribs sealed, and the infection vaporized. The fever and weakened state would linger for a while, but he already felt better.

He scooped Sybil into his arms. "I need to get you to the altar where the magic is strongest," he told the unconscious witch.

Once outside, Umaq grew elated by the vivid scenery. The night sky never looked so rich, a velvety obsidian blanket covered in stars so large and bright it seemed he could touch them. A clear, brilliant moon shone upon the mountain in a magnificent radiance. The cool temperature, fresh air, and soft breeze delighted the senses. The ancient buildings, impressive in architecture and history, comforted him as he reminisced of better times during his past as an Inca.

"We're back home and the first thing you do is take a nap," he chided Sybil. Unresponsive, her head lolled against his shoulder, arms and legs limp. "You're missing a real treat here, so much to see and experience. It's truly wonderful...thanks to you."

Umaq crossed the Sacred Plaza and approached the alternating flights of stairs on a hill leading to the altar, Intihuatana. Sweating from exertion, he climbed several steps and carefully set the witch down on the landing for a breather. Sybil might not weigh much, but his youth had departed long ago, and not to mention feebleness still plagued him after the ordeal in the demon realm.

He wiped his brow and upper lip. Sybil's chest barely rose, her expression pained and covered in dark blemishes from the nether essence. His trembling hand cupped the side of her face.

"Don't give up yet," he whispered. "You fought your butt off to make it this far. We're almost there."

His lower back and knees screaming, Umaq lifted Sybil and climbed. Each step doused his strained

243

biceps and calves in scalding fire. Every movement plunged knives into his tired shoulders and neck. On he went, uttering groans, a steady hiss between his teeth.

Halfway to the peak, he glanced at her. Was she still breathing? Her face had turned white at some point, and he feared the worst. None of his aches and pains mattered. Any discomfort, inconvenience, or obstacle to his own health and recovery meant nothing. Only the girl in his arms had significance. Young or old, his arch enemy and survival partner would live.

"Hold on, Sybil," he panted.

Umaq rose the final step and had to set the witch down for another break. Atop the hill and at the edge of the courtyard overlooking Machu Picchu, he sat next to her, wincing. His arms shook and back spasmed. He rubbed his quivering legs and wondered if he could even walk anymore.

"Come on now," he huffed to himself. "Just a bit further to the altar."

A cold hand grasped his forearm. He looked down in surprise and met Sybil's half-closed eyes.

"Revive Inti first," she whispered.

His jaw dropped. "What? Are you crazy? Death already knocked on your door and has one foot in your living room. I need to eliminate the sickness and restore your youth first."

"No," she countered, her voice unexpectedly strong. "Of a truth, repairing yonder mystical imbalance and setting nature right is more important. I conceive only Inti can accomplish that."

Umaq couldn't believe what he just heard. The poor witch had gone delusional. "I killed Inti and broke nature a long time ago. What's a few more minutes?"

"Every *second* counts," Sybil stressed. "Hitherto your reanimated demon is hunting Marcelo. Restoring the balance shall weaken that creature, I warrant. 'Tis the only chance for Marcelo forthwith."

She tried to sit up as if to argue further. Before she could say anything, he slid his arms beneath the witch and lifted her again. With renewed strength, he marched across the courtyard and past the temple Sybil had emerged from when she ruptured the ley line. He neared the stone altar of Intihuatana and laid her on the ground next to it.

"Fine," he said, caressing her hand. "I'll revive that cursed sun deity first, then make you a bratty teenager again. Inti will more than likely try to kill me, so tell him to wait five minutes so I can work on you."

His smirk faded as he studied her unmoving form. "Sybil?" He touched her ice-cold cheek and frowned at her gray lips and pale face in the moonlight. He moved close and felt a slight breath on his ear. She had lost consciousness again, but how soon until her sleep turned into death?

Umaq slipped a hand into her pant pocket and removed Inti's gold-plated feather. He set the headdress ornament on the altar and closed his eyes. He had spent centuries learning how to open portals, control demons, and manipulate nether energy from the demon realm. The plan to capture and destroy Inti had taken years of study, artifact collection, spell preparation, and practice. Taking the sun god's life had been extremely difficult and painful. Restoring the deity would be just as tough and perhaps unpredictable.

Ley lines now represented the key. No longer requiring dark nether, he needed a life-giving element to serve as a catalyst for the spell. Umaq recalled how ley energy had saved Sybil in the dark gods' temple, an apparent gift from the Earth Mother. It seemed that power had little effect against the black illness inside her, yet he could try and utilize the earth essence to help Inti.

Thankfully his people, the Inca, had deliberately erected the altar on a natural convergence of ley lines. As the carved stone block hummed with the spiritual force, Umaq needed to tap into the blue energy and unleash a torrent—the faucet on full blast.

"Earth Mother, I need you," he uttered for the first time in his long life. As a dealer in darkness and, well…evil, reaching out to the great nature spirit to beg for the power of life wasn't exactly his thing.

"The world needs you," Umaq continued, his eyes squeezed tight. "I am nothing, only a conduit to channel the earth's blood for waking a fallen deity of the sun. Help me restore the balance, Earth Mother. Aid me in…," he opened his eyes and looked down at Sybil, "…in honoring a promise."

Did he hear a woman's distant voice? Unsure, he suddenly noticed an increase in the altar's vibration. The stone sang in a loud drone, a tuning fork struck by the Earth Mother. The gold feather danced across the quivering surface, its light shining bright.

Umaq spread his arms and thrust his mind into the rock, minerals, and soil beneath Intihuatana. His consciousness bored through the mountain and tunneled far below the surface. Thrusting aside compacted dirt and stone, his cognizance drilled deep into a large, subterranean cavern and splashed into a glowing river of ley essence.

The planet's spirit energy surrounded Umaq, but the impression felt different than what he expected. He detected the Earth Mother's illness, the one he had caused by eliminating Inti. Her ailment and suffering, catastrophic for the world if not remedied, resulted from his evil schemes. Reviving Inti and restoring nature's balance would purify the Earth Mother. The act would not cleanse his guilt. However, he did not come all this way to ask for forgiveness.

On the surface, Umaq tilted his head back and cried out. *"Burst from the earth to twist and grow. Shatter ground, split the sky, and crack the heavens so. Roar and sing over death and strife, nourish this sun god and return him to life!"*

Underground, the vast ley essence bubbled and churned. The earth energy spun into a whirlpool of radiant teal light. A large column the width of a door exploded from the mass and barreled upward toward the altar.

Umaq nearly fell as the area shook. He picked Sybil up and transported her to a safe distance in the courtyard. He checked her vitals and sighed in relief at signs of life, though she remained unconscious.

Placing a hand on the ground, he sensed the ley column grinding its way through the earth and rock. It finally reached the large hill and tunneled up to the altar. From beneath, the shiny pillar of ley energy slammed into the stone block and absorbed into it like a sponge.

Intihuatana erupted in a brilliant teal radiance. Umaq shielded his eyes from the strong light and whooped at the spell's success. The hum echoed across Machu Picchu. The earth danced in a steady rhythm.

Soon the volatile energy halted, and everything around lay quiet.

A powerful, supernatural presence appeared on the altar. A wave of heat emitted from the tall entity. It blasted across the courtyard then faded along with the ley energy.

Umaq gazed upon Inti, the sun god of the Incas. The illuminated deity returned a hardened glare from atop the stone surface. In his human form, Inti dazzled wearing gold plates and leather armor. Shiny spaulders wrapped his broad shoulders, his upper arms and wrists covered in gold bands. Beneath the armor, soft vicuna wool fashioned his long, loose outfit cinched at the waist by a jewel-studded belt. Gold earrings dangled from his ears, and leather, fur-lined sandals covered his feet.

Inti's manifestation restored nature's balance and strengthened the waning barrier between realms. A life-long wielder of magic, Umaq sensed a mystical, seismic *thump* reverberating across the planet as the equilibrium returned. In the heavens above, the sun and moon's powerful energy shone in harmony. The Earth Mother would recover, yet Umaq didn't have time to celebrate as he locked eyes with his ancient nemesis.

The sun god's dark eyes pierced in judgement and authority. A long-brewing rage lit his gaze, a raw emotion Umaq knew had been reserved for him. How could it not be, when the two of them had warred for centuries? Umaq had pulled off the final victory by murdering the sun god. After so much time and anger, this occasion provided Inti the chance to even the score.

However, for the moment, Inti reached down and picked up the gold-plated feather. On his headdress, he slid the plume into place among several other decorated

248

feathers from the *coraquenque* bird. With the ensemble complete, the deity hopped off the altar and held out a muscled arm. A fiery glow materialized on his left palm, a devastating weapon. The god stepped toward Umaq, his face twisted into a mask of bloody vengeance.

"At last!" Inti growled.

"Let me heal this woman first," Umaq called. "Then you can—"

Inti ignored the request and raised his hand to cast the spell. It had taken two moon goddesses, a witch coven, a horde of demons, and Umaq to stop the sun god the first time. Alone and in no condition to fight, he waited for the deathblow. Remorse over not being able to cure Sybil burned in his heart. The failure crushed his spirit, the ache inside worse than anything Inti could do to him.

"I'm sorry, Sybil," he whispered.

The burning spell sizzled through the air and raced toward Umaq. A blinding flash of blue-green light suddenly appeared before him and snuffed out Inti's magic. The deity stared in shock, as did Umaq.

Sybil stood between him and the sun god, her arms spread wide. The teal radiance of ley energy surrounded her body in a heavy shield. As in the temple of the dark gods, the witch had once again nullified a deity's attack.

The incredible utilization of earth energy—or how Sybil obtained it—didn't matter to Umaq. What touched his heart had been the act itself, the *why* of her sacrifice and protection.

While traveling with the witch across the demon realm, he had witnessed Sybil's true self under pain, desperation, and duress. Nearing death, no reason for deceit existed between the battered pair. Connected through hardship, they had peered into each other's souls and sifted through a library of one another's thoughts and emotions.

Sybil hadn't leapt in harm's way to ensure his promise of helping her. She didn't rescue Umaq to preserve the chance of regaining her youth, nor risk everything to have him eliminate the black sickness.

No. Sybil Radella Cotterill had saved Umaq because her soul desired to, nothing more. Her mind wished for it. The spirited feelings coursing through her body demanded the gesture. The witch had acted in her truest form, each beat of her noble heart shining in defiance of a god.

Inti remained still. No renewed attack or angry outburst followed. Confusion, and even a touch of awe, filled the deity's expression. His dark eyes never left Sybil. Standing behind the witch, Umaq couldn't see her gaze, but something in her rock-hard countenance held Inti in check.

The sun god finally nodded. No words had been uttered, yet a meaningful exchange had taken place. Inti rose into the air, his form glowing in a bright golden hue. The deity rocketed upwards and disappeared in the sky.

Sybil wobbled and the ley shield disappeared. Umaq wrapped her in his arms and lifted her onto the altar. She smiled weakly, her eyes dull and distant. Whatever light and strength had existed on her face a moment ago was gone.

"You never cease to amaze me," Umaq told her. "Now rest and let me work. You'll be doing backflips off the altar in no time." He had to perform quickly. No need

250

to check Sybil's vitals to realize she only had a few minutes left.

Umaq turned toward the grassy Central Plaza and motioned as if grabbing something from the distant meadow. He repeated the gesture several times until glowing particles of life energy lifted from the grass in a slow drift. Pivoting, he beckoned to the surrounding mountains to collect bits of vigor from vegetation and trees. Gesturing toward the sky, clawed fingers raked across the atmosphere to seize tiny units of moonlight and oxygen.

Shining like glitter, each ingredient streamed from its source and floated to Umaq in long arcs. The mixture of energy and elemental particles swirled into a large sphere hovering over Sybil. The ball flickered and pulsed. It became *alive* as it grew in size and power.

Umaq placed one hand on Sybil's chest and the other on the surface of the sphere. He closed his eyes and chanted. *"Years rewind and body renew, flesh mend and age undo. Earth tremble and Water churn, the Wind rush and Spirit burn. Warm Fire delight and elements unite, I ask the universe to breathe life into this child of light!"*

The throbbing ball descended onto Sybil and absorbed into her body. The life-charging components saturated her skin, soaked her organs, and fused to her bones. The old witch sparkled from head to foot. The enchantment fluttered her disheveled gray hair and torn, dirty clothes.

Satisfied, Umaq stepped back and waited for any reaction. Only a handful of spell casters on the planet could perform this level of magic. Upon waking from her three-hundred-year slumber, Sybil had been able to discover her own method while Umaq had learned this

251

rejuvenating technique over decades. For this occasion, he added a few special fundamentals to not only restore her youth, but to cleanse the black illness as well.

Something should have happened by now. Umaq frowned as the magic dissipated; however, Sybil remained the same. Her skin appeared wrinkled and covered in liver spots. She still had her gray hair, an unhealthy complexion, and no signs of reverse aging.

Umaq kicked the altar in frustration. He paced around the stone structure, thinking. The ritual had been performed while devoid of any flaw. The movements, ingredients, and magical properties had been performed properly. The words chosen for the incantation had been perfect as well. Although exhaustion consumed him, his personal energy and effort had been sufficient to drive the spell.

So why hadn't it worked?

Angry, Umaq slapped his palms onto the stone surface. He completed another circuit around the altar and stopped when a feeble hand gripped his wrist. He glanced down at Sybil laying on the slab.

"Worry not, Umaq," she said in a weak voice. "'Twas not meant to be, truly. But my heart thanks you for trying."

Chapter Eighteen

Sacrifice

Resting on the altar, Sybil gazed up at Umaq as she held his wrist. She had awoken moments ago as he marched around the stone monument, his steps heavy in anger and hands striking the surface out of frustration.

Could he feel the tenderness through her touch? Did he sense her heart and the feelings of warmth in her eyes? As crazy as it seemed, she no longer saw Umaq the Betrayer as a vile enemy. He had received terrible punishment and her vengeance was fulfilled. However, that alone didn't signify her reason for befriending him now.

Tragedy, pain, and suffering brought forth the worst—and best—in people. In the demon realm, Umaq could have left her behind countless times. He could have returned alone without having to complete a single promise. He could have regained al his former power, reestablished the raging demon army, and continued his conquest.

Instead, he had brought Sybil home. He saved her from the dark gods and carried her in his arms. Umaq tended to her health and kept her warm in the cold. He bled for her, shared a meal, and conversed as a friend. Honoring his word, a sun deity lived again, and nature

253

had been restored. In Sybil's view, his promises had been satisfied…even if this final one had not.

Umaq's face melted into grief. Tears filled his eyes, mouth drooped, and he lowered his gaze.

"I don't understand why this isn't working," he uttered in a thick voice. "This is much more than just a deal we made, Sybil. You deserve to be young and well again."

She desired to embrace the man, but lacked the strength. "I conceive of why the spell hath failed." She swallowed, her throat dry. When his eyes widened in question, she continued.

"Umaq," she said softly. "Of a truth, restoring my youth is not simple kitchen table magic. I was born over three centuries agone. Thereof, I cheated death when I took a woman's lifeforce and put her in a coma. Thus, I became young through violent magic, then grew old again in aforesaid time warp below ground. A sundry of abnormal factors exist forthwith. Even using Intihuatana to your behoof, this new attempt may be outside your ability. Truly, do not waste your time—or the world's—on me."

Umaq leaned over the altar and gripped Sybil's shoulders. "You want to find death, don't you? You've experienced lifetimes worth of pain, most of it caused by me. I saved Inti first like you asked me to. Perhaps you saw this opportunity as a way out, a chance to finally rest after ensuring the safety of the world and your loved ones."

Sybil rolled her head away from him. Tears slid from her eyes and wet the stone surface beneath her. Umaq spoke true. Her expression must have been an open book, a visual cue to her distressed feelings. His

254

observant words matched her dark, weary thoughts—she only desired respite. Her love for Marcelo burned strong, yet that wonderful heat failed to overcome the ice wrapping her fatigued, heavy heart.

Umaq suddenly shook her. Surprised, she gazed at his fuming, teary-eyed visage.

"This isn't the girl who battled me across time!" he hollered. "Where's the witch who chased me across Salem and pummeled me in Athens? What happened to the girl who burst from the depths of the earth and crashed into the demon world to save me?" His fist thumped the altar. "You have the right to live, dammit! I'm the one that has to go."

Umaq took a step back and closed his eyes. He took a few deep, calming breaths and pressed his palms together in front of his chest.

"What are you striving to do?" Sybil asked in dread. She attempted to sit up, her pained muscles and deteriorating body useless. She strained to roll over, but couldn't. Her arms refused to respond when she tried to reach for him.

Umaq's lips moved in a silent incantation. Sybil detected a powerful magic at work. The spell stirred around the altar and shimmered the air. Gooseflesh rose on her arms. Her spine tingled. Her heart increased its tempo, quick breath rushing through her lungs.

"Umaq, please halt forthwith!" she begged.

He paused the chant to smile. "I'll show you kitchen table magic."

Sybil struggled to break the enchantment. She raked her mind and dug into her soul for a magical spark, anything. Her abilities still missing, she tried to summon

255

the ley essence, but even that eluded her. She barely had the energy to speak.

"You are mistaken," she cried. "Do not do this!"

Through the spell, Umaq's lifeforce departed his body and flooded hers. Sybil's skin tightened, muscles pulsed, and bones quivered. Her hands opened and closed in rapid fists as vitality poured through her core. Strength surged, the years on her body reversing in a blur. Reinvigorated blood flowed and organs refreshed.

A reborn, eighteen-year-old Sybil flew off the altar. She didn't check her smooth skin or shiny brown hair. She had no interest in her strong heartbeat and toned frame. She ignored her youth and didn't think about the eradicated black sickness.

Her only concern focused on Umaq when he collapsed. She reached him in time to wrap arms around his torso and break his fall. She knelt next to him as he rested on the ground beside the altar, a small smile on his white face.

"You look so stunning," he commented. "Don't ruin it with needless tears, you obnoxious teenager."

Sybil wiped her teary eyes. Her chest hummed in pain, an emotional dagger plunged deep in her heart. "Umaq, I conceive you are the one that hath yearned for death."

"I already died, like twenty times or so," he said through a soft laugh. His face then grew solemn as he took Sybil's hand. "Death changed me, my dear. I am ashamed that only now do I realize my cruelty. I am truly sorry, Sybil. Do not mourn this old, evil man. I saved you feeling gladness in my heart and satisfaction in my soul."

"Umaq, I…" Sybil stroked the back of his hand as she looked away across the courtyard. Several moments passed, the weight of his sacrifice paralyzing her words. He made his choice and she lived, the illness and old age gone. She finally met his eyes, and he offered her an encouraging nod.

"This is why I selected you hundreds of years ago," he continued. "Your raw talent, immense power, and indomitable character. When I captured you in modern Salem and cast my spell, you were to be my greatest asset after Marcelo turned you into an undead. My bloodthirsty, vengeful Witch-General. I dreamt of that for centuries, waiting for your powers to increase while you slept in that coffin.

"However, you got the best of me and right now I couldn't be happier to see you free. I got to experience the real you, the girl with the generous heart and bottomless courage, who pulled me out of the fire. Thank you for being my greatest adversary and my favorite heroine, Sybil Radella Cotterill."

Umaq closed his eyes and breathed no more.

Sybil leaned down and gently kissed him on the forehead. "Thank you, Umaq. You became my hero as well, I warrant. Be at peace forthwith, and may your heart rest easy."

She stood and gazed out over a darkened and silent Machu Picchu, too stunned by everything that had happened to even think. Sorrow, contentment, surprise, distress, relief, solitude…a dozen emotions bled from her heart, an unstable mix that left her nauseous and confused. It seemed she existed outside herself in a false world, the environment dull and deprived of meaning. The breeze had grown stale, the distant moon and stars cold and blinding. The ancient architecture around her became two-dimensional props, empty and misleading.

An odd light suddenly flashed from within the Temple of the Three Windows, grounding her back in reality. A moment later, two shadowy figures carrying lamps ran through the doorway and into the Sacred Plaza.

"Sybil, are you here?" one of the individuals called out in a desperate tone.

Sybil's heart leapt in joy when she recognized Grace's voice. She cupped her hands around her mouth to answer. "Up hither by yonder altar!"

Grace and the other person made haste up the stairs. In the gloom, Sybil now recognized Cessani as the two women approached.

Grace set her lamp on the altar, her face frantic as she threw her arms around Sybil. "I'm sorry we didn't get here sooner, thank goodness you're all right. Look at you! You are well again. I also sensed the renewed mystical barrier, which means Inti has been revived."

"'Tis over," Sybil replied, too weary to sum up the events any other way. Grace's presence further helped Sybil return to her senses. She pulled back and smiled at her beloved friend. "My heart never doubted you would arrive. You are a fair sight indeed."

The sound of a helicopter nearing buzzed in the distance. Covered in blinking lights, the air vehicle approached and landed in the field of the Central Plaza. In the wide glow of flashlights, a knot of armed military personnel emerged, and several red-robed witches followed them. The group crossed the grass, ran into the Sacred Plaza, and pounded up the stairs into the courtyard. The witches surveyed the scene and spoke quietly to each other. The soldiers barked orders and spread out in a protective formation. After receiving

Sybil's letter, Grace had come through as she brought aid.

"Cessani notified her witches ahead of time, and they worked through the night to dismantle the magical defenses here around Machu Picchu," Grace explained. "After I alerted the local authorities, the government provided a military unit in the helicopter as backup. The timing was coordinated, and here we are."

Cessani's eyes darted between Sybil, Umaq, and around the courtyard. Setting her electric lamp down, she finally knelt next to the demon master and clucked her tongue. "You did it, Sybil. Umaq and I were allies once, but in the end, he deserved what he got. He had taken things too far."

Cessani's utter hypocrisy astonished Sybil. The woman had aided Umaq in destroying Inti. Both of them had gone too far. Sybil desired to mention Umaq's redemption, but what good would that do? Cessani's idea of redemption meant blaming the other person and showing up at the last minute to save face.

"Truly, I appreciate you arriving hither," Sybil managed to say, holding her anger. "Please close the portal to yonder demon realm."

"Of course," Cessani replied. "I believe all of us have had enough of demons. My team and I will handle it." She motioned to her coven, and they headed down the steps toward the Temple of the Three Windows.

Grace slipped an arm around Sybil's waist as they watched the group descend into the Sacred Plaza. The woman frowned as she spoke. "That old witch will continue to act as if she did nothing wrong. And she'll probably get away with it."

"I believe she shall reap what she sows," said Sybil. She leaned into Grace and rested her head on her friend's shoulder. "Truly, another day I shall tell you everything that happened hitherto. For now, I must go forth and return to Marcelo. Before I depart, if it pleases you I have a special request."

"Anything, dear," Grace responded. "I'm here for you, sweet thing."

Sybil took the woman's hand and led her across the courtyard to the temple where the ley gate resided. "Umaq was a true Inca and the last member of his kind, I warrant. Thus, please ensure he is buried out in yonder Central Plaza. Machu Picchu hath been his home, and the mountain shall bring him comfort."

Grace appeared perplexed, an expected reaction. Explaining detail would be difficult, as the experience between Sybil and Umaq had been indescribable. The life-altering journey remained etched in her heart and wrapped in her soul, a private affair she would cherish forever. Placing Umaq the Betrayer in a good light and describing her feelings proved to be a challenge. But for now, she hoped her friend would comply.

Grace finally smiled and offered a nod. "I will see it done, Sybil. I surmise a grand, impassioned story dancing in your eyes. But as you mentioned, that will be for another day. Now go. Marcelo needs you."

Sybil hugged her friend, then faced the center of the floor. She waved an arm, and the ground rumbled open to access the ley line. She leapt into the gap and landed softly on a glowing river of earth essence. The Earth Mother's unseen, ethereal presence loomed close and enveloped her in warmth and animated welcome.

My dear child, you are well and have found success. Balance is restored, and my strength has returned. The ground sleeps and trees sing. Mountains dance and the sky celebrates. However, your heart beats heavy. I sense ongoing turmoil in your emotions, and I wish to alleviate the burden. Tell me how the earth may comfort you.

"Oh, beloved Mother." Sybil sighed. "Please do not allow my somber feelings to conceal the utmost happiness I wish to express. My heart is glad you are well and delighted to conceive that the earth is at rest. However, you speak true of my continued unease. So much has happened and much remaineth to strive for. I ought to find Marcelo and fight by his side. Yet I fear it may be too late."

The world is at rest, yet the spirits of nature tremble and I understand what you speak of. Although weakened by Inti's rebirth, I continue to sense Umaq's resurrected demon. Its remarkable power infiltrates even the deep underground. But the creature has not rejoined with its soul. Time remains, child. Open your mind and I will guide the blue ley rivers to your heart's desire.

Sybil closed her eyes. Images and memories of her dearest Marcelo flooded her consciousness. Scenes of his gentle touch, encouraging words, and acts of kindness played out. Joyful moments, knowing smiles, and quickened heartbeats of passion leapt in her mind. She also allowed episodes of conflict to appear during the time of her malevolence—dangerous fighting and spiteful words—as even hardship had strengthened the love between them.

Sybil had been prepared to die an old woman. However, Umaq's gift restored not only her youth, but her confidence. Strength surged within. She sensed her magical ability had revitalized and stood ready to burst. She had torn apart realms, battled the impossible, and defied death all in the name of love. Marcelo waited. Together, they would fight insurmountable odds and crush their enemy under the power of unity.

Guided by the great Earth Mother, the ley river zoomed Sybil across the planet. After approaching her destination, the roaring, blue-green essence lifted her toward the surface in a long flowing arc. Overhead, the ground shook and she passed through the opening. She hopped off the ley line and stepped onto dirt and pine needles beneath a night sky.

The ground closed in a gentle shake of earth. Darkness obscured her surroundings, yet Sybil sensed an approaching dawn. Not good news for wherever Marcelo may be, assuming the ley line had deposited her in the correct spot. She conjured a floating sphere of light to illuminate the area. Rocky outcroppings hid between clumps of trees. The ground sloped beneath her feet, indicating she stood on the side of a forested hill.

The distant roar of an engine told her she hadn't appeared too far from civilization. She moved down the incline between trees and soon arrived at a narrow asphalt road. She walked to a nearby sign that read: Chumash Painted Cave State Historical Park.

"Marcelo!" she called, glancing up and down the empty street.

A realization struck her, and she felt foolish. The ley line wouldn't have taken her to Marcelo's exact location. She had just emerged through a ley gate, a convergence of the earth essence moving throughout the planet to connect many ancient structures, historical landmarks, and natural wonders. Similar to the ley gate on Wizard Island in Oregon, it didn't surprise her to find one here in the ancient territory of the Chumash Indians. Although this gate marked the closest spot to Marcelo, he could still be a hundred yards away or even miles.

The sound of another engine approached. Sybil spotted headlights down the road as she stepped into the lane, waving her arms. The car screeched to a halt and the driver blasted the horn. The window rolled down and a head emerged.

"What the hell are you doing out here? Didn't you hear the news?" a man's voice called. He glanced left and right into the woods, then back to Sybil. "Are you all right?"

The context of the man's words sounded like trouble. Ironically, this appeared as a positive sign for Sybil and a possible clue to Marcelo's whereabouts.

"What is this news you speak of?" she asked. "Please tell me forthwith. I am looking for someone and require assistance."

"I was on my way to work in Santa Barbara when the news came on the radio," the man began. "A demon is on the loose, and a crazy battle is occurring on the highway. The police are warning everyone to stay the heck away from the city. Cars are backed up for miles, and there's panic everywhere. I turned around and am going back home to Santa Ynez. You should do the same."

A demon! That could only be Marcelo and the monster fighting in the distant city. Sybil approached the driver's open window and leaned down.

263

"Please, take me to yonder Santa Barbara," she pleaded. "The person I seek dwells there. You do not have to enter the city. I shall ride till the outskirts."

"Forget it," the man barked. "There's a reason I turned my butt around. I'm not going anywhere near that monster. Now back away from my car!"

Sybil reached through the window and grasped the steering wheel. She ignited a fire in the palm of her opposite hand and waved it near the man's face. He recoiled and shouted in alarm.

"Take me to Santa Barbara or a demon shall be the least of your worries," she growled. "Forthwith this pissed off witch shall be an even bigger nightmare for you."

"G-get in," he stammered.

The vehicle raced down the twists and turns of Painted Cave Road. Likely desperate to escape his passenger and the dangerous situation ahead, the man sped onward until the lights of Santa Barbara came into view. Cruising into the large city, Sybil noticed the abandoned streets and strange quiet. No other cars or people moved about.

The pale, sweaty man halted the vehicle on a bridge crossing La Colina Road next to a residential neighborhood. "The highway is just ahead. Whatever is going on with that demon is up there. I won't drive any further."

"Worry not," Sybil replied.

Through the windshield, she saw fires blazing from the direction of the highway. "Return home with my thanks," she told the stranger before stepping out and shutting the door.

The vehicle turned around and sped off. Ahead, the red and blue lights of patrol units flashed near the onramp. A helicopter soared around using its spotlight.

Sybil jogged in the wooded area on the edge of the road, careful to remain out of sight. She stayed clear of the police blockade and crossed a street named Calle Real that ran parallel to the highway. On the opposite side, she descended a grassy embankment and finally set foot on the interstate.

The ruckus of battle erupted further down the roadway. Heavy metal smashed, glass broke, and small explosions shook the ground. The police had diverted traffic and halted cars far away from the bedlam. Heart racing, Sybil sprinted along a deserted stretch of lanes toward the chaos, a sign that Marcelo still lived. She passed the horrible, twisted shapes of smashed cars and endless debris. Fires burned from spilled fuel and oil. Smoke rolled across the asphalt and stung her eyes.

She charged ahead…and finally saw Marcelo! The avalanche of relief nearly tripped her. Out of nowhere, Johann leapt into the frame and Sybil cried out in joy. No time for a happy reunion. The monstrous demon hovered above and threw a car door at Johann.

The werewolf dodged the hunk of metal. It hit the ground in a shower of broken pieces and sparks. He leapt up high to slash at the beast, but a powerful beat of its wings blasted Johann away through the air.

Sybil approached the wild fight and summoned a cushioned pocket of wind to catch her hairy friend. Landing safely, Johann's wolf eyes widened at seeing her. His muzzle parted in a sharp-toothed smile, and he howled in glee.

A pair of cool, familiar arms wrapped Sybil from behind. In the face of a relentless enemy, Marcelo dared to share a moment of bliss with the woman he loved. Sybil clasped his hands by her midsection and squeezed, the gesture stating her returned love and a thousand words of adoration. She knew he burned to ask questions, not least about her recovered youth, but a critical duel persisted.

"We shall destroy this thing together," she said.

"I sensed Inti's rebirth, no doubt the result of your handiwork," he said in her ear. "The demon has grown weaker since I first encountered it. That's the only reason I've survived this long. But that thing is still deadly and tough as steel. This won't be easy, love." He released her and stepped away, his posture tensed and ready as he focused on the enemy.

The demon swooped down in a mindless charge. The creature gave no indication of strategizing for its new opponent in Sybil. No assessment of the situation or tactical maneuver ensued. The monster's distorted, enraged face and narrowed eyes only showed a desire for violence.

She sprayed a jet of fire from an outstretched palm. The demon flew through the crackling blaze, its muscled arm swiping at her. Marcelo sprinted over in a flash. He gripped Sybil by the waist and whisked her away from the set of razor-sharp claws.

Johann's paws pounded the ground to meet the demon. His muzzle opened wide and clamped down on the enemy's wrist. The monster roared and flailed its arm, but the werewolf's teeth held in a tight grip as he tried to keep the demon immobile. Alert to the opening,

Marcelo grabbed a long piece of metal from a destroyed car and clubbed the beast over its back and shoulders.

Sybil waved both arms and hundreds of broken glass pieces skittered toward her. She manipulated the shards into a tight cluster the size of a basketball and launched the mass toward the demon. Guiding the spell, she maneuvered the barbed weapon past Marcelo and slammed it into the beast's flesh.

The demon grunted, and a renewed swing of its arm flung Johann through the air. The werewolf plowed into the center divider in an explosion of cement and rebar. Marcelo dodged a thrusting wing and a wild punch but failed to evade a hard kick to his chest. He rolled and skidded across the asphalt into the side of a smashed minivan.

The beast scooped up a fallen motorcycle and lifted it overhead. Sybil levitated the piece of metal Marcelo had used as a club and smashed it across the monster's ugly face. Using a powerful wing, the beast slapped a lump of broken concrete and sent it hurling toward Sybil. The dense rubble pulverized her shoulder and collarbone, the blow spinning her into a hard fall.

Still clutching the dented motorcycle, the demon stepped forward and launched it at Marcelo, who had just recovered and tried to stand. Woozy and in severe pain, Sybil screamed a late warning as the bike rammed his body and crushed him back down.

The monster sprinted toward Marcelo. Fighting panic, Sybil rolled to her knees and cast multiple spells using her good arm. Metal squealed as chunks tore from damaged cars and sped toward the beast. The pieces bashed into the demon, unnoticed as it continued. Fire engulfed the crazed enemy to no advantage. Hurricane-strength wind blasted forth, yet the creature lowered its head and shoulders to march onward through the gale. Ice shards pierced its arms and legs, but it did not slow. The crazed beast bellowed in triumph when it neared a facedown, immobile Marcelo.

Sybil's desperate shout seized in her throat as a blast of frozen air numbed her body. An immense, invisible force plastered her to the asphalt, scarcely able to breathe. A pair of bare feet stepped into view next to her. She glanced up in astonishment at the unexpected visitor.

"There's nothing like a grand entrance," Daiyu quipped.

Black Jade, Marcelo's rival and judge in his trial, had arrived. The timing couldn't have been worse. Sybil attempted an incantation, but the intense cold scrambled her thoughts while pressure from Dayu's aura pinned her arms.

"Oh, I'm sorry!" Black Jade commented as she looked down at Sybil. "Didn't see you there."

Of course she had. The ancient vampire had a history of teasing and tormenting those already in pain. Sybil writhed on the ground, then peered in Marcelo's direction. The demon knelt over her lover's body, but its massive wings prevented her from witnessing what occurred.

"M-Marcelo!" she stammered.

"Always whining," said Daiyu. "But I might as well show you why I rushed over here. Maybe you'll stop being such a baby."

The vampire vanished in a blur of speed. Black Jade reappeared next to the demon and swung her leg in a devastating kick. Her foot cracked the monster on the side of its big head in a thunderous blow. The stunned creature rocketed across the highway and thudded deep into the grassy incline lining the road.

Daiyu grabbed Marcelo by the back of his neck and jerked him to a stand. He looked terrible, body limp and face a mess of cuts and bruised flesh.

"When I signal, be ready to attack," Black Jade ordered. She released her grip, and a weakened Marcelo collapsed to his knees.

No longer crushed by the aura and the freezing air gone, Sybil stood and winced from her shattered shoulder.

Daiyu snapped her fingers at Sybil. "When I say, immobilize that beast as much as possible."

Dumbfounded at the sudden change of events, Sybil watched as Daiyu sped over to Johann, who had begun to rouse from the concrete rubble. The werewolf uttered a comical, high-pitched yelp as the vampire pulled him out by the hair on his back.

"You grab that demon's left arm and I have the right," Black Jade told Johann. "Let's go!"

The embankment on the side of the highway rumbled. Covered in soil and grass, the demon emerged from a crater its body had made on impact. The snarling monster charged. Working together, Daiyu and Johann met the beast near the center divider and exchanged a series of blows. The combatants circled and danced in a furious tornado of flying fists and feet.

"Stop trying to be fancy!" Black Jade yelled at Johann. "Take one on the chin to get into position if you have to."

As a live example, Daiyu absorbed a powerful blow to the midsection. She doubled over, then sprang forward to wrap her arms around the demon's right one. She clung like a child on a rope, straining to maintain her grip.

"Hurry!" she yelled.

The beast flailed at Johann with its free arm. The werewolf suddenly morphed into his much smaller human form. In a well-timed maneuver, the naked man ran beneath a punch aimed for a taller opponent. He switched back into the werewolf and clamped on tight to the demon's left limb.

"Sybil!" Daiyu yelled.

Ready to end this lunacy, Sybil had been well-prepared for her moment of action. She stared at the ground beneath the demon's hooved feet and recalled a construction program she had watched with Marcelo. Most asphalt normally consisted of coarse and fine aggregates, various types of minerals, and a sticky substance called a binder to hold everything together.

Focusing all her energy on the spot where the demon struggled, she took a breath and chanted an incantation. *"Spirits of earth leap and dance, elements of fire wake and prance. Temperature rise to melt and burn, I command this surface to boil and churn!"*

Simple but effective, the cracked blacktop of the highway started to heat. The fast-rising temperature in the ground stirred the rock, sand, and gravel. The binder, a gooey petroleum-based bitumen, melted and began to bubble.

The demon sank into the boiling, softened road. The creature roared as the heated material enveloped its feet and calves. A violent flap of wings failed to lift the enemy out of the trap. The monster thrashed in a wild tantrum as Daiyu and Johann fought to hold on.

"Marcelo!" Daiyu called. "Don't wimp out on me now. You're up!"

Sybil held her good arm parallel to the ground, fingers splayed to maintain the spell and keep the beast snared. She glanced to Marcelo, and her eyes widened in hope...and a touch of fear.

Marcelo stood, but barely. He swayed on his feet in a slight hunch, an arm dangling as if broken and useless. His clothes hung in shreds. Black, dead blood dripped from his pale skin in spots. In countless battles, she had never seen him this damaged. Worst of all, the expression on his battered face revealed emotional harm. His vacant and pained eyes contained a hidden mental torment. Sybil couldn't imagine what horror he had gone through tonight. Much like her, Marcelo had experienced his own version of hell during their time apart.

Yet the vampire who was not a vampire, or the "wannabe" as Johann had jested, reached down with his good arm and grabbed a section of rebar. He set his gaze on the beast and charged.

A blur of color sped across the southbound lanes of the highway. Marcelo neared the demon and plowed the rebar into its wide mouth. The metal pole crunched through sharp teeth and exploded out the back of the monster's thick skull. With a ferocious shout, Marcelo reached past the demon's head to grab the opposite end of the rod. Pulling the metal into a hard spin, he twisted the beast's head, and its neck snapped with a loud crack. An extra rotation tore the creature's head off and sent it thudding on the ground.

Black Jade and Johann released their hold and stepped back in stunned silence. Sybil also stared in disbelief. Had the nightmare truly ended? To answer her question, the demon's flesh disintegrated and fell into a pile of flakes. The skeletal remains broke apart at the joints and clattered to the ruined blacktop, the necromancy destroyed.

Sybil approached Marcelo and they embraced, her good arm holding him tight. No words proved necessary. The embattled lovers lived only for this moment, their touch essential and nothing else. She basked within his cool arms, the same hold that had comforted her hundreds of other times before. Whether Marcelo cuddled her in bed, in the car for a quick goodbye, or following an epic battle like tonight, his proximity was all she needed.

"I'm not hugging you," Daiyu said to Johann. "Well, not like *that,* anyway."

Wondering what Daiyu had meant, Sybil pulled back from the embrace and blushed when she saw a naked Johann in human form. Despite the nasty cuts and bruises on his body, the werewolf sported a huge smile. Marcelo laughed, and Sybil also joined in.

"I seem to have lost all of my clothes," Johann observed. "Would you settle for a fist bump?"

Black Jade smiled and held out a fist. "Nice work back there, dog boy."

Wary of Daiyu's aura, Johann darted in, tapped his knuckles against the vampire's, and scurried away. "Thanks for saving our hides."

"Why did you return, Daiyu?" Marcelo asked. "Don't get me wrong, I am forever grateful. But a couple hours ago, you tried to kill me."

Daiyu shrugged. "Supposedly, I stopped at a convenience store on the route to Los Angeles and bought a conscience. You beat my trial, so think of me as a parole officer checking up on you." She looked at Sybil. "Oh now, don't give me such a poopy face, young witch. You're free. Umaq is gone, and this demon is dead. Go celebrate."

Chapter Nineteen

At Last

Three months passed, and there had been much celebrating. However, before the first confetti had been thrown, a proper time of recovery was necessary. A physical mess, Sybil and Marcelo required a period of magical and natural healing. Spells, bandages, and a pill or two had combined with episodes of rest.

Patching up shredded emotions and a trampled mentality had been more difficult. Deep conversations, revisiting dark events, and heavy tears accompanied the long process of improvement. Sybil loved Marcelo and couldn't have recovered without him. Yet at certain times, she desired to be alone. Long walks in solitude, absently watching a movie at two in the morning, or reading a book helped her chaotic mind find peace.

Sybil and Marcelo currently strolled through the beautiful forest of the Illinois River Forks State Park in southern Oregon. They had traveled here to visit Salix's grove and consume a meal with the wonderful dryad. Ample shade protected Marcelo from the autumn sun, though he still sported a wide-brimmed hat and clothing to cover exposed areas.

Carrying a large picnic basket, Marcelo waved to Johann when he appeared ahead. In human form, Johann returned the wave and stood from where he had been lounging against a gnarled trunk. Their friend had journeyed here from Nevada City in northern California to join the reunion.

Holding a rolled-up blanket underneath an arm, Sybil hugged Johann with great enthusiasm. Only a few months had passed since defeating the demon, but she had missed the hairy—and on special occasion—naked werewolf.

The trio continued deeper into the woods and soon entered an area dominated by the willow species of *Salix delnortensis*. Johann led the group to the location where he had buried the catkin grown from the giant weeping willow of Salix babylonica in Athens.

Tears blurred Sybil's eyes as she looked upon a six-inch high sprout of Del Norte willow. Johann had chosen a perfect spot to regrow the dear dryad. Rich, green grass blanketed the grove. Coats of healthy moss grew on nearby trees. Moisture sparkled on leaves of the surrounding willow shrubs. Attractive wildflowers dotted the area amid rays of brilliant sunlight poking through the forest canopy.

Sybil knelt next to the small sprout and leaned over to kiss its tiny leaves. "Hello, lovely Salix," she whispered. "Hitherto how beautiful you are. Truly, I cannot wait to embrace you and hear your laughter once again."

She felt a hand squeeze her shoulder. Marcelo squatted next to her and caressed the leaves of the shrub.

"You'll be with us in no time," he said to the budding dryad. "Keep growing strong, here and in my heart."

Johann took the blanket from Sybil and rolled it out on the grass. "Stop spoiling my little plant face. You're about to make me cry like a fool. I've been checking on the old girl from time to time. Her roots are deep and tough as iron. She's even grown an inch since my last visit."

"You've been quite amazing, Johann, to say the least," Marcelo said. He settled on the blanket and opened the picnic basket.

Sybil joined him and helped set out sandwiches, fruit, and various tasty snacks. "Truly, I agree. Another amazing individual is Grace, I warrant. We spoke yesterday morn, and she provided an update on Salem and yonder cities where Cessani's coven had dwelt. After Inti's revival, her coven hath fractured thus. With the sun and moon now in balance, the witches' overall power hath been diminished. The covens forthwith disbanded on their own, including the group terrorizing Salem. The new endeavor of witch rule proved too much for Cessani to handle, and she hath disappeared."

"She's gone?" Marcelo asked in surprise. "Any idea where?"

"South America," Sybil answered. "Cessani had quite a following yonder. The *brujas* and *chamáns* have been loyal hitherto. The moon goddess, Mama Quilla, is leading the new gathering to their behoof."

"As long as Cessani can play nice, let her hide down there all she wants," Johann commented. "Good riddance." He grabbed a sandwich and bit off a chunk. "What about all the crazy monsters that were running around? I'll never forget how that rabble forced me to fight while moon drunk in Salem."

276

Sybil stroked Johann's back. "Grace mentioned the supernatural beings scattered after aforesaid Inti's light had returned. Forthwith no more berserk creatures frightening normal citizens, I warrant."

"Like I did," Johann said between bites.

"Of a truth, you were the worst one," she joked, grabbing a granola bar.

Marcelo took a soda can and popped the top for Sybil. "Did Grace say anything about demon activity? Umaq had released hundreds into our world, strong ones like Zelaenah. Since he is gone, those beasts are no longer under his control and free to cause havoc."

"She said that most of the demons are hiding forthwith," Sybil explained. "The creature's power hath weakened, and we all ought not feel disquieted about them."

"What about the moon Maiden?" Johann asked. "I expect that deity has no one to associate with now. She abandoned the Mother and Crone, and Cessani's flock is no more."

A crunch sounded as Sybil bit into the granola. "Truly, can you believe the Maiden hath returned home? The unpredictable deity with the persona of a teenager ran back to the Mother and old Crone. The Triple Moon Goddess hath been reunited, and thus the ancient archetype restored."

"Well, I'm glad the Maiden is fickle," Johann replied as he finished the sandwich and picked up another. "She provided you the ingredients to help me overcome the moon sickness. Was it Grace who told you about the moon deity going back to the way things were?"

"I actually conversed with the Maiden about it some days agone," Sybil answered. "Persephone hath a fancy to meet me and get ice cream." She shrugged and took another bite. "Forthwith, I have an appointment with a deity when we return home."

The friends continued their picnic, munching good food, exchanging banter and a few laughs. An immense relaxation filled Sybil. She couldn't recall the last time she felt so calm and free of stress. Intense joy also surged, another emotion she had longed for, and at times, questioned if she might ever experience the feeling again.

The hour grew late, and the time had arrived to depart. Sybil and the others said goodbye to Salix. After cleaning up the area, the three strolled to the edge of the woods and exchanged farewells. Johann hopped into his vehicle and drove off to Nevada City. Sybil and Marcelo hit the road for the long drive home.

***

A few days later at their house in Avila Beach, Sybil flopped on the couch and stretched. Marcelo had just cooked a wonderful meal, and she looked forward to tomorrow's leftovers.

"Truly, that lemon chicken was so tender," she commented. "My heart wonders if you miss eating things like that. Thereof, does it feel odd preparing food while knowing you shall not consume any of it?"

"I don't remember much about the actual taste of food," Marcelo responded. "However, the delicious smells do trigger wonderful memories of my mother's cooking. So in a way, I'm also enjoying the meal." He

278

joined her on the sofa and draped an arm around her shoulders.

"What *moovy* shall we watch forthwith?" she asked, always excited to experience a new one.

"We're almost through the entire list of Clint Eastwood westerns, which you adore. You haven't seen *Unforgiven*."

"Oh, yes! I shall enjoy another western."

Marcelo hit the button on the remote to start the film. As always, Sybil watched in fascination. These modern moving pictures, with their amazing effects and heart-pumping action, had thrilled her greatly ever since waking in the twenty-first century. Best of all, she had Marcelo at her side to share the moments and explain things she didn't understand.

The relaxation and happiness had carried over from their visit to Salix. After so much chaos, pain, and tears, she finally felt at *home*. The film played on, yet try as she might to stay awake, drowsiness soon crept in. She stifled a few yawns and sank more against Marcelo, then at some point closed her eyes…and took the best nap of her life.

About the Author

Alexander Fernandez was born in Santa Monica, CA and grew up in Rancho Cucamonga. Retired from the United States Air Force after serving 24 years, he lives with his wife Helem in Roseville.

Alex has been writing fantasy and paranormal stories since early childhood for both school and for pleasure. He hopes to make a lasting emotional impact in his readers. He thrives in the exhilaration of creating memorable characters and adventures that become a part of the reader's life.

ADDITIONAL BOOKS BY THIS AUTHOR IN EPIC FANTASY:

Lonely World Trilogy

Book One: Tears for a World
Book Two: Tears for Love
Book Three: Tears for Life